THE FOURTH BOOK OF THE SMALL GODS

WHEN RAVENS CALL

BRUCE BLAKE

When Ravens Call

The Fourth Book of the Small Gods

Bruce Blake

<u>Comments?</u>

<u>Contact Bruce at: bruce@bruceblake.net</u>

Visit Bruce online at www.bruceblake.net for FREE SHORT STORIES, signed copies, and to stay updated on new releases

ISBN 978-1-927687-23-9

Prologue

FLAKES OF GRAY SNOW fluttered out of the sky, covering everything with despair and hopelessness.

Rak'bana gasped a breath into her singed lungs, inhaling the burnt world across the tip of her tongue and edging out from under the archway, head tilted back to watch them fall. Snow hadn't fallen on the land since the time of her youth.

But the world didn't hold the crisp, fresh essence of snow, and the flakes were the wrong color. Instead of the invigorating scent of first season, the stink of fire and death filled her nostrils. A sigh escaped her lungs, releasing the rank air from her chest.

The exertion and stress of their flight caused her muscles no discomfort; her flesh did not scream in agony from the flames that had devoured it. Only the ache of her heart registered. The kingdom she knew lay in ruins, changed beyond recognition, and her brother—her world—gone along with it. Nothing would be the same again.

Not for her. Not for anyone.

Hand held out, red and blistered palm facing the sky, she watched a large flake land on her burnt skin. But it didn't melt, for this wasn't snow. The chunk of ash fell to pieces the instant it touched her, becoming a darker shade of gray as it mixed with the dampness of her flesh.

The kingdom is on fire.

She'd seen this day in her dreams, but foresight couldn't prepare her for the reality lying before her. Despite the visions Goddess sent her, the direction and instructions given, the sight of her smoldering world shocked her. Not even the Mother of Mothers readied her for Ine'vesi's treachery. She curled her fingers, closing her hand into a fist and grinding the wet ash to paste. The angry response to the memory of his betrayal did nothing to quell her disappointment and rage.

Rak'bana lowered her arm, let her gaze fall across the ruined courtyard. The Pillars of Life lay in pieces in an apt representation of the devastation laid upon the world; steam rose from the river as though a giant had boiled it to make his tea and it hadn't yet cooled. Stepping into the yard, her bare foot crunched in charred grass. Her ears heard the sound it made, her mind knew it should be sharp and painful on her scalded soles. She experienced nothing, her ability to decipher sensation left behind in the fire.

She picked her way through the rubble, attempting to discern the Pillars: Faith, Love, Courage, Healing, and the rest of the nine. But they stood no more and, when the columns fell, they'd shattered into an unrecognizable mess. One chunk of fractured stone appeared no different from the next.

Halfway across the courtyard, she stopped without knowing why. Nothing she spied caused her to halt, no sound gave her pause; a shiver, a vague sense of place. It started in her broken heart, forcing the ache aside, filling her with a sensation reminding her of—though it couldn't have been—hope. It prompted her onward, pushing her toward the river.

Burnt debris bobbed along with the current—charred branches and heat-curled leaves, blackened chunks of wood torn from structures, shreds of things Rak'bana didn't want to recognize. The bits and pieces of ruined lives floated past, garnering an instant of her attention before flowing water ferried them on their journey to end up caught against the rusted metal grating or, if a piece passed through, making its way to the sea to be lost forever.

One column had toppled toward the river and shattered against the edge. Half lay destroyed on the ground, jagged chunks of marble strewn across the courtyard, the rest of the monument gone in the depths of the running water.

The debris' resting place suggested this to be the Pillar of Faith. She'd spent so many mornings kneeling at its base and sharing her thoughts with Goddess, her knees wore patches in the grass. Everyone in the castle of Draekfarren knew the prayer spot of the Priestess Rak'bana. She remembered most every instance when Ine'vesi joined her because they numbered so few; he preferred to indulge his faith alone in the chapel, closing a door on the world. At the time, she didn't understand her brother's preference but, given the way the kingdom met its end, she thought she now understood.

He wasn't speaking with Goddess, and he didn't want me to know.

The realization led to a question she neither wanted to ask nor answer.

If not Goddess, with whom did he commune?

She shivered and her burnt flesh prickled. With the sensation came pain; where she'd experienced no sensitivity, the priestess' body became clothed in a tight-fitting outfit fashioned of agony. Her step faltered, and she gasped sharp breaths, waiting for the torment to cease. It slithered across her shriveled skin, tightening her muscles, which made the torment more intense. Rak'bana went to one knee, breath rasping along her raw throat. An instant later, the gooseflesh passed but left a throbbing ache in its place.

She took time to gather her energy, discovered it difficult to find. Her breathing calmed, and she became used to the irritation crawling across every bit of her flesh. She got to her feet and set out again, taking slow, deliberate paces toward the fallen Pillar. The hopeful sensation in her chest grew as the torment of her body subsided. Whatever attracted her in this direction, each step brought her closer to finding out. She skirted a deep depression in the blackened lawn left by one of the massive fireballs, then saw what drew her here.

Although the fire had reduced the legs protruding from beneath the fallen pillar to nothing but charred bone, Rak'bana realized to whom they belonged. She crept toward them, sadness choking her, and fell to her knees when she reached the burnt corpse.

"Vesi," she whispered, her dry throat throttling the word so it came out an indecipherable croak. It didn't matter; no one remained to hear her speak.

Is this what brought hope to my heart? My brother's death?

The thought disturbed her, but she realized the truth in it, and her disturbance turned to guilt.

Why should her emotions betray her by being anything but sadness and remorse at the loss of Ine'vesi? He'd lived his life with her, for her, and she for him. Goddess meant more to her than he, no other. Their births came one after the other, they'd grown up together, become priest and priestess at the same time. They'd relied on each other in good and difficult times... always. Even over the last few turns of the season, when she recognized doubt growing in him, she'd stayed with him, believed in him. How could his death instill in her any relief or hope?

Because it means he didn't make it out of the castle.

Despite the grief in her heart, she cast her gaze around the charred ground, searching for any vestige of the burnt parchment. She realized the impossibility of differentiating it from the ash fallen from the sky, the scorched grass and clothing, her brother's seared flesh, any surviving scrap carried away on the wind or deposited in the river. After a moment, she hung her head, her eyes unintentionally finding the reddened skin of her bare and scalded legs. Angry blisters covered her, many oozing fluid. She looked at her hands and arms enveloped with the same singed tissue, touched her fingers to her skull where once she'd have found hair. None of this distressed her, for Goddess willed it.

Sorrow grew from her reaction to losing her twin. Surely Goddess' will did not make her experience happiness at the death of her brother.

She let her head droop again, chin touching her tightening chest, throat knotting, but she didn't cry. The fires of Goddess' wrath had made steam of her tears.

How she wished she and Ine'vesi had parted under different terms, but how could they unless he'd acted out of faith? She considered his defiance unforgivable. The larger scale malaise of the kingdom had caused this devastation, killed countless people. She'd warned everyone who took the time to listen something like this could happen, but few heeded her words.

And now they're dead and gone.

The ache in her chest expanded, filled her. She hoped for it to end soon, for death to claim her and resolve this life's suffering without ceremony. Then she'd walk with Goddess. Once, the thought might have dispelled her despair, but she doubted it could be enough after what she'd seen, after what she'd endured. And she wouldn't be with her dear Ine'vesi. Wherever he'd ended up, it wouldn't be with Goddess.

Weariness overtook the priestess. Her shoulders sagged, her hands fell onto her thighs and a jolt of pain shot through her, catching her off guard and startling a gasp from her lips. She pulled her palms away, but the hurt spread, crawling up her arms, digging itself under her reddened skin with the care and sensation of shards of wood jammed beneath a fingernail.

Rak'bana threw her head back and cried out toward the sky. Never in her life had she wished for death.

Until now.

"Priestess."

The word cut through her pained howl as though someone spoke it with lips pressed to her ear. It brought a prickle across the top of her flesh like a thousand insects crawling along her blistered skin. The sensation balanced on the edge between tickling and torment, flirted with making her forget the anguish in her heart.

She stopped screaming, pulled her gaze from the sky.

Two figures stood on the far bank of the river, their features disguised by a rolling mist and smoke drifting from fires not yet extinguished. Her pain didn't disappear when she saw them, but it ceased to have meaning in her life. She unfolded herself one piece at a time, mimicking an awkward plant striving to reach the sun. The agony in her limbs and torso should have been unbearable, but she made her way to wobbling legs, knees waiting for an excuse to fail.

"G... Goddess?"

"You have served me well, Rak'bana." The voice emanated from everywhere, not from the misty figures. Rather than hear the words, they sank into her, a salve absorbed by her seared flesh.

The priestess diverted her eyes from the figure, feeling as though she shouldn't gaze upon Goddess. A body floated past, carried on the river's current, and she tried to shut her lids but they refused to close. Did she still have eyelids?

"I failed you. Look at what my failure forced you to do."

"The cleansing became necessary with or without you, Rak'bana. Your role never meant for you to prevent it. Your part was to plant seeds to keep it from happening again."

The priestess raised her eyes to the base of the swirling mist, thought she saw the shapes of bare feet disguised within.

"The scroll," she whispered, a hiss of breath so quiet she hardly understood the words herself.

"Yes."

"But my brother. He defied you, took part of the holy parchment for his own purpose."

"As I knew he would. As I needed him to."

Rak'bana leaned back, teetering, struggled to her feet with the last of her energy. Her gaze trailed up the silhouette hidden in the mist. She opened her mouth but found it dry and useless.

"Balance must exist, Priestess. They have insured the world's safety for the foreseeable future. I won't step in to this degree again. What will pass will pass."

Rak'bana's breath shortened and pain filled her chest, making it difficult to draw air into her lungs. Her heartbeat sped, hammering against her insides, and her gaze moved to the indistinct shape at Goddess' side.

"H... h... who...?"

"This." The deity gestured to the silhouette beside her. "Many turns of the seasons hence, this one will save the world. Because of you."

"The firstborn child of the rightful king."

The mist dissolved, and the figure became more distinct: a youth who'd seen the seasons turn twenty times, give or take. Clothed in the garb of a fighter, the person stood with an air of confidence, legs spread and arms crossed. The last of the haze faded from the unknown figure's face when a seizure quaked through Rak'bana. Her head flew back and her knees failed. She hit the ground, her body exploding with torment: the pain of her wounds, grief over the loss of her brother, despair at what had happened to her world. Unseen fingers wrapped themselves around her heart, squeezed it, prevented it from beating. A fat drop of rain struck her cheek, its coolness too late to offer respite. More raindrops fell, pattering against the charred earth, hissing in still-burning fires.

The priestess Rak'bana gasped a final breath, tasted ash and burnt grass on her tongue. Then Goddess stood at her side, holding her hand, stroking her forehead. Relief flowed into her, inserting itself between her and the pains and regrets. A new feeling replaced them, an invigoration, a suspicion of things to come. It was early, but she knew the time to begin preparations was already nigh.

The other figure accompanying Goddess had disappeared, leaving her alone with the Mother of Mothers. Peace filled her and life faded away.

For now.

1 - Teryk - Saved

*W*ATER SPLASHED OVER HIS head, filled his mouth and eyes, nose and ears. The waves tossed Teryk around, the current tugged, the combination turning him over and over so he lost the ability to discern up from down. He worried he'd never surface and draw breath again.

The tight panic growing in his chest took him back to the river under the castle and being trapped under the bars intended to keep people out. How long since that happened? As he struggled in the freezing ocean, the finding of a scroll written an eternity past for someone who may not have been him seemed an age ago.

The more seawater entering his throat, the less likely it became he'd fulfill the prophecy.

The prince's head broke the surface, thrusting him from the bitter sea into the driving rain. He coughed and gasped, drew a partial breath to relieve the burning in his lungs before the next wave washed over him and the current dragged him under again.

Briny water stung his eyes, but he refused to close them. A beast lurked in the depths; he'd seen the flat skull topping a long, curving neck rise above the ocean, its gaping mouth lined with ferocious teeth. Seeing it coming wouldn't prevent the inevitable outcome, but knowing the end approached might be better than having it come upon him unsuspected.

His head bobbed above the surface again. The storm roared in his ears, water splashed in his face, but he kept himself from going under again. Driving rain and sea foam swirled around him, twisting his body and forming shapes that shouldn't resemble anything, but did. Amongst them he spied his father's likeness, the firm resolution of his brow. Had he listened to him, heeded his words, he'd not be waiting to discover if he'd die by drowning or between the teeth of a god.

Teryk drew another breath, then another. Were the waves abating? In response, a swell pushed him up toward the sky, holding him above the world to peer into a trough between it and the next. The sight convinced him the size of the undulations hadn't decreased, but the opposite. He breathed again while the opportunity existed.

Before he crested the surge and descended into the furrow, a shape at the bottom caught his eye. At first he thought it the God of the Deep on its way to devour him in one bite like in the story of the sailor and his cat Nanny told them in their youth—Danya's favorite, but not his. It gave him a fear of the ocean until he'd seen the seasons turn for the tenth time.

In the tall tale, both seaman and feline survived. The cat rode a stream of water out the whale's blowhole while the sailor crawled between teeth the size of boulders while the whale napped. He didn't know if whales slept—or if they were more than mythical beasts—but he doubted his survival should a monster of the sea ingest him.

As he slipped down the swell, the wave buoyed the thing he'd spied up the other side. It wasn't a creature swimming in the roiling ocean but a chunk of debris. Teryk stroked hard to keep himself above the surface, to get closer to the unidentified object, but briny water washed over his head and the current took him under again. This time, instead of allowing the sea to have its way with him and leaving him hoping to find respite before his air ran out, he thrashed with his legs, pulled against the tide with his arms. His numb limbs fought the ocean's drag, and he concentrated on what floated above him, not what might lurk below.

If his efforts had any effect, he couldn't tell.

His muscles took on the characteristics of waterlogged wood as he struggled to find his way back to the surface. His chest swelled with the strain of keeping his air. If he released it, he didn't think he'd be able to stop himself from drawing another breath and filling his lungs with salty water.

How did this happen?

He thought of his mother, of Trenan, and of his sister. So much living yet undone, multitudes of things to see, places to go, and none of it to be, his future given up for a scroll filled with unintelligible words. For all he knew, Danya might have planted it, the prophecy made up from whole cloth, a lark for them to have fun. A joke on him gone too far. Why hadn't the possibility already occurred to him? The end of his life approached because she considered it funny for him to believe himself the savior of the world.

The thought drained the last of the energy from his limbs, and his struggles ceased. He floated in the sea, letting the current take him where it may as the first of the air escaped his lungs in a crowd of bubbles. He watched them rush up and away toward a surface he'd never see again.

Where will my body wash ashore? A ragged beach for someone to find me? Will my parents hear of my death? Trenan? Danya?

More breath seeped between his lips; he fought his body's natural urge to breathe in, replace what left. His head throbbed, his chest felt as though it might burst into flames. He let his lids slide closed, shutting out the dark nothingness of the sea.

His foot touched something solid for an instant, but then it disappeared.

It startled the last of the air out of him, leaving his lungs shrunken, depleted bags dangling inside him, longing for breath. The prince opened his eyes, jerked his head side to side. Had his sole brushed the bottom?

The inky depths stretched out below him, an impenetrable void as far as his vision allowed him to see. His throat tightened, his skull felt empty and buoyant—light enough to aid with flotation. The urge to suck water into his lungs parted his lips.

The solid thing under his foot returned, but this time, it stayed. It exerted upward pressure, bending his knee, then he sensed movement. Teryk forced his mouth shut again, swallowed the need to breathe. His chest screamed for air and darkness swirled at the edges of his vision threatening to take away his sight.

He became a rag doll in the ocean, his limbs trailing out behind him while an unseen presence propelled him upward. The pressure in his ears eased, water leaked between his lips and into his mouth, salt touching his tongue. He wanted to cough it out.

An instant later, his head broke the surface. Wind and sea roared around the prince, but he didn't understand what it meant or what to do, then his natural instincts took over. His chest spasmed, drawing air and seawater, making him hack and spasm. The replenishing breath returned energy to his limbs, and he stroked with his aching arms, pulling to keep himself afloat. The pressure against his foot remained.

Teryk finished clearing his lungs of water and drew a whooping inhalation. A new panic flooded through him and he flapped his hands, twisting to see what brought him back from the brink of death.

A dark, indistinct shape loomed beneath him, too big for him to figure where it began or ended. His nanny's story of the whale came to mind again, and he pushed off from whatever his foot rested on, propelling himself away.

A sleek, gray hump slid across the surface of the sea and disappeared. A current rushed around Teryk, swirling him in a whirlpool. He glimpsed a wave looming over him, an unidentifiable chunk of debris carried upon it. The thing fell on top of him, pushing him under again and stealing his consciousness.

—ᴇᴇ—

The pain came first.

It might have been easier to name the parts not causing him discomfort than to list all those involved. Salt and struggle left his throat raw, knots bound his muscles, his head throbbed.

Sound returned next—the swirl and lap of water, the creak of boards, the cry of a gull. The sharp tang of the salty ocean stung his nostrils. Light shone red through his eyelids.

Am I alive?

He made the effort to open his eyes, but the lashes had stuck together, gummed shut. An attempt to raise his hand to his face resulted in more pain and no movement. Air sighed out of his mouth, the tiny gust brushing parched and chapped lips. Despite the added discomfort, he took delight in breathing; it wasn't so long ago he thought he'd drawn his last breath.

Teryk allowed his mind to stray back to his time in the water, the numbness in his limbs, the struggle in his chest. Frigid, icy, he recalled. Although the sun now warmed him, his body shivered in response to the memory. Other memories followed: the solid mass beneath his foot lifting him to safety; the smooth, gray flesh breaking the surface of the sea; the shape sliding away into the depths.

Where am I?

The story of the sailor and the whale flashed through his mind again, panic close on its tail. With an effort, Teryk pried his eyelids open. A good part of him expected the darkness inside a great fish's belly to greet him despite the sunlight and warmth touching his cheek.

How a whale's guts might appear, he didn't know, but this wasn't it.

Water stretched on to a distant horizon, as smooth as he imagined possible for the ocean to ever be. He lay on his side, one arm kinked beneath him, the other stretched out in front. The tips of his fingers dangled over the edge, brushing the surface of each small wave. He gulped the few drops of saliva his dry mouth created, thankful to be safer than when currents and waves tossed and tugged him around the God of the Deep's home.

Teryk shifted his weight, rolled onto his chest so his cheek pressed against what turned out to be a slab of wood keeping him afloat. Its edge lay a mere finger's width from the tip of his nose, the act of rolling having dunked his protruding arm into the water. A movement tickled his fingertips, so he found the energy to lift his head and peer into the sea.

Of course, the prince had seen many fish before, most arrayed on a fishmonger's cart or beheaded, flayed, and cooked on his plate. Because of this, the small creature toothlessly nibbling at his fingers surprised him with its color. The bulk of its scales were yellow, but two thin blue stripes—one behind its gills and another before its tail—provided a striking contrast. Part of Teryk realized he should take his hand away, take away its chance to cause him harm. But its colors brought him a joy and comfort of a kind he hadn't experienced in a long time.

He raised his eyes and looked at the sea stretching on to a distant horizon with nothing between. No ship, no land, not a single object to break the ocean's near-smooth surface. The nothingness should have caused panic and fear, but the relief of being alive usurped fright's power.

Teryk returned his gaze to his hand dangling in the water and the colorful fish nibbling his fingertips, found a second joining the first. The green of this one's scales made it one shade from invisible against the ocean's depths. He wouldn't have noticed it but for the red dot atop its head.

With a smile on his face, Teryk wiggled his fingers and watched them skitter away before returning to reapply their fishy lips to his flesh. He chuckled at their persistence and let them continue their nibbling as fatigue weighed on him. He allowed his eyelids to slide closed but popped them open again, repeated the action.

The second time he opened his eyes, a glimmer of light caught his attention. Normally, he'd have written it off as the reflection of sun on water, but it winked back to life again a few heartbeats later and he realized it shone from below the surface. It came closer, moving in a zig-zag pattern, mesmerizing Teryk. Colors flickered in the curious glow, though he couldn't tell if the luminescence itself caused the spectacle or if the waves flowing over it created the effect.

It caught the finger-nibblers' attention, too, and they ceased their attempts at dining on his fingers. They maneuvered themselves around, tails lashing back and forth to hold their place against the ocean's current. The hypnotic light moved side to side, inching closer, and Teryk readjusted himself, leaning nearer to the water. At first, it appeared to be floating of its own accord, a lost star fallen from the sky and unable to navigate its way home from beneath the sea. The prince found himself able to identify with the sentiment. The two fish watched, entranced along with him.

When the bewitching glow came within an arm's length, he discerned a vague shape below it, nothing more than a darker patch on a dark background. The light didn't illuminate whatever hid below it, making the outline too dim for him to recognize. He leaned closer, close enough a large ripple kissed his chin.

The light's forward motion ceased, and it bobbed and swayed in place with the ebb and flow of the waves. The two fish edged toward it, moving in a quick, darting way a short distance at a time; curiosity tempered by caution.

A sudden dread insinuated itself in Teryk's chest, the innocence of the disembodied light countered by the ominous shape lurking below it. The desire to warn the fingertip-nibblers overcame him and he shifted again, freeing his arm from beneath himself. His hand and forearm prickled with the touch of a thousand pins unfelt by his numb fingers. The muscles in his shoulder seized and, before he moved to slap the water and scare the predator off, the thing attached to the glow darted forward.

It swam fast for a creature of its size. A horn jutted off its head; the luminescence affixed to it winked out, and a mouth lined with spiky teeth gaped. It took both fish into its gaping maw at once as it broke the surface, the saw-like fin on its spine narrowly missing Teryk's outstretched hand.

The prince gasped a surprised breath into his lungs and jumped away, setting the wood he floated on rocking and pain shooting through his body.

"Settle, boy, or you'll send us tumbling back into the sea."

Teryk twisted toward the voice, startled again. While watching the fish, he'd heard nothing to suggest he wasn't alone floating atop the ocean.

He stared at the master of the Whalebone across the chunk of wet deck once a part of his ship. The man sat with his legs stretched out, the block of wood where once a foot lived twisted at an odd angle. Beside him lay a second sailor facing away from Teryk so he couldn't see who.

"C... Captain. What...?" He paused, eyes scanning the makeshift raft, then the endless sea before settling back on Bryder. "What happened?"

"The storm took us," he said, voice quiet and regretful. "Worst squall I ever seen. Too much for the Whalebone."

He sighed, breath catching in his chest.

"Me and Rilum Seaman are the last two left, and I'm surprised to find you alive."

Teryk wiped a hand across his face and glanced at his white shirt, wet and stuck to his skin. He felt the urge to run his hands over his body, to search for injuries, but the pain he experienced came from knots and aches, not broken bones. No blood stained the fabric of his clothing.

He closed his eyes, remembering the rain and wind, the waves towering over the ship, the monster he'd seen jutting out of the sea. He opened his lids again, fixed his gaze on the captain.

"It wasn't the storm. It was the God of the Deep."

"That thing ain't nothing but a story to scare those who shouldn't find themselves sailing on this harsh mistress."

Teryk shook his head. "I saw it," he said then swallowed hard. "It saved me."

The captain's expression turned stern. "I saved you. Waves threw your noggin against this chunk of ship. I grabbed you and yanked you aboard before you sank."

The prince opened his mouth to relate the firmness under his foot responsible for pushing him up out of the depths and the gray flesh sliding across the ocean's surface. The look on the captain's face stopped him. His taut-pulled lips, his forehead and the corners of his eyes creased—a man who wanted to hear nothing of gods and monsters. "Th... thank you."

Captain Bryder nodded and diverted his gaze toward the distant horizon, his expression remaining unchanged. Teryk did the same, taking in the expanse of ocean.

"I never expected it to be so huge," he said.

"It goes on until it touches the sky in every direction around our home."

"But what of the land across the sea?"

"Hmph. As much legend as your God of the Deep." He faced the prince, intensity written on his brow. "What you know of the sea you learned from tall tales and bedtime stories."

A blush rose in the prince's cheeks as he again recalled the story of the sailor, his cat, and the whale. Might such tales, the God of the Deep, and the land across the sea, be merely fancy? Didn't stories have their genesis in truth?

If the land across the sea doesn't exist, neither does the man from across the sea. If the man doesn't exist, the prophecy is another fable.

The prince opened his mouth to argue the point, but Bryder continued before he spoke.

"This water be a dangerous beast without the help of stories and lies. You experienced it yourself; it devoured every soul aboard the Whalebone except for the three of us."

Teryk sensed the captain's intent to disguise the sadness and guilt in his voice, but it spilled over despite his best effort. He dropped his gaze from the prince's, choosing to stare at his off-kilter wooden foot instead of looking him in the eye. The prince glanced from Bryder to Rilum Seaman's back where he lay on the makeshift raft.

"Is he all right?"

The captain pivoted to glance over his shoulder at the other man. "As good as anyone who's lost his father on the Devil and his son on the Whalebone. He's been lying there since the sea calmed. Best not to expect more of him."

Teryk nodded. "And how are you?"

"My foot's crooked." He tilted his head toward the wooden block. "Otherwise, I made it through."

"I didn't mean—"

"I know what you meant," the captain snapped. "But you don't want to be asking the ship's master how he feels after losing his crew."

Bryder glared, but the prince refused to divert his gaze this time. He nodded once so he knew they understood each other, then allowed the subject to fade into the still ocean air. They continued looking at each other, the day suddenly heavy with the captain's mood.

"I know who you are. I recognized you the first time I saw you."

The declaration startled Teryk, and his eyes widened before he got his surprise under control. He looked away to prevent his expression from confirming the other man's suspicions.

"What are you talking about? My name is Taylor. I fell asleep in a crate and—"

"You're the prince of the Windward Kingdom, next in line for the throne. I met you once on the Devil before your father decided I'd become too old to command his precious flagship. Don't you remember so many turns of the seasons in the past?"

For a time, Teryk debated in his head whether to admit the truth or continue on with the ruse. He glanced out across the vast sea. Did it matter anymore?

"I remember," he whispered before looking to the captain. "If you knew, why didn't you take me back?"

Regret twinged in his gut; if Bryder had returned him to Draekfarren, he'd be home instead of floating in the middle of the ocean accompanied by two sailors and no hope.

And my quest to fulfill my destiny would have ended.

Bryder shrugged. "Maybe the king sent you to keep your eye on me, to make sure I could handle captaining the Whalebone." His gaze slid to his hands resting in his lap. "I guess I proved I wasn't worthy."

"We could do nothing. The storm was too much. The..." His lips shaped to say God of the Deep, but good sense prevailed. "The waves. Besides, that's not why I found myself on your ship."

"Then why did you?"

"My story isn't far from truth. I had no intention of being on the Whalebone."

"Aye, you didn't appear a man who got aboard out of a want to sail."

Teryk huffed a staccato laugh. "Nor did I intend to end up in a crate. And I never got my sea legs; not much of a sailor, I'm afraid."

"That be truthful."

"I'm sorry for what happened to your crew. If you'd taken me back—"

"No point thinking what might've been. Only thing matters is what is—them being gone. It's on me, not you. If you weren't aboard, we'd have ended in the same place."

"I guess we both wish things turned out different."

"That be the truth, too."

Beside the captain, Rilum Seaman stirred, pushed himself to a sitting position. His concentration on Bryder, the prince had nearly forgotten the other man.

The sailor raised his arm, extended a shaking finger to point across the calm sea. Teryk squinted against the glare of the sun, shielded his eyes with a flattened hand. The ocean stretched on, the same as in every other direction, but with one difference: the horizon appeared closer.

He leaned forward, staring hard at the dark spot jutting out of the water.

"Land," he whispered. "We're saved."

II - Danya - Merchant Road

*T*HE SUN CRAWLED ITS way across the sky, not yet high enough to mark midday. Droplets of sweat ran along Danya's back and chest, prompted by the thick wool of the red tunic heated by the day's warmth. More than once she'd suggested removing the garment, but Evalal disagreed. Though they'd seen no traffic all morning—wagon, horse, or pedestrian—the girl remained cautious.

Why should I listen to her? She's but a child.

Not many turns of the seasons ago, people might have said the same of her. If they swapped their current ages, she'd likely not be half as responsible as Evalal or worthy of such trust. For this reason, she followed her instruction; the Mother of Death put her faith in this girl to lead Danya and her precious cargo to wherever they needed to go. Who was she to question a woman through whom the Goddess spoke? Though her parents raised her with other views, things she'd seen in the past days went a long way toward convincing her of the veracity of these women's beliefs.

"Where are we going?" She wiped a line of perspiration from her forehead.

Evalal shrugged. "Pay attention to the Seed of Life. It will guide you."

Danya frowned and rested her palm against the pouch hanging at her waist. The hard egg-shape pressed against her, separated from her by soft deerskin. If she didn't know better, it might have been a rock she carried. It offered no guidance and no suggestion of possessing the ability to do so. The princess sighed and let her hand fall back to her side.

"It does nothing."

"Be patient."

"But how will I know?"

"You just will."

"How will I understand what it wants me to do?"

As soon as the question left her mouth, she realized how ridiculous it sounded. She carried a seed, an inanimate object. She'd seen it change colors—unusual, to be sure—but shifting its appearance didn't give the thing the power of communication.

"You'll understand."

Evalal's words set a tight knot in Danya's gut. What sorts of answers were these?

No answers at all.

The princess stopped walking, the lump in her belly growing into anger and frustration. She'd left her home, risked the wrath of Trenan and her parents, lost her brother, and for what? To carry a color-changing seed to who-knew-where in the company of a child? She pressed her lips together, peered at Evalal from under her brows, aware that, an instant before, she'd understood why they trusted the youngster. For that moment, she believed in the Goddess and the mysterious task laid before her. But now exasperation washed it away. Part of her wanted to stop it from happening, but she'd lost control over it.

"Those are not answers," she snapped. She didn't mean for her words to sound so harsh, but her mouth operated without her consent. "Not another step until you tell me where we're going."

Evalal faced her, the expression she wore not what Danya expected. Not an air of upset or displeasure, but the aspect one might see worn by a nanny having to explain a simple concept to a child. Her head tilted, a corner of her mouth bent up in a placating smile. The shine in her eyes, the cast of her features infuriated the princess further. She stepped toward the girl; they stood close in height, but Danya took full advantage of the slight difference. She pulled back her shoulders, puffed out her chest. She'd seen Trenan and other soldiers act in this manner when they wanted to appear threatening.

"My brother is gone," she said, the words forced between clenched teeth. "I've left my family behind. The time for platitudes and vagaries is done. Tell me where we're going, what we're meant to do."

Evalal's smile disappeared from her lips, but the softness of her countenance didn't change. The princess interpreted what remained in her expression as pity.

"The Mother of Death told you everything we need to know. The Seed of—"

"Do not say the bloody seed will guide me," Danya snapped, cutting the girl's words short. She glared at her, hands clenching into fists, her thoughts coiling into one she didn't recall ever having before:

If she mentions it again, I'll strike her.

The sentiment caught her off-guard; in her life, she'd never hit anyone other than in practice or jest. Teryk's shoulder often received both gentle and not-so-gentle punches—as his love taps bruised hers—but she'd never struck a single soul out of anger, nor did she remember having the desire to do so. Why should she now?

"Tut, tut, ladies. Is this a polite way to converse?"

The voice startled Danya. After traveling the entire morning without seeing anyone, she expected no one within leagues. Evalal's posture stiffened. She diverted her gaze from her companion to the speaker, her usual languid nature absent from the movement, replaced by the woodenness of trepidation. The princess pivoted to see who'd spoken.

She'd never seen the man before. He wore a thick and unkempt beard, a thin twig caught in it at one side like a rabbit in a trap. His hair—what remained of it—dangled limp upon his shoulders, and the smile he cursed them with lacked at least one tooth, perhaps more. Despite the grin and the calm tone of his voice, the princess suspected this to be someone they didn't want to meet alone on the road so far from help.

Danya reached for the hilt of her sword, but the thick wool garment thwarted her attempt to grasp it. When fashioning a cloak meant for the sick, ease of drawing a weapon wasn't a consideration.

"Is it a blade hidden beneath your shawl? Not what I'd expect from someone dressed in the garb worn by the Goddess' tribe. Better move your hand away."

She dropped her arm, fingers balled into a fist. Why hadn't she considered the difficulties wearing the garment might present? What good were those seasons of training with Trenan if she couldn't draw her blade when necessary?

"In fact, it be best you take it off. Seems too warm a robe for a sunny day."

"Do you know what this cloak denotes?" Evalal asked, though she didn't wait for a reply. "We're bound for Ikkundana where my companion will live out her last days."

"Ikkundana, is it? Sad for such a youngster." He glanced along the trail, then back the other way. "A shame this road don't go near the place. Take off the woolly cloak."

He lifted his hand, rested his fingers on the short sword hanging at his waist. No scabbard held the weapon; his belt pinned the bare steel against him like something he'd found and possessed no other way to carry it. Danya thought he'd most likely cut himself or the belt if he drew it in haste. Still, with her own blade hidden beneath the unwieldy tunic, she stood no chance to counter him should he attack.

Danya stole a glance toward Evalal, saw the confidence of her ruse fade and her shoulders sag with it. She possessed no more plans to get them safely away; it fell to the princess to save them.

She nodded and untied the bows holding the robe closed at the front, unwound the garment from around her and let it fall to the ground. As it slid off, her sword hand darted for the hilt of her weapon. The fellow standing before her reacted by shaking his head and laughing.

"Tch, tch. I don't think you'll be wanting to do that."

An instant later, Evalal cried out, startling her. She jerked her gaze toward her companion.

A second man had sneaked up on them while the first held their attention. Much bigger than the girl, he'd grabbed her around the middle, pinning both arms to her sides, and pressed a short blade to her throat. To Danya, it didn't appear any more than a sharpened butter knife, but enough to open the artery in her companion's neck. The girl's expression of terror drained any thought of defiance from the princess and she let her hand drop from her sword.

The man holding Evalal grinned, his attempt at a smile proving more gap-toothed than his counterpart. Besides two extra missing teeth and a twig for his beard, they might have been the same person.

Twin thieves.

"We got 'em, didn't we, Jon? Got 'em good," the second fellow said.

"That we did, me brother John." Now the first man took the time to draw his weapon. He inserted the fingers of his free hand between his skin and the belt, ensuring he'd pull the blade without severing it or cutting himself. "Lose the sword belt, lass."

Danya gritted her teeth, her pulse beating at her temple. She'd never been in a real fight before, only sparring with Teryk or Trenan or one of the other soldiers. Part of her felt nervous at the prospect of engaging this man, but the possibility of testing her training excited another part. It took one more glance at the panic in Evalal's eyes for her to give up the thought. She used two fingers to draw her sword, held it dangling in front of her to show she posed no danger, then let it drop to the ground.

"Don't hurt her," she said, staring at the first man, the point of his short sword directed at her with the practiced ease of someone who passably knew how to use it.

"We won't, but you will have to prove you can listen better. I said to take off the belt. I've a feeling whatever be in your pouch is more likely what we'd be after."

A chill crawled across Danya's skin, prickling goosebumps on her arms. The seed was the reason for this journey, why they'd left the castle and ended up on this dangerous road. It featured in the prophecy along with so many other things she didn't understand. Belief in the ancient scroll meant a link between the fate of mankind and the Seed of Life. Wasn't it worth more than the life of one young follower of the Goddess?

The second man squeezed Evalal tighter, soliciting a frightened squeak from the girl's throat. The princess didn't look toward her, but hearing her reaction brought a tightness to her chest and gut. She drew short, shallow breaths through her nostrils as she rubbed the back of her teeth with the tip of her tongue.

What would Trenan do?

A simple answer: he wouldn't have put himself in this situation.

Resigned, Danya reached down and unbuckled the sword belt, took it from around her waist, and held it out toward the man, dangling it from her fingers. She looked at the pouch drooping off it, imagined the seed inside, how its surface changed colors before her eyes, the trial she'd been through to retrieve it. Was it supposed to end this way? She might hold the fate of the world in her hand, and she was about to give it up to two toothless, unkempt brigands in the middle of nowhere.

"Don't—" Evalal whispered, her word cut off by her captor squeezing her tighter.

No one else spoke. They stood for a long stretch of heartbeats, the belt swaying in Danya's grasp as the first man stared at the pouch and she watched him staring. They might have remained stationary longer if not for the interrupting crunch of a boot heel on dirt.

The brigand diverted his gaze down the road toward the sound, then Danya did the same.

She recognized the tall, slender fellow right away. They'd met the weapons merchants before leaving the inn. Which one was he? Fellick or Ive?

And where is the other?

The princess cast her gaze behind him, looking back along the dirt track, but saw nothing. No wagon bearing swords and axes, and no stocky partner standing in the lane.

"Halt yourself where you are," the man holding the short sword said. He'd developed a quiver in his arm enough to shake the tip of his sword. "Ain't a thing here concerns you. Turn around and walk away."

The tall fellow continued toward them for ten more paces before halting. For someone who looked far from imposing and dangerous and appeared to have no weapon, he carried himself with a great deal of confidence.

"I beg to differ. I presume the two of you must be Jon and John? What other set of twins does one find along this stretch of road?"

"Aye, that we are," Evalal's captor said, pride noticeable in his tone. "You've heard of us."

"I have," he conceded. "And do you know who I am?"

Twig beard nodded. "You're the weapons merchant. You pass this way often."

"I do. And what's my name?"

His gaze held the man with the short sword as though he looked right into the fellow instead of at him. The subject of his intensity swallowed hard, throat clicking.

"Ive."

"Correct. Of Fellick and Ive. Do you understand my meaning?"

Danya wasn't sure what she was watching transpire. Her gaze trailed from the weapons merchant to first the one Jon, then the other. Both men's eyes flickered away, searching along the road or into the forest beside it.

"I'll happily answer for you, gentlemen. It means Mr. Fellick is near. My friend and business partner is never far. You'll not want to anger him, I believe. He's a good man, but I'm afraid an ill temper is a shortfall of his." Ive shook his head and clicked his tongue. "He has such trouble controlling it."

The weapons merchant wore a bemused smirk; despite being outnumbered, he knew he'd won the exchange by mentioning his partner. The two brigands appeared resigned to end the standoff, but they both remained a measure too wild-eyed for Danya's liking. Would they let it finish with a whimper, skulking away with nothing to show for their efforts, or leave in a splash of blood and chaos? Though the knife the second man held was small, it looked sharp, its point deadly. The muscles in her body tensed, turning her rigid; she clenched her fists so tight, her nails dug into the palms of her hands. Her knees bent, ready to launch her toward Evalal should he make the wrong move.

But the girl must have noted the change in Danya's attitude. She caught the princess' eye and shook her head ever so slightly. The air crackled briefly with the indecision of the two men, then the first lowered his arm, the tip of the sword drooping until it pointed at the ground. The bit of his cheeks visible above his beard had turned red, and he appeared to find it difficult to keep his gaze on one subject for more than a second.

"Let the young ladies go and take your leave and I'm sure Mr. Fellick's mood will not sour."

Jon with the sword looked to his brother, nodded once, and backed away. He didn't raise his weapon again, but neither did he return it to its place at his belt. His companion lowered his knife, pushed Evalal from him as he followed his twin's retreat. The girl stumbled, but Danya got to her before she fell, catching her under the arms and keeping her on her feet. The sudden action with her body already so tense forced a knot beneath her shoulder blade. She winced at the pain, but the relief of her companion's safety made her forget it.

After retreating five or six paces, the two would-be thieves turned and ran, veering off the road and into the woods. They thrashed through the brush, their figures disappearing amongst the foliage long before the sound of their passing faded.

"Are you alright?"

Evalal nodded as she stood upright and brushed off the front of her smock with the palms of both hands. "Goddess protected me, as she does."

Behind them, the tall man snorted. "No one has called me a Goddess before."

The girl's mouth tilted in a smile reminding Danya of the patient expression of a parent explaining something to a child who couldn't understand. The princess strapped her sword belt back around her waist as her companion took the time to set the weapons merchant straight.

"No, you are not a goddess, Mr. Ive, but, whether it is within your awareness, Goddess' will brought you here."

"I am a merchant. This is a merchant road. Look close enough and you'll find the tracks of my wagon's wheels in these ruts."

"Of course. But to be here today, at this moment—Goddess' work."

Ive waved his hand, dismissing her assertion. "Yes, yes. Goddess looks out for her sheep. And yet it's common to have mutton for dinner, isn't it?"

Evalal's smile did not fade, but the princess saw a change in her companion's eyes. Not resignation—a man of the weapons merchant's ilk couldn't sway her faith—but a weariness Danya didn't expect to see in a girl so young.

"My compatriot is waiting around the next bend, guarding our wares. You've seen Mr. Fellick; he's exceptional at protecting things. We can make room in the wagon for you."

His gaze held Danya's as wind rustled through the trees and a crow flew overhead, cawing at them. The princess wanted to respond—and the weapons merchant's demeanor suggested he expected the same of her—but how she should do so failed her. All she thought to do was stare at the man.

"It's this particular skill of Mr. Fellick's that brought me here," he continued, sensing they needed further explanation. "While you'd certainly say Mr. Fellick is the brawn in our partnership, the fact leaves the brains to me; I do my best to accept this mantle with humility." He chortled a laugh as dry as his humor. "It occurred to me: if I have ever seen two souls in need of protection, they belong to the young ladies standing before me."

A smile crept across his lips. It held none of the comfort Evalal offered when she smiled, but neither did it suggest menace. His grin sat squarely in between, as though painted by an artist unsure what to do with the mouth. The princess glanced at her companion; if his demeanor set her at unease, she didn't show it.

"Thank you for your concern," Danya responded, "but we have no need of an escort. We appreciate your offer of protection but it's unnecessary."

"I understand how one might believe such to be the case." He lowered his chin, gazed upon them from beneath his brow. "Your response is what I'd expect of someone who has never traveled this road, but you have seen what dangers it can hold. Jon and John are the least of the perils you may encounter. This is a merchants' route, a fact well-known by the lesser element of our society. This is why I travel with Mr. Fellick." Ive leaned forward, spoke in a quieter timbre. "It's not for his social graces and pleasing conversational skills, to be sure."

"We will be safe, Mr. Ive." Danya's tone hardened a degree.

"I'd never forgive myself if Mr. Fellick and I left you to your own devices and ill befell you. Then we'd shoulder the fault as much as the perpetrators."

Heat rose in the princess' cheeks. Part of her—the part experiencing gratitude for Ive's presence having negated the threat to Evalal—thought it might be a good idea for them to have protection. But the other part—the larger part—argued they knew the weapons merchants no better than the twin brigands who'd accosted them. Then pride weighed in. She was the kingdom's princess, trained by the best fighter in the king's army—she needed no one's help.

"We—"

The tall man's smile melted from his face. "Please don't make me insist. I am not enamored with forcing aid on others. It is so much more pleasant to give it to those who accept with grace."

Danya glared at him, the knot in her back making its presence known again. She resisted the urge to roll her shoulder to relieve the pain, using it instead to fuel her anger at the man's suggestion of their inability to take care of themselves. She opened her mouth to speak but stopped when Evalal laid her hand on her forearm. The girl turned away from the weapons merchant, leaned closer to her companion.

"I think we should accept his offer." She spoke in a whisper.

As Danya's brows angled toward the bridge of her nose and the frustration she'd felt at Evalal before the twin brigands appeared returned, a tickle on her leg distracted her. She shifted to assuage the irritation without success. Evalal whispered again before giving her the opportunity to reply.

"Sometimes Goddess makes the path clear."

The irritation in Danya's thigh grew until it became less a sensation and more a vibration. She reached her hand down, meaning to use her touch to calm it, when her fingers encountered the pouch dangling at her belt. She realized the quivering didn't begin in her leg, but emanated from within the doeskin bag. Startled, Danya felt her breath catch in her throat at the realization.

It's trying to communicate. What does it want me to do?

Evalal watched her companion touch the purse. "What does the Seed tell you?"

Danya's resistance and anger dissolved and, for an instant, she forgot the other two people standing with her on the dirt track. Memories flooded her mind: Teryk, the scroll and its prophecy, the Mother of Death and her proclamations. They didn't clarify the meaning of the Seed of Life's vibrations but brought focus to her thoughts; the world needed saving and, like it or not, she'd become linked to it. No matter what it took, accomplishing her tasks—whatever they may be—must be more important to her than everything else.

"We accept your offer, Mr. Ive," she said, her voice cracking. "Please forgive our resistance; sometimes pride stands in the way of common sense. Traveling with you and Mr. Fellick in a wagon full of swords and axes sounds a much safer choice than walking through treacherous areas alone."

The weapons merchant relaxed, the not-quite-a-smile returning to his lips. Danya swallowed hard. Was this the right decision?

"Excellent," he proclaimed with a clap of his hands. "Mr. Fellick will enjoy having someone other than myself for company, I'm sure."

He gestured along the road with a sweep of his arm. Danya turned her attention back to Evalal, found the girl bearing a satisfied expression. The princess moved a step closer to her, leaned in until her lips brushed her ear.

"If you are wrong about your Goddess, this may be the death of us."

Danya bent, retrieved her sword and smock from the dusty road, and started down the track toward the corner ahead where a wain lay hidden, the stocky, formidable man waiting with it. The sensation in her leg ceased, the seed returning to being nothing more than dead weight thumping against her thigh as she walked. Did its quietness mean she'd made the right choice, or she hadn't?

They'd find out soon enough.

III - Trenan - Ikkundana

TREES AND BRUSH CAME to a sudden conclusion, a straight and stark line marking the end of the forest and the beginning of barren ground.

Trenan reined his horse to a halt, and the beast snorted its relief. He'd pushed it hard through the night, an evil air of death chasing them as he fled with Dansil lashed to the saddle behind him. Even in the light of day, the sensation of being pursued remained, but he took time to allow his steed to catch its breath while he surveyed the land stretching out before them.

In the distance, bland, gray walls rose from the parched earth, reaching up toward the sky, never to achieve their goal. They stood featureless and implacable, their lack of windows or murder holes making the slabs of wall more imposing.

"Neither easy to defend nor a pleasure to attack," Trenan muttered. Dansil groaned from his seat behind him on the horse.

The forest ended near a league shy of the fortress, the earth between the last tree and the city of Ikkundana bare and dead—appropriate, by Trenan's estimation. When a past king converted the stronghold to house the sick and dying of the Sisters of the Goddess, they'd hacked away the trees nearest the walls, razed the rest. It left no means to sneak up without detection—a byproduct of its actual intent: to make sure no attempted escape went unnoticed.

Trenan allowed his steed to recover a bit longer as it nibbled at the sparse grass growing along the border between lush forest and dead earth. Anxiety coiled within the muscles of his legs. He knew he should put heels to his horse and cross the dry ground to the fortress ahead, but what man in his right mind went to Ikkundana? A visit to the city of the sick was to invite suffering and death—no way for a lifelong soldier to die. When his time came, he'd decided it should happen with a sword in hand, gazing into the eyes of his killer.

He hauled a deep breath through his nostrils, the smell of this place an odd mix between dusty ground and green foliage. Again he delayed in coaxing his horse to advance.

Why do I need to go there?

A lack of medical aid likely meant Dansil's death. The thought reminded Trenan of the queen's guard leaning against his back and it set his teeth on edge. He didn't enjoy being within eyesight of a man of his ilk, and knowing Ishla's safety fell to him nauseated him further.

I could leave him.

But aid for Dansil wasn't the only reason for visiting Ikkundana. When last he'd seen Danya, she'd been wearing the red robe of the Goddess' sick. But did the vestment mean they'd be taking her to the much-feared city? Too obvious. Had he planned the princess' escape, he'd use the garment to dissuade the curious, to keep anyone from peering beneath the cowl. If he put the robe on Danya's shoulders to flee Draekfarren, he'd make the city of the sick the last place he'd take her.

The master swordsman's eyes narrowed, and he noticed the man leaning against him, his breath stirring the short hairs at the back of Trenan's neck. The touch of both prickled through him, spreading anger and disgust through his body. No one would call the world worse less a fellow of Dansil's character.

Trenan dropped the reins and turned in the saddle, enough movement to displace the queen's guard had he not lashed him in place. All the better—it meant once he loosened the knot, unseating became easy.

His fingers found the first knot and worked the rope. He couldn't see what he was doing and fumbled it, cursed, tried again. He twisted farther, straining to look over his shoulder and past Dansil's waist to lay eyes on the fastening he now wished he hadn't tied so well. It had just loosened in the grip between his forefinger and thumb when a rattle of leaves caught his attention.

The horse nickered and raised its head, ears pricked, and Trenan stopped, held his breath. No wind caressed his cheek, so a breeze didn't cause the sound. He scanned the thicket behind them but saw nothing other than greenery, trunks, and branches at first. His gaze darted from one forest shape to another, tree to bush to rock, until they ran together and other shapes coalesced amongst them: a silhouette in a robe, face hidden in the shadow cast by its cowl, a second figure beside him, this fellow with no legs and one arm.

Without warning, the horse reared and bolted. Trenan reeled, the sudden move throwing him backward, the efficient knots holding Dansil fast the only things between him and a dangerous fall to the ground. He reached forward, grasping for the reins as his steed's hooves beat clouds of dust out of the parched earth. When he found them, he straightened himself in the saddle, regained his equilibrium, but the animal refused to heed his commands to slow its pace. It raced across the bare expanse as though a devil from hell nipped at their heels.

Trenan pivoted, glancing over his shoulder toward the woods they'd left behind, but the dust cloud of their passing choked the air, obscuring any view of the figures he'd spied amongst the trees, leaving him doubtful of their reality. Had Stirk found his way back to hunt him?

Impossible.

The horse thundered across the barren ground, headed straight for the fortress. Its walls grew taller and more imposing as they neared it, the gray surface seeming to swallow the sky. He did his best to calm the frightened animal, trying to coax it into slowing its pace, but his seasons of handling horses did no good. Whatever had scared the steed did so well enough it refused to pay attention to him, ignoring the things for which its trainers raised it.

Trenan hunkered, Dansil's limp form leaning against his back, as he resigned himself to letting the horse run itself out. With two armored men astride the animal, it wouldn't take long.

In no time, they'd crossed half the distance to the city of the sick. The master swordsman lay flat against the horse's neck, the muscles and tendons in his body tense and tight as he compensated for the stallion's erratic gait, the dead weight of Dansil's swaying form throwing it out of true. Trenan kept his eyes straight ahead, saw a flash of sunlight on something metallic. He squinted, resisted the urge to sit upright and peer past the steed's head to figure out what he'd seen.

The animal's long strides gobbled up the distance and the walls loomed before them. Another glint and the sword master thought he spied shapes, but the horse faltered beneath him and his stomach lurched. He gripped the reins tighter, but it didn't matter. The beast's feet tangled, and it fell, throwing Trenan over its head. The swordsman contorted in the air, twisting himself to land on his shoulder. He hit with a crunch of metal and a clack of teeth. The impact jarred through his bones as his armor dug a furrow in the ground and sprayed dirt in his face.

Inertia dissipated and his body settled to a halt. Trenan didn't move at first; few times in his life had a mount thrown him, but it had happened. When you've sat a horse as much as the master swordsman, seen as many battles, you were bound to lose your seat now and again. He'd learned that, unless something threatened your life, it was best to take a moment to assess the damage rather than popping up without consideration.

He unfolded his arm. Pain lanced through the shoulder on which he'd landed, but nothing appeared broken or separated. He sighed a breath from his lungs, his face close enough to the ground for his air to disturb the parched dirt. The discomfort held his scrutiny for a few heartbeats, then he turned his attention to untangling his legs, a feat he accomplished without trouble. He rolled onto his back, eyes closed, and exhaled again, wondered how Dansil fared being both unconscious and tied to the steed. His search for the princess might have proven easier if he'd left the queen's guard lying in a pool of his own lifeblood, but he was a soldier of the king's army. Many turns of the seasons past, Trenan swore an oath he held above everything, a vow by which he lived his life. The pledge included not leaving behind a wounded man. The act of living with honor proved far more difficult some days than others, but perhaps a horse's fear both solved his problem and allowed him to keep his virtue.

Sun warmed the soldier's cheeks and, for a brief instant, he considered lying where he'd landed for a longer time. It felt like an escape from everything: Dansil, Teryk and Danya missing, unrequited love, his severed arm. Dallying offered an added benefit: every passing moment meant Dansil's life was less likely to continue.

Is that any different from leaving him behind to bleed to death in the forest?

To some, it might be, but his age-old sense of duty niggled at his mind again, tightening his chest. None knew the reality of what transpired, but that meant nothing, for honor and character are what one does when no one else knows.

Trenan inhaled and released another deep breath, preparing himself to stand, and opened his eyes to stare at the tips of five pikes.

—ele—

They rode in silence into the shadow of the fortress, a rope round Trenan's wrist tethering him to one of the mounts as he jogged along behind. The horses' hooves clacked on the hardened ground, bouncing back to them from the face of the flat wall. None of them said a word from the moment he realized their presence, but he couldn't fathom how he hadn't heard the approach of the eight soldiers now escorting him toward the City of the Sick. With the walls looming over them, blocking the sun, the temperature cooled and, after a short time for his eyes to adjust, Trenan scanned the colorless surface. No windows, no door, no gates, and no sentries peering from a high parapet. He scowled, unimpressed they'd have to circumnavigate the place to gain access; walking so close to a horse's ass wasn't his preferred style of transportation.

The master swordsman looked over his shoulder, identified the featureless heap that was once his steed lying on the bare ground. He squinted but saw no sign of the queen's guard, so directed his attention back to his footing, not wanting to trip on an unseen rock or clump of weeds because of his own inattention.

"Who are you? What have you done with my companion?"

Referring to Dansil as such set his teeth on edge. He didn't care what had happened to the man, but the silence of his captors weighed on him like a stone. He hoped hearing an explanation might help lift it, though the sound of his own voice did not.

Not one of the helmeted heads so much as tilted in his direction.

They rode on, hooves kicking up dust, armor clattering, their pikes held pointing toward the sky. Whoever these warriors were, they appeared well trained. But from where had they come? Why were they here? And by whom had they been instructed? Their armor bore no marks of local nobility, and they weren't soldiers of the king. Trenan knew the deployment of all the kingdom's army detachments.

Or do I?

He raised his eyes again to the blank wall. Now they were closer, he spied scars made during an ancient battle breaking the wall's uniform smoothness at irregular intervals. No other features marred its surface, as if builders had carved the fortress out of a single great piece of stone. As a military stronghold, Ikkundana was formidable, near impenetrable. How it fell from the army's grasp into the hands of the Goddess worshipers, history had forgotten. It had been so since the time of the Small Gods and no one dared challenge it; no soldier desired to risk their lives for a city full of the diseased.

So why are these soldiers here?

He opened his mouth to demand an explanation, readying the tone he used to get what he wanted from the men in his charge, but stopped short of speaking.

Ahead, a patch of the stone faded to a lighter gray. Anyone else might have overlooked the subtle difference, but so many turns of the seasons training and fighting had honed Trenan's observational powers to a higher level than most—it kept him alive when other men perished. His escorts rode toward it, their captive in tow.

When they drew within the length of ten horses from the fortress, the leader halted his steed, and the others did the same. Trenan continued forward a few more paces, pulling even with the horse to which they'd tied him. The rider atop it leaned his pike over until it touched Trenan's chest, prompting him to stop.

The master swordsman did so, staring ahead at the wall. He doubted he'd have noticed the minute color change if the sun shone on the surface. The uniform edges started at the ground and climbed to the height of three men. Another straight line connected them at the top to form the shape of a gate. Trenan clamped his jaw tight; he'd come here to find the princess and the end of his journey could lie on the other side of the barrier, yet what lurked within might kill him. He didn't recall anyone he'd known going to Ikkundana, certainly no one returning to tell stories of it.

He glanced from wall to riders. None of them moved. If not for the occasional huff from a horse's nose or impatient whip of a tail, they might have been detailed statues fashioned by the most talented of hands.

"What now?" Trenan demanded.

His words fell against stone and died, unheeded by any ears close enough to hear them. He thought of the scars he'd seen on the smooth surface, remnants of attacks gaining no more success than his greeting.

Trenan swept his gaze along the top of the wall, searching for the slightest movement, or a head peering over the edge. A place such as this received infrequent visitors—likely none other than supply deliveries and the ill arriving from every corner of the kingdom. They may not have reason to mistrust him in particular, but he supposed the rarity of strangers explained their wariness of any who approached the refuge.

But who'd come to the City of the Sick without good cause?

He couldn't imagine why anyone might risk disease and death. If not for the possibility of the princess being here, and then his honor demanding his concern for Dansil's miserable life, he'd never have found himself here, either. All of it begged more questions: why did this place need soldiers to guard it? Who were these men who risked their lives guarding the deathly ill? Where did they come from? If the king's command stationed them here, why didn't he know of them?

The distinct sound of rock scraping against rock fell on his ears and the rectangle in the wall ahead of them moved, sinking into the fortress, then shifting to the right, creating an entrance in the barrier. Trenan's eyes widened; he'd never seen such an ingenious system for ingress and egress. The riders started forward, but Trenan stood his ground, legs tight with apprehension at what lay beyond. He'd fought in battles, one on one, and in tournaments, experience making fear a rare emotion in the master swordsman, but he'd stared into the faces of his opponents in each of those situations, known the danger. Disease and sickness were dangers unseen, impossible to fight or prepare a defense against. Since those condemned to Ikkundana were the sickest of the sick, any breath or touch might be deadly.

Trenan wanted to reach for Godsbane's pommel but knew he wouldn't find it where it should be; his sword belt hung from the saddle of the same horse to which they'd tethered him. An instant later, the rope around his wrist tightened, forcing him to follow the rider toward the gap in the wall. His lips pressed into a thin line. From his youth, he'd known he'd likely not die an old man. He'd always imagined coming to his end on a battlefield or at the hand of a swordsman who bettered him in a duel. The thought of dying from an unseen virus had never crossed his mind.

The rider's pace quickened, forcing him to increase the speed of his own steps to faster than a quick walk. His shoulder tensed, the muscles in his arm knotted from the strain of the rope pulling at his wrist. He tried to ignore it, splitting his attention between ensuring his footing and the widened space in the wall. Would a robed woman step into the opening, perhaps wearing a red robe to warn of her sickness? Others must live in Ikkundana to care of the ill. He didn't know how any of them survived living with the mortally sick. Or maybe no one did.

Hoof beats and the song of armor filled his ears, hiding all else from his notice. So it was he wasn't expecting the solitary rider who stepped into the opening in the wall.

The lone horseman's chestnut steed looked bred for carrying an armored man, but the horse itself wore but saddle and blanket with no barding of any kind. The rider's sword remained sheathed as he sat the animal like a veteran, all ease and comfort, but did nothing for a few moments. From behind a visor preventing the master swordsman a glimpse of his features, he surveyed Trenan and his escort leading him to the City of the Sick.

The riders reined up a few horse-lengths short of the new arrival and again, no one spoke. The swordmaster bit hard on his back teeth, the muscles in his jaw flexing. Was Ikkundana filled with mutes?

The solitary soldier dismounted with the clack and thud of leather and mail. Half a dozen strides brought him in front of Trenan where what turned out to be the most diminutive warrior the master swordsman had ever seen tilted his head back to gaze up at him. In other circumstances, their size difference might have girded him; not so much when his foe carried a sword, and he did not. The blade's bite cared not about a man's stature.

The soldier reached up with both hands, grasped the sides of his helmet and removed it. Brown hair fell past the rider's shoulders. Dark, intense eyes bore into Trenan.

A woman!

She glared at him, her mouth curled into a snarl, and he sensed she awaited his reaction. He knew better than to give away his surprise.

"Welcome to Ikkundana, swordmaster Trenan."

The rider spun on her heel, returned to her horse, mounted, and led them behind the walls of the City of the Sick.

Trenan followed.

IV - Teryk - Serpent

To Teryk's eyes, the strip of green perched on the horizon neither grew closer nor drifted farther away. It felt as though the chunk of deck on which they floated awaited the distant shoreline's approach or flight, but the land proved hesitant.

The three men watched, waited for the sea or the shore to make their decisions. No one spoke for an age—Teryk rarely heard the other two draw breath. He endured the silence for as long as possible; when they continued not to speak, he took it upon himself.

"The day is too calm." He looked from one to the other, waiting to gauge their reaction, but neither showed any. Anger rose to his cheeks; he hadn't survived a beating and a ship sinking to die floating atop a piece of wood within sight of land. He bit hard on his back teeth and spoke through his clenched jaw. "We'll never reach the shore if we do nothing."

Still no response. How long floating here before his chance to fulfill the prophecy passed him by? What might happen to the world if the firstborn child of the rightful king died? He fought the urge to stand, yell, jab an accusatory finger toward the listless men. They'd lost their crew, and Rilum his son, so Teryk tried his best to be compassionate, but the effort grated on him. Who mourned a few dead compared to the end of mankind?

"Aye, you have a point," Rilum said after a pause. "But maybe it be for the best."

"For the best?" Teryk's voice rose in volume and pitch as his brows dipped toward his nose. "What do you mean? How can it be for the best?"

The prince cast his attention to the surrounding ocean, lips pressed tight as he searched for a reason for the sailor's response. He spied nothing but the hint of green on the horizon ahead and the endless sea everywhere else.

Did Rilum know something he didn't? If so, he in no way acted eager to give up his secret. Frustrated, Teryk forced his rage back into his chest, cleared his throat, and made another attempt.

"What are you talking about?" He faced the other man. "Captain, what does he mean?"

Bryder stared straight ahead, face slack, eyes hollow. His lips parted, quivered. Teryk's frustration and anger wound themselves into a ball in his gut as he realized the man wore an expression he'd never seen on the old seaman, not even during the rageful storm. He held his eyelids wide open, and he chewed his nails without appearing to realize he did so. The unexpected shore lying on the horizon appeared to have spooked the lifelong sailor.

"That..." Bryder spoke in little more than a whisper, then paused and swallowed hard, the saliva clicking in his dry throat as if the one word had taxed him. "...Is the land across the sea."

Teryk's gaze snapped back to the green strip; it suddenly appeared menacing despite the distance between their bit of wood and the shore.

"We've gotten turned about." The prince shifted, craned his neck to peer over his shoulder, and set the makeshift raft rocking. He saw nothing but ocean around them before returning his gaze to find both the other survivors staring at him. His voice trembled as he spoke again. "Home lies ahead of us. We're saved."

"Calm yerself or we'll end up in the sea again," Rilum growled.

"But maybe it's home, right? You might be mistaken."

Bryder shook his head before Teryk finished speaking.

"Can't a landlocked fool see where the sun hangs in the sky? Don't you recognize we're past midday? The sun is to port; if the Windward Kingdom lay ahead, you'd find sunset to starboard."

"Go easy on the lad, Rilum." The captain's quiet voice lacked the authority Teryk had become used to hearing in it.

The prince watched Rilum's face redden, his eyes narrow, before he replied.

"Easy?" he blurted. "I lost my son. You, your ship and crew. The worst stroke of luck ever to strike the Whalebone with but one thing different on this voyage from every other." He raised his arm, extended a finger toward Teryk. "This lying whelp."

The sailor's accusation sent nervous and fearful energy prickling across the prince's skin. He opened his mouth to protest without having a clue what he might say, but Bryder interrupted, relieving him of the burden.

"He's no more to blame than you or me, Rilum. Leave him be."

Teryk watched the seaman's glare slip from him to the captain. The prince had become accustomed to reading angry expressions after dealing with his own father for so long, and he saw more reflected in the sailor's eyes: the grief of losing his son, his friends.

"If it's not his fault for being bad luck, who else is to blame?" His words carried the sting of a whip, emotion dripping from each syllable.

"What are you saying?"

Rilum's lip curled. "You know what I'm saying. If you can't blame luck, blame the skipper."

Bryder's sudden, explosive anger pushed him to his feet, a movement made more difficult than expected by the listing of the raft and his wooden foot left askew, its support not in the location he'd anticipated. Rilum Seaman jumped up in response, too, sending the raft's delicate balance out of true. The chunk of deck tilted and Teryk lunged to his right, pressed himself against the wood, as the other men lurched over the side.

Frigid water splashed against the prince's skin, his muscles going taut as he prepared to plunge into the sea again. Instead of flipping, the sudden displacement of the other men's weight sent the raft slapping back against the ocean, jerking a shock through Teryk's cheek where it contacted the wood and jarred his head. It stunned him for an instant and he lay chest down until the chunk of deck settled.

Behind him, splashing and shouts boiled up out of the sea. The prince blinked, stared at the spot where his face rested, taking in its grain, jagged splinters protruding in places, a black mark where flame had burned its surface. He released his frightened breath from his chest and pushed himself up on his elbows.

As the noise suggested, the other two survivors of the Whalebone grappled in the water. Whether out of anger or in an attempt to help each other out of the sea, Teryk didn't know. He dragged himself across the chunk of deck toward the edge nearest them, careful not to upset his haven's balance. A sliver inserted itself into his right hand. He jerked away, breaking the embedded piece of wood off, breath hissing between his teeth.

A drop of blood welled up around it and he resisted the urge to put the tip of his finger in his mouth.

"Stop it, both of you."

He moved toward the side closest to the men, but without their weight to counterbalance his, the raft lurched again. Teryk flattened himself against the chunk of wood once more, legs spread behind him, arms thrown wide before him. His hands extended right to the edge of the deck, fingers wrapping around it as the ripples and waves created by Bryder and Rilum Seaman splashed against them. Brine stung the small wound where the sliver remained lodged in his finger.

The other survivors continued their struggle, each grabbing the other by their shirt front. They pulled and pushed, each one occasionally dunking the other under the water to come out sputtering a few heartbeats later. Teryk thought he might have found the scene humorous if it weren't for the fact they represented his best chance of surviving. If they brought about each other's demise, he'd float alone on the sea with no way to make shore and no hope of fulfilling the destiny laid out for him in the ancient scroll. He inched himself closer to the edge, the muscles in his jaw clenching as the raft listed farther.

He glanced back over his shoulder at the green strip on the horizon. Bryder and Rilum thought it the land across the sea—and who was he to dispute their navigation skills? They'd spent their lives using the sky to find their way while the prince sometimes got lost in the castle he'd lived in since the day of his birth—then fate pointed him in the right direction. He'd learned the prophecy possessed its own plans for how things should occur, despite what he may think he should do.

Teryk turned back toward the others, pulled himself closer to the edge, muscles tensing, knotting as the chunk of deck tilted a little more. Bryder shouted sailorly obscenities at Rilum, and the sailor responded, words garbled by seawater splashing into his mouth. He coughed, spat, dunked his captain's head beneath the surface and held him under.

"My only son," Rilum said. The captain's arms thrashed, fighting to emerge. "First the sea took my father, and now my only son."

Panic tied Teryk's gut into a tight knot. His mind flashed back to the day he and Danya found the scroll, when he'd gotten caught under the grate at the bottom of the river beneath the castle. His body recalled the alarm of needing to draw a breath but knowing doing so meant his death. Did

Bryder experience the same distress? The prince's air grew short, as though it was him unable to breathe; anxiety burned in his limbs and chest. He pulled himself closer to the edge, the raft tilting enough his arms slid into the water halfway to his elbows.

The tilt of the piece of deck redirected his gaze away from his fellow survivors and toward the sea. A flash of color near his hands caught his attention.

Fish.

Half a dozen finger-sized ocean dwellers maneuvered around him, fighting to find space. Fascinated by the reds, blues, yellows, and greens of their scales, the swishing movement of their fins and tails, Teryk forgot the two men struggling in the water. He wondered if the shape of the raft floating above their home drew these types of fish out of hiding. In response to his thoughts, he felt a smooth, toothless mouth brush against his fingertip. Such a gentle touch shouldn't have hurt, but it sent a mild jolt along his nerves—the little creatures attempted to feed at his wound.

They're attracted by my blood.

The realization yanked the prince from his distraction. He raised his chin, looked toward Rilum and Bryder.

The sailor had released his captain's head, and the skipper blustered and coughed, spewing equal parts seawater and profanity from his lips. As he watched them continue their pointless struggle, fear rose in Teryk, filling his chest and flowing into his limbs. He jerked his hands out of the water, setting the raft rocking.

If blood attracts small fish, what else might it attract?

His head filled with an image of the God of the Deep rising out of the waves to sink the Whalebone and his breath caught.

"Get out," he said, the fear in his chest turning to terror and squeezing his lungs so the words came out but a gasp.

He swallowed hard, cleared his throat and opened his mouth to warn them again. A shape broke the ocean's surface behind Rilum and Bryder a mere three horse-lengths from them. Sunlight flashed on smooth, gray skin as the coil of a monstrous serpent pulled through the water. It ended in a pointed tail flicking droplets of sparkling spray into the air before disappearing beneath the sea.

"Get out," Teryk screamed, finding his voice. "Get out now!"

The two men ceased their watery squabble and directed their attention toward their companion. He waved his arms, frantic to get them moving and out of the water. He didn't know if they'd find safety on the raft, but it must be better than being in the sea with whatever monstrosity lurked beneath the surface. Despite his efforts to make them realize the danger, they both merely stared at him.

"Something's after you," he shouted, beckoning them.

Bryder half-smiled and waved a dismissive hand, as if to say a land-bound stowaway didn't understand what the sea held. He'd captained a ship since before Teryk took his first breath. But the captain hadn't seen the slick, gray coil, nor the way the smaller fish so greedily consumed his lifeblood. Might the ocean around this foreign place hold things a seasoned sailor never dreamed of?

Rilum appeared to take Teryk's warning at face value, or he no longer wanted to be near his skipper. He drew one hand out of the water, threw it over his head scattering sparkling droplets in the sunshine, then plunged it into the brine, stroking toward Teryk and the chunk of ruined deck.

"Coward." Bryder splashed water at the other man the way Teryk might have done to his sister as children playing in the river.

The captain leaned back, floating atop the salty sea with his eyes directed upward to the cloudless sky. The panic in Teryk's gut coalesced with a familiar frustration he'd felt so often when speaking to his father. How many times had he wanted to tell the king things, only to experience dismissal the same way he did now at the hands of the captain? More than he'd ever hope to count.

Rilum reached the edge of the last surviving bit of the Whalebone, leaned against it. Teryk flattened himself against the wood before realizing he'd need to help the man out of the water. The prince inched back toward the middle of the piece of deck, got to his knees and held out a hand. The sailor grasped it, using the assistance to leverage himself up and onto the raft. It bobbed and rocked under his weight but Teryk kept his position. With Seaman safely aboard and the chunk of wood settled, Teryk clambered back to the side.

Bryder continued floating in the same place, gazing skyward without a care in the world. For an instant, the prince's frustration waned. The captain had lost his entire crew; the prince couldn't imagine how it must weigh upon the man. If anyone deserved respite, Captain Bryder did.

Beyond the captain's prone form, the water swelled.

Teryk's eyes widened and panic flooded through his body. He waved his arms above his head, opened his mouth, but his voice refused to issue the warning perched at the back of his throat. The swell moved toward the skipper, the smooth coil closing in on him without his knowledge. The prince slapped his hand against the water, hoping to draw Bryder's attention. It didn't work, but it brought Rilum to the edge of the raft.

The chunk of wood tilted under his weight, making Teryk think he'd plunge into the sea with the beast stalking Bryder. Rilum Seaman stopped short of the side, a man used to where to place his feet when afloat on the ocean.

"Bryder!" he called in a deep and booming tone.

Teryk watched the captain turn his head the direction of the sailor's voice. A shadow fell across the prince and he knew without looking Rilum had raised his arm to point at the creature. The swell lengthened, grew, drew closer to the floating man. Bryder looked to the spot where Rilum indicated, saw the ridge of water moving toward him, and rolled onto his front, stroked for the raft.

The prince got to his knees, the chunk of deck tilting precariously. Rilum shifted to keep his footing, placed his hand on Teryk's shoulder, no doubt expecting the normally land-bound lad to have trouble staying put. Truthfully, if the man hadn't steadied him, Teryk would have ended up in the sea with Bryder.

The captain splashed in the water, legs throwing droplets high in the air. The block of wood he wore as a foot proved an ineffective flipper, slowing his progress toward the chunk of the Whalebone's deck. Rilum crouched, held his arms out to his captain.

"Hurry. It's closing on you."

Teryk glanced passed the struggling man. A snout broke through the surface of the water at the leading edge of the swell. Two black eyes stared out of the wide, flat head. A mouth split it from one side to the other, rows of sharp teeth lining both the top and bottom jaws. A menacing thing, but not the God of the Deep he'd seen tear the Whalebone apart; this thing appeared a worm in comparison, but big enough to pose a mortal threat.

Bryder closed on the raft as the creature edged closer to him, the two of them locked in a race for their goals. Rilum shouted at his captain, exhorting to go faster, to swim harder. Teryk watched, transfixed by the captain's struggle as compared to the smooth ease with which the animal cut through the ocean. Despite the many turns of the seasons he'd spent commanding ships floating on the turquoise brine, he was no more made to be in it than a bird or a horse. His arms splashed, the shape of his body slowed his progress, he fought to draw air into his lungs. Behind him, closing fast, the sea creature opened its mouth. Streaming water cascaded past sharp teeth, over a pointed tongue.

The length of three men separated the captain from the raft. Teryk shook himself from the beastly distraction and leaned over the edge, held out a hand for Bryder to grab. The fingertips of his other scraped against the wood, digging for purchase to keep him from tumbling into the sea.

The tips of their fingers brushed, and the captain ceased swimming, concentrating instead on grabbing one of his rescuers' hands. The sudden stoppage pushed his head under the surface and he swallowed a mouthful of the briny water, then resurfacing, sputtering and coughing. He waved his arms, reaching out, desperate for someone to save him.

Teryk caught hold of his left hand as Rilum nabbed the other. The prince leaned back, eyes closed, pulling as hard as his position allowed without slipping off the chunk of wood, but the water-logged sailor weighed as much as a war horse. The sounds of thrashing and splashing assaulted Teryk's ears. He bit down, the muscles in his jaw knotting. A grunt escaped his throat as the captain cried out; Rilum called out his name, an unsettling tone in his voice making Teryk not want to open his lids.

Somehow, the skipper jerked back as though trying to escape their grasp. The action threatened to pull the prince off balance, but he held on and kept from being yanked off the raft. He dug his heels in, pulled harder. This time, Bryder slid so easily from the sea, Teryk fell over backward still holding onto the captain's hand. He lay on his back listening as the turmoil of churned water dissipated, his own heavy breath loud in his ears. He opened his eyes, sat up, parted his lips to ask the captain if he was all right.

The words died on his tongue. Nothing but a pink streak in the sea and the arm attached to the hand Teryk held remained of Captain Bryder. He stared at it for an instant before panic seized him. With a jerk of his wrist, he cast the disembodied limb away and scuffled backward from it, desperate to distance himself from the appendage.

The raft tilted, his palm reached the edge, slipped off it, and Teryk tumbled into the deadly sea.

V - Horace - Alone

*M*ORE O' THE STREAKS o' light shot across the nighttime sky. It might've been pretty to get a peek at if it weren't for the fact they was ancient baddies fallin' to the earth.

Horace did his best to keep pace with Ivy but even her short, little legs carried her faster than his ol', tired ones. It seemed like ev'ry step he stumbled o'er a bit o' branch fallen from a tree or a rock what found his toe. None of 'em made him hit the ground, but they sure as hell did a fine job o' slowin' him down.

"Ivy," he called after her, but the wind whippin' through the trees took his voice and tossed it away.

They was closer to the glowin' green o' the veilish barrier and he began wonderin' what they'd do when they arrived. Ivy must've had a plan o' some sort, 'cause this'd been where they was headed, windstorm or no.

But why did she call out the name o' her brother?

Maybe she thought he'd summoned the sudden breeze. Horace'd seen the little feller do some unusual stuff when they was travelin' together, but he hadn't a recollection about no wind caused by him. Didn't make it impossible, and he figured she must know her own kin better'n him, but he still didn't think it proved nothin'.

The ol' sailor struggled o'er a log and paused on the other side. He leaned against the fallen piece o' tree, hand restin' in a cool, soft patch o' moss as he stopped to catch his air. He watched Ivy continue on ahead o' him, the muscles in her bare, gray buttocks flexing with ev'ry step she took.

Why don't them little folk use their magic to make themselves some breeches?

He sucked in a heavy breath, hopin' it'd bring energy to his legs the way the girl's touch did, then started out after her again, cursin' to himself. His limbs gave him immediate grief, knots startin' in his calves and workin' their way up; he pushed on anyway, forcin' one foot in front o' the other though he knew Ivy took three steps or more for ev'ry one he did. He begged them to move quicker lest the small one get too far ahead, but it seemed all the stress and strain o' the time what'd passed since the dunce Dunal put him o'er the side o' the Devil filled him with rocks now.

His gut flipped at the memory o' what he'd done to the poor feller in the name o' savin' his own skin. And look where it'd got him. He hated his life upon the sea, but at least he'd known what it were and what people expected o' him. Now, he didn't know if he'd survive from sunrise to sunset and back.

The brush grew thick as he neared the veil o' green and his feet became tangled in the runners and creepers, the branches and twigs. At first they slowed him, but then they stopped him, as though the forest itself made a grab for him, not wantin' him to go on. He did his best to pull free, but the tight grip o' the plants got the better o' him and he tumbled to the ground.

Horace landed with a *whoof* o' breath what might've come outta some dog's mouth. Weren't no dog around, though—least he hoped not—so he knew the sound must've been his own. He followed up the realization by tryin' to breathe in but didn't have no success with doin' so. The rocks what'd been weighin' down his limbs seemed like they spilled into his chest, cloggin' it to keep air from findin' it's way in.

Panic surged through the ol' sailor, settin' the hairs on his arms and the back o' his neck on their ends, makin' his skin all prickly. The thought o' gettin' to his feet passed through his mind without a second look as he concentrated on breathin' again instead. He lay on his front, elbows pressed into deep loam, its moisture soaking through his sleeves, as he wheezed and hacked. If anyone'd come across him, they'd like have assumed he'd eaten a big chunk o' pork what'd got stuck in his throat. He felt his eyes bulgin' and his cheeks goin' hot and worried this might be the end and he'd never draw another breath again.

But such weren't the case. It took a while, but some air squeaked through his windpipe and into his chest. The little gasp of it offered the tiniest bit o' relief from the terror o' death takin' him away from the world. He gulped more air down his throat, lungs thankful he did so and its presence forcin' them exhaustion rocks out and back into his arms and legs. Didn't so much like them there, either, but at least havin' limbs full o' that weighty feelin' weren't goin' to kill him.

Down near the ground, the air tasted o' moss and dirt, held the flavor o' long decayed needles and leaves, a hint o' death what hid from his eyes. Some part of it he liked more'n he'd ever liked the scent o' the briny sea, but somethin' else in it made his toes curl and his nostrils flare. Couldn't place a finger on exactly what it were, but didn't really want to, neither.

When his breathin' returned to a reasonable approximation o' normalcy, Horace got himself up and outta the brush, pushin' himself to stand on wobbly legs. His heart beat hard in his chest, knockin' against his ribs with a desperate rhythm like it tried to find its way out. Bendin' at his waist, he rested his hands on his knees and stared down at his feet while he sucked in the forest air and did his best to convince the fast-beatin' thing not to bust out. To him, it seemed to take about as much time to calm the racin' muscle as it had for him to regain his breath after the fall. The two might've been related, he guessed, but it weren't important.

He straightened up and sighed, happy to be breathin' and possessin' what might pass for a regular heartbeat. The relief lasted for the brief time it took his eyes to scan the forest ahead o' him and find it empty o' his gray-skinned companion.

"Ivy?"

He took one step then stopped, unsure if he'd picked the right direction. The ol' sailor cocked his head back, searchin' through the leaves and boughs hangin' o'er him, seekin' the sun to give a little help. It stayed hidden, and the shimmery green curtain what kept him trapped in this place appeared to be in a different spot than it'd been when he fell.

Did I get turned about when I stumbled?

He spun a tight circle, one foot firm on the ground while the other propelled him around. Trees, leaves, bushes, the veil to his right instead of the left where he expected to find it. Nowhere did he spy a gray derriere in need o' a pair o' breeches. A shiver shook his spine and chattered his teeth.

"Ivy?"

He spoke her name louder, but the word fell off the end o' his tongue and tumbled to the forest floor, floppin' once or twice before dyin' amongst the ferns. No answer from Thorn's sister, nor from the trunks o' the trees surroundin' him or the sky hangin' somewhere up above. He sighed and did his best to suppress the tremor seekin' to make its way into his arms and shoulders. He'd already spent enough time alone in this place, waitin' for some animal to devour him or them faceless things to find him and grind his flesh against their fleshy mouths. Neither appealed to him, and he hadn't worried about them when he walked with Ivy beside him.

With no other option, he positioned himself to put the translucent green wall to his port side, where he thought it oughta be, and set himself to trekkin' again. He hoped for the little gray one to eventually realize she'd left him behind and come back for him. Accordin' to her, he were part o' some prophecy; she couldn't let him die.

Could she?

Horace shuddered and wished the God o' the Deep'd decided to eat him instead of draggin' him ashore.

VI - Teryk - Swimming

*T*ERYK SAT IN THE center of the raft, knees pulled up to his chest, uncontrollable shivers shaking his spine and rattling his teeth at irregular intervals. He stared at the spot where the creature took Bryder, at the disembodied limb lying near the edge of the chunk of the Whalebone's deck—the last remains of the captain perched on the final remnant of his ship. Rilum had been quick to pull the prince from the sea when he fell in, but neither of them hurried to venture back to the raft's edge, or to touch Bryder's arm.

Though he'd been concentrating on saving the captain and hadn't seen the beast's teeth sink into the man's flesh, Teryk couldn't help imagining it. The ragged end of the captain's arm and a splash of red soiling the deck painted a picture in his mind of dagger-like fangs flashing in the sun, blood spurting, shimmering as if streams of liquid rubies. The ocean had long absorbed any trace of him, and neither he nor Rilum spoke in the time since, except when the prince thanked him for pulling him out of the sea. His last remaining companion didn't respond and the silence between them reigned so complete, he wondered if the sailor might have slipped over the edge when he wasn't watching.

Worried, Teryk suppressed the latest quake threatening to jar his bones and diverted his eyes from the empty sea and to his right.

Rilum Seaman knelt in the spot where he'd plucked the prince from the ocean, but he didn't gaze where Teryk had been. Instead of staring at the macabre remnant of their captain or scanning the water for signs of the thing that killed Bryder, he peered over his shoulder, looking toward the land across the sea. He wore an expression so intense it compelled the prince to do the same.

He craned his neck, tight muscles threatening to cramp. The pain disappeared when he realized what so captured his companion's attention.

The prince gaped. How had they come so much closer than before?

It must have happened when the sea creature took the captain. Its emergence and subsequent disappearance created the largest wave they'd seen since the end of the storm, pushing them nearer to shore as they mourned their friend. The lush green shoreline stood tantalizingly close yet, with a deadly monster lurking in the depths, the space seemed as insurmountable as if it remained a mere dot on the horizon. Short of washing up on the beach, any distance requiring they enter the water where the ravenous beast lurked was too far away by Teryk's estimation.

As if he'd heard the prince's thoughts, Rilum shifted himself around to face the land perched on the near horizon, mocking them with its proximity. He struggled to his feet, listing and leaning, setting the chunk of deck rocking under his shifting weight. The movement forced the prince to place his palms against the wood to steady himself. Bryder's severed arm rolled nearer to the edge.

"What are you doing?"

"Fuck this," Rilum spat. "I'd rather die in the sea than stay floatin' here until I wither away to nothin'."

He shuffled a half-step closer to the brink and drew a deep breath.

"Rilum—"

Before Teryk spoke further, the sailor lunged forward, belly-flopping into the ocean. Water splashed, and the chunk of deck tilted without Rilum's weight for counterbalance. The prince collapsed, spreading himself flat against the rough wood. The raft lurched, and he pressed himself flatter until the tilting diminished. He remained stationary, not wanting to raise his head and find a toothy creature making a meal out of the last man he might ever see alive.

The rhythmic splashes of a swimmer floated through the afternoon air. Teryk steeled himself, awaiting Rilum's scream as dagger teeth tore into his flesh. He waited. And waited.

The screams didn't come.

By the time the prince raised his head, his shipmate had covered more than half the distance to the shore. Incredulous, Teryk propped himself up on his elbows to watch.

Droplets splashed and sparkled in the sunlight; Rilum's kicking churned the ocean white in his wake, spreading ripples out across the water behind him. Teryk's gaze strayed from the man, following along the line of waves he produced. They reminded him of the creature and the captain's screams; he shuddered.

Other than the shallow swells created by the sailor's escape from the raft, the surface remained smooth and peaceful.

Is the sea ever this calm?

Nowhere did he spy the hump of water pushed ahead of an onrushing serpent. No fish leapt, no gulls wheeled. Everything appeared as though the entire world ignored the sailor swimming toward the shore. Teryk gulped a mouthful of saliva. Left alone on the raft. Survive or die, his choice.

If his future included surviving to fulfill his destiny predicted by the scroll, he must follow Rilum's lead.

He inhaled, tasting salt on the air as he continued watching his companion's progress. His mind knew he should stand, dive in, and follow Rilum to safety, but his limbs disagreed. He remained in place, picturing himself standing, preparing, launching himself from the chunk of deck into the sea. During his life, he'd only swam in the river under the castle and lakes near his home until he found himself submerged during the storm. The thought of it returned the salty taste of brine to his tongue, and his throat closed. His last two times in the water had both come close to costing him everything.

"I'll die if I stay here." *I may die if I leave.*

He scanned the ocean around Rilum, between him and the shore, but spied nothing unusual. Teryk shut his eyes, pictured himself swimming, sun sparkling on droplets thrown up by his hard-working arms. He imagined himself trudging onto land, water streaming from his clothes. Trenan had spent many sessions teaching him the visualization technique, but he rarely remembered to use it. Perhaps this time it might prove its usefulness.

He sighed again, filling his lungs to capacity before letting his breath go all at once. He repeated this over and over, searching for courage in the salty air, but his search proved fruitless. One did not find the virtue of bravery externally, but within, and it pained him to realize he lacked this ideal at the most important times.

Rilum continued splashing shoreward, his strokes as strong now as when he'd first plunged in. Teryk wondered if he'd have the same stamina to make it to land. Pondering it made the shore appear farther away, and doubt crept into his mind. The choice belonged to him: did he prefer to die on the raft or in the sea?

"I haven't died yet."

He shook his head, attempting to dislodge his fear. After being stabbed, left for dead in a crate at the docks, threatened with being thrown overboard as a stowaway, and surviving the raging storm when everyone else perished, how could he imagine himself not protected by an unseen source? It had been so his entire life if he took time to reflect. Like any other youth, he'd placed himself in many precarious situations, maybe more than most, given the adventurous nature of his sister. He'd survived with nary a scratch, and the same held true now.

Did his presence in the prophecy ensure his survival? Whatever hand inscribed those archaic words also plucked him from danger when required and set him on his necessary path.

I have courage in me.

He gritted his teeth, glanced back over his shoulder to make sure the sea behind him remained as free of deadly serpents as the water ahead of him appeared, and gasped a shocked breath into his lungs. In his concern for Rilum and his own life, he hadn't noticed his foot touching the captain's severed arm.

Without consideration, Teryk kicked at it, sending the limb spinning across the piece of deck and over the edge into the sea. He scrabbled to his feet, took a quick step forward, and jumped. He slipped on the wet wood, and he entered the water ungracefully, the surface slapping his face with the force and shock of the open hand of a jealous lover. The cold penetrated him at once, forced the sting from his flesh.

With his head underwater, panic flashed through the prince, his body recalling the struggle in the stormy sea. It held on a few extra heartbeats after he resurfaced an instant later, gasping for air with the voracity of a man deprived for far longer than he had been. Satisfied with his ability to breathe without having to fight to fill his lungs, his racing heart slowed, and he set himself to stroking toward shore.

In his youth, both Trenan and Danya—who'd learned to swim at a much earlier age than he—attempted to teach him the proper method to ensure the most efficient use of one's energy while swimming. It involved keeping your face in the water and exposing it to draw breath every few strokes. Try as he might, Teryk had never mastered the technique. His lungs despised any attempt at holding his air. He found it easy when diving under the surface, or with his face out of the sea, but not how it suited his present needs best. For whatever reason, attempting to do so brought on extreme agitation.

So Teryk swam, head tilted back, and noticed he no longer saw Rilum Seaman as he had when standing on their raft. He thought he detected the wake left by his passing, but couldn't be sure. Now submerged in the sea, it didn't seem so calm as before.

The prince stretched his neck to peer over his shoulder, scanning the watery expanse behind him for the piece of deck which saved their lives. A gentle roll of waves had developed, alternately hiding the chunk of wood from him the same way it kept Rilum from his line of sight, then heaving it into view. He noted something else in the water beside it. At first, this presence concerned him, but he soon realized what it must be: Captain Bryder's arm.

Seeing it again caused a twinge in his chest. Grief? Regret? He hadn't known him well, but he must have been a good man to rise to the rank he did. As he stroked and thought about it, Teryk understood it wasn't a sense of loss causing the feeling behind his ribs. A memory floated into his head, mimicking the limb floating on the sea, and he recalled the sliver in his finger, blood in the water, the way it attracted fish.

Teryk's eyes widened. His strokes faltered.

Where did these waves come from?

He returned his attention to the shore ahead and the task of reaching it. His breaths came in short bursts as his arms plunged into the increasing swells. The nature of the sea remained mysterious to him, but he guessed sudden and unpredictable changes might be the norm. The thought did nothing to quell the sliver of panic inserting itself in his chest.

The shore—more accurately, the line of trees beginning after the ocean ended—appeared no closer than before. To keep from losing heart, he diverted his focus away from his goal and the creatures potentially finding their way to dine on Bryder's arm, instead counting his strokes. He decided on forty as the right number to complete before directing his gaze landward again.

He concentrated on the count, resisting the compulsion to gauge his progress or look back. The effort of swimming returned the pain and tightness to his shoulders, and doubt about his ability to make it to shore crept into him. He knew the shortness of his breathing contributed to this fatigue, but struggled to slow his inhalations.

Thirty-eight. Thirty-nine. Forty.

The waves grew, though they remained but rolling bumps of water. As he rose on one, he glimpsed Rilum stumbling out of the ocean and onto the shore. A measure of relief flowed through him—if his companion made it, then he could, too. He returned his attention to counting his strokes.

One. Two. Three.

Seeing the sailor drag himself out of the sea shot a dose of energy back into Teryk's limbs, and the second forty count passed quicker than the first. After completing the final stroke of the set, he looked shoreward again, found it noticeably closer. The recognition encouraged him, brought warmth to his cold and tired body. Feeling it increased his confidence, girded him into believing in his ability to reach his goal.

Forty strokes went by so quickly, he didn't stop, instead continuing to sixty.

When he raised his head the third time, he'd gotten close enough he estimated two more counts of forty before his feet touched bottom. If he held on until he counted to sixty last time, perhaps he'd hold out until eighty the next and finish with this swim. Before returning to the count, he spied Rilum on the beach waving his arms in the air.

At first, it seemed he meant the movement as simple encouragement, like he thought the action might make the prince move more swiftly through the water. He'd have continued thinking this the case if not for the strained expression twisting the sailor's face. Teryk stopped stroking and kicking and, with the near silence of the open sea falling around him, heard Rilum's voice, small and distant.

"Behind you! Hurry!"

A jolt coursed through Teryk and he jerked around in the water, sending a fresh ripple of waves rolling away from him, their momentum negated by larger ones rippling toward him.

A coil of smooth, green flesh slid along the surface of the sea before disappearing back into the depths.

Teryk turned for shore, paddling and thrashing with every scrap of his strength to save his life.

VII - Trenan - In the City

*A*s *Trenan suspected,* the streets of the City of the Sick lay empty. The quiet became an oppressive force weighing on him as he sat where they'd left him lashed to a wooden chair set against a blank, white wall. He gulped a shallow inhalation, not wanting to draw the air of Ikkundana into his lungs, but each tentative sip of breath proved fresh and clean. He imagined the same wasn't true of the chambers hidden within the surrounding walls. What atrocities might he find should he wander the dim-lit halls? He pictured desiccated bodies wasted away to living skeletons, weeping sores, rheumy eyes, pus and blood and puke. The thought made his stomach roil, gave him and appreciation for being bound outside in the silence.

Are you here hidden among the sick, princess?

The question sent a shiver along his spine. He doubted the possibility of someone hiding amongst the infected—or being held—for any length of time without becoming ill themselves. The red robe worn by Danya suggested Ikkundana may have been her destination, but it proved nothing. Part of him hoped it was because it meant the end of his quest drew near, but he also didn't want her to have to be in this place. Either way, he blamed Dansil for his current predicament. If he hadn't needed to carry the near-lifeless queen's guard, he'd not have ended up here.

He didn't know what they'd done with the man, whether he'd survived or perished. With any luck, he'd met his end. That, too, might complicate his life given the man's threat of revealing his secret. Considering his position tied to a chair with no real clue who his captors were, the master swordsman had more pressing issues, though.

It made sense there'd be people in the city who weren't sick. He harbored no desire for the job himself, but someone needed to take care of the ill and dying. Why have armed soldiers, even if only women? Ikkundana was likely the most impenetrable fortress in existence and filled with those no one wanted to confront; why waste resources protecting those who didn't need protection?

Past midday now and the sun sloped between the walls, shining on Trenan and causing sweat on his brow. A bead of water rolled from his temple and along his cheek; he longed to wipe it away but the knots they'd used to secure him to the chair held firm. Instead of fighting against it, he tilted his head back, resting it against the wall behind him, and let his lids slide closed. The sun's warmth on his face threatened to make him forget his predicament—the rope binding him, the missing prince and princess, the love he could never reveal. If only after closing his eyes he might open them again onto a world where these problems didn't exist, a world where he was home, with his lover at his side, and their children safe. A world without deceit and lies, a world with two arms.

Trenan sighed, opened his eyes, and lowered his chin. The three women standing before him startled him into gasping his air back into his chest.

"How...?"

"Be quiet, swordsman. No one has requested you to speak."

He recognized her as the rider who'd met him and the squad who captured him at the gate, the dark intensity of her eyes unmistakable. She gestured and the other two women moved forward. One placed the point of her pike within a hair's width of his throat while the other crouched and untied the knots binding him to the chair. As they loosened, the blood flow return to his hand and feet. He curled his fingers into a fist and released it, flexing them while being careful not to move his body and risk the pike's tip pricking his flesh. When the ropes were undone, the second woman stepped back and brought her own weapon to bear on him, too. Trenan directed his gaze toward the leader and waited.

"Goddess has brought you to us. It may be part of her plan, but it doesn't mean we must welcome you." She crossed her arms, exhaled. "Stand."

Each of the pikewomen took a step away, giving him space to obey her command without opening a vein in his throat. He did so, wiped sweat from his brow with the back of his hand. The leader stood taller than the others, and the way she held herself suggested not merely pride and a touch of defiance but spoke of more than a little training. But how was it possible for a woman to learn the arts of war in the Windward Kingdom without Trenan's knowledge?

The answer came on the heels of the question: she didn't learn her craft in the Windward Kingdom.

How did their enemies infiltrate so far into their homeland?

The woman's gaze roamed to his feet and back up again, resisting like a thing dragged against its well. Upon completion, one side of her upper lip curled in an undisguised expression of disgust.

"I do not deign to know Goddess' mind, but this..." She pursed her lips and spat on the ground as though attempting to expel something she found distasteful. She didn't finish her sentence, didn't need to say more. Instead, she spun on her heel and strode along the avenue, turning her head to cast a final word over her shoulder. "Come."

The pikewomen responded in unison as if they'd practiced many times. One stepped back, moving her weapon from his path but keeping it close to the side of his neck. The other shifted hers behind him, tapping him on the shoulder blades with the shaft and prompting him to follow. He did as they wanted, doubtful they'd hesitate in skewering him if he did not.

The woman leading them walked five paces ahead, her leather armor creaking and her boots crunching on the pebbles spread across the road. Hearing this, and the steps of the women behind them, Trenan wondered how they'd crept up on him before. Could it be he'd fallen asleep?

Impossible.

Too much training and too many desperate situations had squelched any possibility of unplanned dozing from him long ago. No, something had aided them in their stealth.

They traversed the streets in silence. No one watched their passing from high windows, no pedestrians, horses, or wagons shared the avenues with them. The woman led them, walking with confidence as she took corners and navigated roundabouts. Trenan didn't bother to glance back to confirm the business ends of the two pikes remained directed at him; he practically felt their pointed tips pricking his flesh. The softness of their tread made them stealthy warriors, but did they know how to wield the weapons they held? Their stances and bearing suggested yes, but many men believed females weren't meant to take lives, only to give them—as mothers, nurses, caregivers. Trenan didn't count himself amongst those who agreed with this opinion; he'd seen Danya's skills grow beyond her brother's too quick to doubt other women might not possess the same capability.

By the time they rounded a fifth corner, Trenan's patience wore thin.

"Where are you taking me?"

The lead woman stopped, turned, and closed the distance between them with a swiftness to her pace. Trenan considered taking a backward step, but he assumed doing so meant the tip of a pike or two penetrating his flesh. She halted a hand's breadth in front of him, tilted her head back to stare up into his eyes. Her gaze held not a modicum of fear, nor any respect.

"Do not mistake my silence as permission to speak, male." The words squeezed out between clenched teeth, weighted with disdain and distaste. "I do Goddess' bidding and no more, so do not test me."

She spun away again without giving him any chance to respond. An instant later, he felt the jab of a pike at his back, encouraging him to follow. He did, his own jaw clamped tight. In other circumstances, he'd be searching for the first opportunity to relieve one of them of their weapon and make his escape but after finding their way deep into the heart of the city, he realized he didn't know how get out of the place.

Three more turns and Trenan detected sounds other than footsteps and armor-song for the first time. It sounded an uncertain tumult, one which might have been made by any number of sources. But as they rounded a last corner, they came onto a straight avenue running straight to its end at a pair of wooden gates. Though some distance of dirt road lay between them and the portal ahead, he recognized the noise emanating from behind them. He'd heard the clang and clatter of weapons too many times not to recognize it.

His step hesitated and the cold metal of a pike tip brushed his neck, prompting him to continue. He did, a curse for the weapon-bearer teetering on the edge of his pursed lips, his arm tensed as he strained to keep from striking out at her. No doubt he'd best any two of these women in a fight—maybe all of them—but the matter of their weapons and his lack of the same changed the likely outcome.

Her response came in the form of the clop of hooves and creak of leather. The woman leading their party didn't bother looking back at him. With surprise on his side, he might take out two or three of them before the business end of a pike penetrated his body, but no doubt it would result in his blood wetting the dirt road. Best to wait for a better opportunity; one always came.

"You seemed as though you awaited my arrival," he said, defying the leader's most recent admonition, but if he couldn't fight, keeping quiet wasn't an option. "How did you know I'd be here? Is the princess here?"

His last question finally begat an answer. The woman came to an abrupt halt, faced Trenan with an impatient and humorless expression upon her face. The swordsman halted, too, this time without the touch of cold steel on his bare skin.

"Worry not for Princess Danya. She is not here, but she is under our care. She has her own part to play in this."

"So she is safe?" The heaviness in his chest and limbs eased by the weight of a fly.

"She is. I imagine you will see her again soon."

Tension the swordmaster hadn't noticed creeping into his muscles relaxed; he breathed a deep sigh. "And Prince Teryk?"

The woman hesitated. "His path leads him to a different place. A darker place."

"But he's alive?"

Another pause. "Of a fashion." She turned away, resuming her route toward the gate at a quicker pace than before.

Trenan's heart jumped a beat. For all the turns of the seasons he'd trained the royal children, he always did his best to treat them the same, at least in terms of emotion if not the effort he asked of them in practice. But no matter how hard he tried, he knew things tilted one way more than the other. Yes, he loved Danya and respected the woman she'd become—a source of pride for him—but he'd never share the same connection with her he had with the prince.

'Of a fashion?' What does she mean?

He parted his lips to press her further about the prince's whereabouts, his condition, but the warrior behind Trenan pressed the shaft of her weapon against his back, jarring him forward. The master swordsman stumbled, righted himself, and spun on the woman, his teeth clenched tight. Before he said or did more, the tips of four pikes hovered within a finger's width of his face and throat.

He froze, the muted sounds of clashing weapons floating along the avenue from behind the wooden gates. After an instant, the distinct crunch of boots on gravel joined the commotion, and he sensed the leader at his back.

"Mind yourself, swordsman. Goddess brought you here for a reason other than your death, but it doesn't mean my warriors won't defend themselves."

She'd stepped so close behind him, her breath touched his neck as she spoke. He suppressed a shiver and a portion of the instant rage left him. Careful of the pike tips hovering near him, he pivoted slowly toward her. When he faced her, he found she stood four paces away from him. Had he so misjudged her place, the feel of her air on his skin? Or she performed the same stealthy magic as the others did when they discovered him? Either way, he stared at her, perplexed and unable to respond to her threat. A corner of her mouth tilted upward in what one may have considered a smile, then she turned her back to him once more, returning to their trek.

The gate was much closer now, the noise tumbling out from behind it louder. Trenan walked again, frowning. Why did a community meant to house the sick and dying have such arms and armor as to create this sound? He might have suspected a tournament in progress, but it lacked cheers accompanying the clatter of combat. An actual battle, then? Inside the city walls?

The woman halted when she came within five paces of the gate. The tap of a pike shaft on his chest prompted the master swordsman to do the same as another of the pikewomen hurried past. She stopped short of the gateway and rapped on it with the butt end of her weapon. Completing this task, she returned to her position without waiting for a response.

Five heartbeats later, both sides of the gate swung open.

The commotion of sounds increased in volume as the wooden baffle opened. Trenan leaned to his right, looking past the shoulder of the leader standing in front of him. Beyond her he spied a practice yard, dozens of soldiers within honing their techniques with sword and shield, spear and polearm. A few wore leather and chainmail like the pike-wielders, the others in nothing but white cloth hanging at their waists, their chests bare and gleaming with the sweat of their efforts.

And every soldier a woman.

VIII - Ishla - Queen's Guard

*E*RRAL SLAMMED HIS FIST on the tabletop, setting it shuddering and the flagon upon it wobbling. It settled without tipping. The king rarely took counsel or messages at the table instead of the throne room or meeting chamber but, when the queen heard of messengers bearing news of her children, she'd insisted they not wait on tradition.

"The princess escaped him and still no sign of the boy?"

Ishla winced at the king's choice of words. She hated when he referred to either of their offspring as 'the boy' or 'the girl,' but she worried most when he neglected to use Teryk's name. It wasn't possible he'd guessed the truth, but part of her harbored fear he suspected. What might happen if he found out? The thought frequently made her shudder.

The taller of the two soldiers—she didn't know him but recognized him as an acquaintance of her queen's guard, Dansil—practically hopped from foot to foot, a ludicrous grin on his face. His expression angered her; did he find the fact of her missing children amusing? The older soldier, she was familiar with—Osis, a compatriot of Trenan's. The veteran fighting man glared at him out of the corner of his eye, embarrassed by the man's demeanor and not attempting to hide his anger.

A shadow fell across the king's face. "When Trenan returns, I'll—"

"He doesn't matter now, your highness," Ishla interrupted. Using her husband's title rather than his name added to her discomfort, but the soldiers' presence demanded it. "The safety of our children is paramount. Considerations of reprimand can wait."

She paused, awaiting the king's response. As she watched his thoughts reflected in his expression, she suppressed her own nerves and trepidation. Worry didn't gnaw her stomach only for her children, but for Trenan, too. The seasons had turned many times since he'd sacrificed his arm to save the king. Though he'd proven himself a true and loyal adviser in the time after, Ishla suspected their children's disappearance wore thin her husband's patience for the master swordsman. Each instance of his anger showing made the queen wonder if he might have guessed the truth. If he did, his tenuous patience and any forgiveness his friend's sacrifice may have earned him would disappear like a layer of dust blown by a strong breath.

A few tense moments passed, everyone in the room silent. Ishla watched her husband but sensed the gazes of the other men shift from her to the king, to each other. Being a seasoned soldier, Osis would be assessing the situation and preparing for the king's orders, ready to do whatever his ruler asked of him. She couldn't guess the other man's mind or intent. Did it matter?

Erral rubbed his hands on the front of his breeches, removing the sweat from his palms. He cleared his throat and raised his arm, pointed a finger at the older warrior.

"You. Gather a squad—ten men at least. I shouldn't have allowed Trenan to go with such a small deployment. Take them to where you last saw the princess, track her and Trenan and return them to Draekfarren."

Osis bowed at the waist but missed his chance to respond as Strylor jumped on the opportunity to insert himself.

"You can count on us, your kingliness. We'll have your daughter and the incompetent swordsman back in no time."

Ishla opened her mouth, a reprimand for the way the man spoke and how he referred to Trenan teetering on the tip of her tongue, but she caught herself. It wasn't her place, not in the king's presence.

Erral turned his gaze on the excited soldier, raised an eyebrow. "You'll be going nowhere. With Den... Dan..." He glanced toward the queen, set a questioning mask atop the ire that pinched his features.

"Dansil," she finished for him.

"Dansil. With the queen's guard traipsing around the kingdom with Trenan, my wife's complement is one short. Since her safety is the kingdom's safety, you will protect her in his stead until his return, however long it might be."

Concern flickered to life in Ishla's gut. The soldier's eyes widened and his lips quivered to disguise the thrill handed to him by the king's proclamation. The queen looked from him to her husband, her stomach tightening. Erral's gaze slid to her, and for an instant, she thought she saw the corner of his mouth tilt up in a tiny grin, as if assigning this unqualified man to her detail amused him. He returned his attention to the soldiers before she determined the smile real or merely fancy.

"Why are you still here?" the king snapped, startling Ishla though he didn't direct his words at her.

Osis reacted at once, bowing lower this time and spinning on his heel, heading out of the chamber to gather his squad. The other man—Strylor, she reminded herself—slid his feet along the floor, shuffling closer to the queen.

"What are you doing?" she asked, incredulous.

He appeared surprised by her question, though the ghost of a smile remained. "The king assigned me to look after you. It's what I'm doing."

Erral cleared his throat but Ishla raised her hand, stopping him before he spoke. Because the man was now her personal guard, she knew her husband would allow her this leeway. She took two steps toward the soldier, moving close enough to reach out and touch him if she wanted to; she did not.

"Do you think I am not safe alone in the king's company? Do you not consider my husband able to protect me?"

Strylor's eyes widened, his cheeks blushed red, and the hidden smile disappeared abruptly. He shook his head with such haste, Ishla took a step away for fear saliva might fly from his lips.

"N... no, my queen. I—"

"Then get out."

He bowed too deeply, bending far enough forward he appeared in danger of tipping. The queen crossed her arms, glared at him. When he straightened, he wore a sheepish smile as though he considered the entire thing an amusing little game, then spun and exited the chamber, closing the door behind him. Ishla faced her husband.

"Why—?"

"Hush yourself, woman. With the other one gone, you need another Queen's Guard. What matters now is having Trenan return to answer for his incompetence."

"No, what matters is getting our son and daughter back safe."

Erral waved his hand. "Of course. But the master swordsman will face consequences for his failure."

Ishla's cheeks grew warm as anger filled her. Was it possible he placed more importance on punishing a man who'd served him so well for so long than on finding their children? Whatever might have happened, the queen knew Trenan enough to realize he'd done everything in his power to protect the prince and princess.

"You make it seem as though rescuing our children is not of the highest priority."

He glared at her, the knuckles of his hand turning white around the handle of his flagon of ale. "Of course it's important," he said through clenched teeth. "But I have a kingdom to run and defend. Things happen you do not understand because I protect you from them. I see no need for the weight of the kingdom's affairs to squash you."

"But our children—"

"Will be found." He emphasized the last word by slamming his mug on the tabletop, but it did not fare so well this time; the clay shattered, spilling ale everywhere. He continued as though he didn't notice, the flagon's handle still held in his hand. "I understand the importance of finding them; one of them is the heir to the throne. And if Trenan had accomplished what I meant him to rather than being distracted by his own affairs and feelings for the children..."

One of them...?

Ishla took a step toward the table. "Do not blame Trenan for this. It wasn't his actions that drove them out of the castle."

"It's my fault? For discouraging their interest in the ridiculous scroll?"

His eyes darted away from hers for an instant but, in the brief space of time, she became certain he kept something from her. She didn't speak, didn't so much as move her head, but knew he'd understand her intended response.

"Despite your choice of words, they are children no more. If their mother realized this and treated them accordingly, maybe they wouldn't be chasing a fanciful dream."

The queen's hands clenched into fists and she opened her mouth, but stopped herself. He may be her husband, but he was also her king, and some things shouldn't be said. She closed her lips, inhaled a deep breath, and reset her thoughts.

"Don't blame Trenan for this," she said. "He'd do everything in his power for Teryk and Danya."

Erral opened his hand, allowed the handle of the flagon to roll off his fingers and clunk down on the tabletop, then wiped his palm on his trousers. He stared at his wife before responding.

"Be careful in your defense of the master swordsman, my queen, or I might wonder why you are so adamant about his innocence."

A shiver ran up the queen's spine and she struggled to prevent distress from showing on her face. Old worries clambered into her mind, ones she found always with her but she tried to keep buried. They resurfaced whenever the three of them gathered in the same place. Did he see unintentional looks between them? Did he recognize the slight resemblance between their son and the swordmaster? With an effort, Ishla forced the worry back into the pit of her stomach where she'd carried it for so many turns of the seasons. She'd have to deal with it another time. Now, more important matters demanded her attention.

"Find my children. Please."

The instant she spoke the words, a thought entered her mind.

Because if you don't, I will.

She remained where she stood for a moment longer, ensuring she made her displeasure obvious without speaking before she turned and strode to the door. It required more concentration than she expected to keep her legs from shaking. A tremor quivered through her fingers as she reached for the door handle. Anger at her husband? Nervousness about what she might have to do to get her children back? Worry for their safety? All of it.

Ishla squeezed her hand into a fist and held it tight. When she opened it again, the quaking had stopped, so she grasped the handle and pulled the door open. Before stepping across the threshold, she shot a final glance over her shoulder at Erral, but the king had returned to other things, his attention diverted from his wife and, in all likelihood, from his children. She clamped her teeth together and stepped out of the room and closed the door behind her, intentionally too hard. She turned to the right and found her new guard leaning against the hall's stone wall, a finger buried in his nose to the first knuckle. When he saw her, he yanked it out, wiped whatever came along with it on the front of his trousers, and straightened.

"Are you yet here? I thought I told you to leave."

"To leave the chamber, your highness. You did. And now you've left it, too, and no longer have the king to protect you. This is where I come in."

She felt not the patience to suffer this fool; she sighed, set her jaw, and approached him. When she came close, she leaned in to speak and unintentionally caught a whiff of him—it had been a long while since he last bathed.

"I don't need your protection."

She remained near him, holding her breath and intending her proximity to be threatening. The soldier swallowed hard, but the way his gaze darted from her eyes to the front of her dress and back made it clear threat wasn't what he felt. Disgust clogged her throat, and she almost forgot herself and drew some air. Despite his actions making the skin on her arms crawl, she didn't move away.

"Soldier?"

She spoke the word harshly, its sound surprising him; he jerked his gaze from where it had fallen on her bodice again. She set her expression to chastise and accuse him, but he only smiled.

"Yer my job, your highness, and I aim to take good care of you."

Frustrated, the queen sighed and swept by him, careful not to touch him as she passed. She stared straight ahead, trying not to think about the soldier and his intended actions, but she heard the ruckus of him hitching up his sword belt and following her. One more thing to worry about: if she was to find her children herself, she would have to lose her guard.

IX - Teryk - Shore

*T*ERYK GASPED FOR BREATH, inhaling a splash of water as he did. He gagged and coughed, the unrhythmic jerking motion slowing his strokes. His shoulders burned and the urge to peer back threatened to overtake him; the desire to see if the sea creature swam right behind him, mouth agape and dagger teeth ready to shred him swelled in his chest. He resisted, instead keeping his eye on the shore and Rilum waving him on frantically. The sailor's action told him everything he needed to know of the monster's proximity.

Waves lapped around the man's knees as he yelled desperate encouragement. The splash of his hands and feet in the water and the rush of blood in his ears prevented Teryk from understanding his companion's words. It didn't matter. If he intended to tell the prince the creature gave up the chase and he should relax, he'd behave far differently.

The wish to stretch his legs toward the bottom, discover if his soles might touch, burned stronger than the impulse to peek back. He couldn't walk faster through the water than his ability to swim, but he'd find the knowledge of the earth below his feet for the first time in longer than he recalled reassuring.

Reassuring means nothing if I'm dead.

Despite his intent not to, Teryk stole a glance over his shoulder. A long, smooth line bisected the waves behind him, curving side to side like a dark river flowing through the surface of the sea. It stretched out to the length of many men, but nowhere near the size of the God of the Deep he'd seen looming when the Whalebone met its end.

Not a god, but a fish looking to feed.

He redoubled his efforts, focusing on the shore ahead.

I'm the chosen. The firstborn of the rightful king.

He clamped his jaw tight enough it hurt his teeth, but the panic at the hungry creature behind him forced the discomfort from his mind. He did as Trenan taught, plunging his face into the frigid water as he swam, turning his head to draw breath every fourth stroke. When he looked up again, he spied Rilum splashing toward him, not too far off, in the water up to his waist.

Teryk paused his kicking, letting his feet sink until his soles touched. The sea reached to his mid-chest, but the softness of the sandy bottom under him made him forgo swimming as the better alternative. He churned his legs under the surface, pumped his arms. Silty sand flowed from beneath his toes, slowing him, and the ocean greeted him with great resistance.

"Swim, Taylor! Swim," Rilum hollered, his voice plain now Teryk wasn't splashing and stroking. The desperation in his tone suggested the nearness of his pursuer.

He knew he shouldn't look back, should plunge into the water once more and kick toward his companion as fast as possible. But knowing and doing are different things, and he glanced over his shoulder once more despite the knowledge. The top of the serpent's head stuck out above the surface, the bulbous eyes set atop it fixed on the prince. In the brief instant their gazes met, he saw hunger blazing in them.

Teryk spun toward shore, lurched forward and kicked as hard as his tired legs allowed. Salty water went up his nose, onto his tongue, in his eyes. His feet churned the sea, and he sensed the beast closing on him, the bubbles of its exhalations heating the ocean at his heels. In his mind, his progress ceased, as though something grasped him by the ankles, preventing his escape so the monster might catch him.

It swims faster than I do; why hasn't it caught me?

He didn't mean to ponder the question—his focus should have been on escaping intact—but knowing so didn't stop it from entering his head. Any creature made for swimming could do it swifter than he, yet he'd stayed ahead of the serpent as its coils slid through the waves without resistance. It followed him so far and held back its attack.

A firm grip took him by the wrist; his first reaction was to pull away but, when he did, he felt no razor teeth dig into his flesh. Instead, fingers tightened their hold and pulled him along.

Teryk raised his chin to find Rilum holding onto him, propelling him forward, pushing a wave ahead of them and leaving a wake behind. The prince stopped kicking and contorted to get his feet on the ocean floor again, stumbling and twisting as he did. In his effort, he glanced back, saw the serpent swimming with its head and neck out of the water, mouth open revealing three rows of small, sharp-looking teeth. The length of four men separated them.

He found his footing and stumbled along beside the sailor, Rilum's hand gripping his wrist. The sea receded around them, moving from waist to mid-thigh, to knees. How shallow did they need to be before they reached safety?

With waves lapping at his calves, Teryk heard powerful jaws snapping shut. His muscles tensed, awaiting the pain he expected to follow, but none did. When the water touched only as high as their ankles, he looked back again as Rilum continued pulling him toward the beach.

The creature writhed, its thick body half-submerged, but its forward progress halted; shallow water prevented it from swimming any closer. The serpent-fish snapped its jaws again and again, the small, sharp teeth clicking together, but it made no other noise.

With seawater covering the top of his feet, Teryk stopped and pulled his arm from Rilum's grasp. The sailor took two more steps then halted, joining his companion in staring at the monstrosity. It gnashed its fangs once more, raised its wide head in the manner of a land snake readying to strike. The prince faltered back from it, thinking it might do exactly that. His feet tangled, and he fell on his backside, splashing in the shallow water and jarring his teeth. The serpent twisted its body and slammed its length against the ocean's surface like an angry, petulant child. Salty water sprayed into the air as it flicked its tail and slid away, disappearing into the ocean with the smallest of ripples.

Teryk sat with waves washing around him. He drew heavy breaths and waited for his thumping heart to slow, and Rilum let him. When he heard the splash of his companion's steps carrying him out of the sea, the prince tore himself from his trance. He climbed to his feet, fingers sinking into sugary sand as he pushed himself up, then turned to follow the sailor. He took one step before the sight before him stopped him in his tracks.

A beach made up of sand so white it threatened to blind him in the afternoon sun stretched out to his left and right. When his eyes grew accustomed, he saw lightning bolts of black streaked through it at irregular intervals. Teryk plodded forward, feet splashing in the shallow surf, and bent to examine a wide, dark streak. It appeared simply to be sand of a different color.

"I've never seen anything like this," he said.

"No one has, lad," Rilum replied. "This be the land across the sea."

X - Danya - Inn

THE SHARP AROMA OF mutton and spices wafted from the kitchen behind Krin, the odor overpowering stale beer scent always emanating from the stained wooden bar. With his patrons now satisfied, the barkeep rubbed at one of those stains, knowing full well no amount of elbow grease possessed the power to erase it. He stopped, inspected his work, flipped his cloth over, and got after another, smaller mark to the left of the first.

If the marks could be removed, Krin wasn't sure he'd rid the bar of them. Each told a story, even if he couldn't remember their details. He knew most of them came about during good times—ale slopped during an energetic toast, or splashed from a cup knocked over by a grand gesture. Only one stain did he wish to remove, the one not made by a spilled beverage, and certainly not created out of goodwill or merriment. His eyes slid along the bar's length until his gaze rested on the dark, ugly mark at the corner—the one stain whose origin he'd never forget though he wished to.

Krin paused in his cleaning and stared at the near-black patch of wood, sudden emotion roiling in his chest. But why should it? How many times had he wiped his bar, exactly as he did now, without feeling overcome? The turning of seasons proved no better at erasing the memory than at removing the stain. He wrenched his eyes away, sucked a deep breath between his lips, the air tasting equally of fresh stew and old beer. Just then, the door swung open on squeaking hinges.

They need oiling tomorrow.

The barkeep forced a smile on his face and readied a greeting. He'd be damned if he let the stain of blood spilled long ago prevent him from offering a bit of friendliness to his guests. For a breathless moment, no one entered; Krin's grin faltered. Had the wind picked up and blown the door open? Normally, if it gusted so hard, he'd have heard it groaning in the chimney, rattling a loose shutter, whistling in the roof; he detected none of these.

"Greetings."

The word entered before the dark figure, outlined in the sun's glare. The tightness Krin experienced before returned at the sound of the voice; his hand holding the cloth clenched into a fist. Tall and slender, the shape crossed the threshold into the tavern, two more smaller ones following close behind. The speaker proved exactly who the barkeep thought it to be.

Ive.

His heart plunged into his stomach as he awaited the slight man's stocky partner entering after him. He resisted the urge to glance back toward the ugly stain as he forced the even more false smile onto his lips. The weapons merchant crossed the threshold and closed the door behind himself, no Fellick following him. Krin let out his air.

"To the bar, please," Ive said, prompting the two girls forward, partially under his breath.

As they crossed the room, feet scraping against the dirty plank floor, the patrons who'd stopped to assess them returned to their conversations, their meals, their ale. A few continued watching as they made their way to the rough wooden bar. Ive put his elbow on the edge and leaned in with the familiarity of someone used to performing such an action.

"Mr. Ive," the barkeep said. He nodded at the weapons merchant but couldn't stop his gaze from flickering toward his unusual companions. "I dare say Mr. Fellick appears less intimidatin' than usual today."

Ive creased his face with a fake-looking smile—he rarely offered better—and chuckled an empty laugh. "Mr. Fellick is watching the wares, as always, while I see to feeding my niece and her friend. Can you supply four bowls of your infamous stew?"

"Aye, the missus has a fresh batch ready to go. Will you be wanting ales as well?"

"Tch, tch. When have you ever seen myself or my companion imbibe, Mr. Krin?"

"Never, and it be damn curious. Man's got to ask, though. They say sometimes people flip their leaves to a new side, whatever that means.

Besides, how else am I going to make me some coin?" Krin cocked his head to call over his shoulder. "Four bowls, mother. And be sure they're hot."

He moved to the other end of the bar, busying himself again scrubbing a part of the wood unneeding of the attention to avoid making conversation with the weapons merchant. The man made his skin desire to shrivel up and peel off. Ive turned to the room, cleared his throat, and raised his arms. With his height, his fingers brushed the underside of the thick ceiling beams. Krin waited to see what he'd say, caught the older of the two girls watching his unnecessary cleaning. Her expression gave him pause.

"Ladies and gentlemen, and everyone else in attendance at Krin's Glorious Home of Food and Drink, please note: Fellick and Ive have arrived. We come to satisfy all your weaponly needs. Did you bury the hatchet and need a new one? Have you lost your edge? Sales and repairs of every type of weapon. Well, hand-held weapons; if you're having troubles with your trebuchet, you may have to look elsewhere for assistance."

A murmur of laughter swept through the room as everyone trained their gazes on the stick-like man. He paused, enjoying the attention, then lowered his arms and pointed toward the door.

"On the other side of the portal stands Mr. Fellick. Don't let his appearance or demeanor dissuade you; he is gentle as a newborn piglet... unless you short-change him. He will attend to your needs, great and small, so hurry yourselves outside for the wares of Fellick and Ive, the best weapons in the Windward Kingdom."

Chair legs scraped the wooden floor and a few people clapped their appreciation. Ive turned his back on them, pleased with the result of his oration as he canted himself against the bar once more. Barely enough time passed for his elbow to touch wood when Krin's wife approached with four steaming bowls of stew teetering on her arms. The barkeep hurried over to take them from her and pass them out lest they topple from their perch. The stew was so thick, the spoon handles stood at attention. When he put one in front of the older girl, she leaned forward and inhaled the aroma; he thought her stomach growled its approval and wondered how long since Ive's "niece" and her friend last ate.

"D'you want me to take Fellick's bowl out to him?" the barman asked.

"Mr. Fellick is busy taking money from your patrons. Leave it here. I'll bring it to him shortly."

Krin nodded, spun on his heel and started toward the far end of the bar before Ive called him back.

"Before you go."

The barkeep peered over his shoulder, and Ive gestured for him to come closer. He did so, and the thin man stood straight and leaned partway across the rough-hewn wood.

"Has Birk been in?"

The question caught him off-guard, but Krin did his best to conceal his surprise. Why did the weapons merchant want to know about that cretin? He screwed up his face as if struggling to recall, and his gaze fell on the two girls. The elder one glanced up at him without pausing in her acquisition of sustenance. It seemed to him her eyes widened at him, if only minutely, as though trying to tell him something, ask him something.

For help?

He pulled his gaze away, admonishing himself for letting the mention of Birk's name send his imagination running off to such strange places. Still, he sensed an odd familiarity about the girl.

Krin turned his attention back to the spindly merchant.

"Not for a while. Took a stranger under his wing, I heard. Also understand he's got a beef with Juddah, who lives near the water, but I know little about it."

Ive frowned, rubbed his chin. "A stranger? Tell me about this fellow."

Krin wondered how much he should say. He put a finger to his lips, as though the gesture helped to recall a happening too long ago to be fresh in his memory, but he didn't need the pause. One of his best qualities as an innkeeper and bartender was his ability to remember faces. As he opened his mouth to reply, he noted the girl leaning closer, listening in a way Ive wouldn't have noticed.

"An old salt, man of the sea. Never laid eyes on him before. They shared a meal and an ale, then Birk took him away to the doctor. Word is he killed a fella at the doc's—another stranger—then disappeared."

"Perhaps the reason for the disagreement with this Juddah fellow?"

Krin leaned back from the bar and wiped his hands on his apron, fought the urge to raise an eyebrow. "Don't know. Might be you'd want to ask him yourself."

"Might be." Ive spoke louder, added a pleased tone to his voice. "Where do I find our man Juddah?"

Krin tilted his head forward, toward sunset. "He's got a place right next to the shore. Careful if you go see him, though." His gaze flickered to the girls, then back. "He ain't the friendliest of sorts."

"Appreciate the advice, Krin, but you forget I travel with the redoubtable Mr. Fellick."

"Yes, you do."

A droplet of sweat slipped from the barkeep's hairline and rolled along his temple. He raised his arm and wiped it away on his wrist. It wasn't particularly hot, so he wondered what about Ive's words or visit squeezed a drop of nervousness from his brow; wasn't like he'd make him go to Juddah's place. The older girl noticed him do it, so he wiped his palms on his apron again and gave her a half smile. She didn't return the expression, and he understood his cleanliness didn't concern her; she also speculated about his nerves, perhaps had some of her own.

Ive stood, took two coins from a pocket in his coat, and threw them on the bar. They clanked against the wood, one of them landing flat, the other hitting on its edge and spinning in a wobbling circle before falling. He hadn't taken a single bite of his stew.

"For the delicious repast, and for your troubles." He scooped up the two full bowls. "I'll take Mr. Fellick his lunch and enjoy mine with them. We will bring the dishes in when we're done. Finish up, ladies."

"Keep 'em," Krin said with a wave of his hand. "Drop them back next time you're passing through."

Ive nodded. "Fair enough. Come on, girls."

The younger of them, who hadn't looked up from her meal for an instant during the exchange, picked her bowl off the bar and held it to her lips, scraped the last of the stew into her mouth. The older girl appeared to have lost her appetite. She lifted the spoon one more time, then dropped it back into the vessel and pushed it away.

Ive paced toward the door, and Krin took a quick step to his right, putting the two still-seated girls between himself and the weapons merchant. Unexpected concern swirled in his gut, nothing more than a feeling without a solid base.

"Enjoy the stew, did you?" he asked in a voice he realized to be too loud for the circumstances as soon as the words left his mouth. He leaned close, his belly touching the wooden serving surface, and spoke so quietly, he wasn't sure if they'd hear him at all. "Be wary of this one."

His head tilted toward Ive, then he straightened and moved a step back from the bar, bowls in hand. At the same instant, the weapons merchant stopped and faced them.

"Ladies?"

The smaller girl slid off her stool first. Her companion didn't follow right away, instead keeping her seat and staring into the barman's eyes. In that heartbeat of time, Krin's renowned recall for faces finally brought a memory back to mind, solidifying the familiarity he'd felt. He recognized her from many turns of the seasons past, during one of his trips to the Horseshoe. She'd been younger then, a child; she and her brother, both.

Before Ive asked again, the first girl touched the arm of the second, prompting her to follow. She slid off the stool and forced a smile onto her face.

"Delicious, thank you. Our compliments to the cook."

She took one backward step away, her eyes holding Krin's gaze, and her lips moved, formed words making no sound.

Help us.

She turned and followed the others, leaving Krin grasping the dirty bowls, staring after them as the blood drained from his face and his cheeks went cold.

Ive opened the door, waving his charges through with a characteristically grand swing of his arm. The barkeep squinted against the sun streaming through the opening, but didn't move nor speak until it swung closed again. After the latch fell, he set the dishes aside, scooped up the coins left by the weapons merchant, and came out from behind the bar. He blinked to restore his vision, then scanned the tavern until he found the man he searched for sitting at a table by the fireplace. He strode across the room and helped himself to a seat beside him.

"People say you have the fastest horse in town, Gihl."

The fellow pursed his lips, peered at Krin through slitted lids. "Do they?"

"They do. Is it true?"

"I'd put her up against near any nag in the kingdom, I believe."

Krin nodded. "Then I need you to do a thing for me."

Gihl leaned back in his chair, propping it up on two legs. The action made the barkeep cringe—he'd seen too many of his chairs broken when someone overbalanced, but he said nothing. The horse owner wasn't a bad man, but bore the reputation of one who didn't take kindly to sharing his possessions.

"Why the sudden interest in my horse?"

"Because I need your help."

Krin threw Ive's coins on the table, then dug in his own pocket and pulled out five more. He set these beside the others and waited. Gihl lowered the front legs of his chair to the floor and leaned forward, eyes fixed on the money. The barkeep might have accused him of counting it if he thought Gihl guilty of being capable of doing so. After a time long enough to count them several times, the horse owner looked up.

"What is it you need?"

"For you to ride to Draekfarren as fast and as hard as your nag will carry you. Tell them we know where the princess is. Tell them they have to come if she is to live."

XI - Teryk - Shooting Stars

A SHOOTING STAR STREAKED across the sky, its ghostly trail of light cutting through Teryk's vision. Of the few fond memories of his father from his youth, one came on an unspoiled night such as this. The two of them stood atop Draekfarren's wall, their faces lifted toward the heavens.

"I see another," young Teryk cried. He'd seen the seasons turn but six times by then, if he recalled.

"And more." The king raised his hand and pointed.

Three more lights chased each other across the darkness, followed by a fourth, a fifth. The prince gasped aloud; he'd never experienced this type of display of nature. Its beauty left him short of breath, but part of him wondered if their being exposed to this might be a poor idea. The things his nanny told him about the stars made him frightened of being outside alone at night. With Erral at his side, he controlled the fear tonight, but worry gnawed at the lining of his belly, nonetheless.

"If you make a wish when you see one, your desire will become truth."

Surprised, Teryk tore his gaze from the light show to stare at the king. Why would the evil stars grant him a wish? His father didn't notice his disbelieving expression.

"Look, another. What will you ask for?"

His mind spun, leaving him nothing for which to wish. "Nanny says the lights in the sky are bad. Goddess put them there because they didn't follow her rules. They're..." He searched his young memory, trying to recall the name she'd given them, but it eluded him. Tiny Gods? No, but similar. "They're mean."

Now the king looked away from the firmament and Teryk wished he'd said nothing. A crease appeared on his father's forehead between his eyes, the way it always did when he became unhappy. The prince cowered in case he should raise his hand, though he didn't know why he should; he'd simply mentioned what Nanny told him.

"What else did she say?" The flat tone of his words formed a perfect reflection of his expression. The combination made Teryk forget any fear he might experience at the pinpricks of lights in the dark.

Small Gods, he remembered. She called them Small Gods.

"She said Goddess was unhappy with the Small Gods and banished them to the sky to keep them from hurting people anymore. That's all."

"Rubbish," the king snapped. "There's no Goddess or Small Gods. They are naught but stories to make scare children. Are you a frightened little child?"

Teryk shook his head—the answer he knew his father wanted. But he realized the words 'frightened little child' most accurately described him. He struggled to keep his knees from trembling, his teeth from chattering, thoughts of Nanny and Small Gods gone from his young mind.

"Priests teach you of gods, not your nanny."

The king pivoted from the parapet and strode toward the stairs leading into the castle, leaving his son behind. Despite his effort, a shudder ran through him, and he lifted his gaze to the sky. Two stars shot across the firmament, the light trails left in their wake ominous, threatening now he stood viewing them on his own. Nanny's stories flooded back to him; they foretold the return of the Small Gods one day. Had the time come?

Fright clogged Teryk's throat, sent tears to perch on his bottom lids; they blurred his vision and smeared the stars into ugly, scarier shapes. He wiped his face on his sleeve and sprinted after his father, desperate the man not leave him.

The next morning, when his nanny normally came for him in his chamber, it wasn't her, but Trenan, his father's master swordsman. After breaking his fast, his training began, and he never saw the kindly lady with the tall tales again.

Lying on the sandy beach of the land across the sea, Teryk tracked another star crossing night's black canvas.

Not such a pleasant memory, after all.

He heaved a sigh and swept the thoughts back into the recesses of his mind with the other times he failed to live up to his father's expectations. Sometimes he suspected he might need a second head to contain every time he disappointed the king. He closed his eyes, expecting the shooting star to run its course and disappear but, when he opened his lids again, it remained. He pursed his lips.

On the night with his father, the stars they'd seen crossing the sky lived but short lives, flashing to existence, streaking partway through the darkness, then disappearing. This one started out high over his head, a dot of light brightening and growing before it moved. It did so slowly at first, its momentum increasing, but its path didn't travel left to right as those on the seasons-passed evening standing beside the king. Instead, it appeared to plummet toward the earth.

Teryk pushed himself up on his elbows, the old fear brought on by his nanny's stories and reignited when he and Danya found the scroll creeping in to tighten his muscles. They'd have been nothing to him—a silly childhood memory lost with so many others of the same ilk—if not for the words his sister recited from the parchment written in a language she had no right to understand.

Should the Small Gods rise, man will fall.

A shiver rattled his spine as the star's arc continued, its brightness growing as it appeared to hurtle downward. It grew in size and Teryk climbed to his feet, entertaining the compulsion to track its trajectory. He did so until he saw it no longer. Did it slip past their world and out into the dark unknown beyond the sky? Or did it plummet into the ocean? Perhaps it struck the earth somewhere?

The Windward Kingdom?

He stared at the sky's reflection in the ocean's surface, the counterfeit stars trembling and shaking as waves disturbed their image; the moon's glow cut a swath across the sea, separating it into two broad, dark canvases. He continued staring, expecting to see the mirror images of more light streaking through the sky, but he saw none. The ripples disrupting the picture of the stars broadened, transformed into shallow swells so the visual echo became akin to the snapping fabric of a waving banner.

Its appearance reminded Teryk of the dark streaks running through the otherwise white beach, and his gaze trailed away, came to rest on the dual hues of this alien shore. A sharp line differentiated them with nary a speck or grain out of place. Light-colored sand took on a glow in the moonlight while the black patches might have been places where the world disappeared. If he dared set his foot on one, he'd likely slip inside this foreign land, lost to the life he knew.

Rilum slept on the ground behind him, deep snores rumbling in his chest loud enough to disguise the hiss of waves rolling onto shore. His body rested on a stretch of white, as though in sleep the sailor also worried the blackness would engulf him. Teryk wished for the man's noise to stop so he could experience the night in its fullest. Perhaps the sound of the sea—unhindered by creaking boards or flapping sails—might well bring him peace.

When did I last feel peaceful?

The prince slouched back onto the sand to ponder the thought, selecting a breadth of white to avoid disappearing into the earth. How long since he'd left Draekfarren? The answer eluded him, the gap in his memory hiding it from him. He remembered the woman with the space between her teeth and the men who ambushed him, nothing else after but vague sounds and cloudy images until he found himself inside a crate on the Whalebone. How he got on the ship and what happened in between remained a mystery he'd likely never solve.

Another star overhead brightened and grew as though collecting energy for its journey. As before, it began above him and, like the preceding dot of luminescence, the brightening light drifted at first, picking up speed as it went. Its movement followed a similar path to its predecessor, falling from the sky rather than traveling across it. Teryk climbed back to his feet, held his breath as he watched its descent.

It grew bigger, taking up more than its fair share of the night. Instead of continuing the same direction as the first shooting star, where it might have fallen on his home's distant shore or continued past into the vast beyond, its course veered toward the land across the sea.

It's heading straight for us.

Teryk faltered back a step, his still-wet boots squelching in the sand. A bright, fiery tail trailed out behind the hurtling star, and he'd have sworn the crackle of the flames reached his ears.

His eyes wanted to continue watching the fireball, but he tore his gaze away from its brightness, glanced backward at the dense forest crowding the shore. Even if the glare of the falling star didn't compromise his vision, he'd be unable to see anything between the tightly packed trunks of trees. What lay beyond them in this foreign place filled with nothing but the unknown remained more of a mystery than the missing days of his life. Heart beating faster, the prince returned his attention to the bright path of light. It closed the distance between itself and the world with incredible speed, its size increasing as it neared. He stumbled back another step, then froze. He looked at his boot; the edge rested the width of the finger from a stretch of black sand.

"Rilum."

Teryk held his ground, afraid to move and topple into the void created where night met colorless beach. He raised his gaze again to the falling star, now as big—if not as bright—as the sun. It didn't light up the sky, but it threatened to blind him. The prince threw his arm in front of his face, blocking the glare while still watching it, impenetrable forest at his back, chasm at his feet.

"Rilum!"

The sailor's rhythmic snore broke apart, punctuated by one loud snort, but then resettled into its natural cadence without further response from the man. Teryk clenched his jaw, lips pressed tight, and swallowed the sudden flood of saliva filling his mouth; it might have been a rock for how it scraped his throat going down. He narrowed his eyelids, lowered his arm.

At the last breathless instant, he realized it wouldn't strike the land across the sea, but it came close.

The ball of light fell to the horizon, its glow reflected on the surface of the water before it disappeared much more abruptly than it began. It did so in silence, as though he'd watched someone blow out a candle at a distance. The tension in his shoulders and legs eased, he inched his feet away from the ominous line between pale and dark, inhaled a lungful of briny night air. Its disappearance extinguished not just his fear, but also an excitement tickling his chest. The land across the sea, stars falling from the sky—here were the clues to prove the veracity of the scroll, proving him to be the savior of mankind. He glanced upward, searching for another, desperate for the validation of more Small Gods plummeting to the ground.

A few heartbeats later, the sound reached him, a crash like none he'd heard before, not even when storm and monster pummeled the Whalebone. The tumult of star striking sea buffeted his ears after being slowed by space and the salty air between them. Distance diminished it from the eardrum-shattering impact it must have been to a rumble, felt as much as heard.

Teryk looked to the ocean. The frequency of waves rolling onto the beach increased, the size of each growing. Beyond, the sea lay black like the night brought to earth, but the horizon had changed, grown darker. No stars hung low in the sky. He squinted, a knife point of concern jabbing into his chest.

From what he made out of it, the top edge of the horizon appeared irregular, the stars above twinkling, some disappearing then reappearing, others winking out and not returning. They simply disappeared.

The first wave splashed against his boots. He glanced down, stared at them, his sleep-deprived mind struggling to cobble together what he perceived as disparate pieces. Another swell rolled up the beach, this one more than kissing his sole. The next struck his foot with enough force to send drops of seawater splashing.

Realization dawned and Teryk stumbled back a step. His gaze returned to the darkened horizon, but now he realized it wasn't the sky empty of stars. A wall of water blocked the heavens from his view. A wave as big as any mountain.

The watery barricade rushed toward land pushing ever-growing waves before it, each successive one finding its way farther and farther up the seashore. The beach rippled beneath Teryk's feet, and he stumbled back a step, forgetting the sharp line between light and dark. When he stole a look down and found his foot crossing onto the black sand, vertigo spun his head. He whirled his arms beside him but couldn't find his balance. He threw his hands out without expecting them to impact anything solid, sure he'd be sucked into the ground instead of being washed away by the monstrous wave.

Rather than disappearing into a void, he landed with the softness of striking his down-filled mattress, chest splashing against the wet sand.

Rilum!

With the falling stars and growing waves, he'd forgotten his companion asleep behind him. He'd neglected the one person who knew where he was, the last of the Whalebone's crew who might help him fulfill the prophecy. Scrambling to his feet, he spun from the sea and lurched back toward where he'd left the sailor, traveling but a single step before stopping.

He stood atop a dune of white sand, the waves washing against its sugary substance without eroding it. Another mound gathered beneath Rilum, lifting the sleeping man up to a level equal to the prince's height.

How—?

A taller wave touched his sole and the sandy hill heaved upward, throwing him off balance, but this time he kept his feet. His head spun, trying to understand what was happening, but through the fog of confusion and sleeplessness, he realized the one thing he needed to do above all others.

Get to Rilum.

Without a backward glance, the prince sprinted for the second growing mound and his companion prone atop it. With each step, he expected his boot to splash in foamy surf, to lose his equilibrium and tumble into the wet, perhaps sucked away into eternal dark. What would it be like trapped in the black powder? Would he live? Would he understand what happened to him? Would he miss the world he left behind?

But he didn't find out. Each time he lifted a foot and set it ahead, a stump of sand rose to meet it. The muscles in his legs threatened to cramp, his forward progress slowing as though he ran on the same down mattress that had caught him a moment ago. Seawater flowed all around him, burbling and rushing, begging him to return to the sea, threatening to take him. Behind it, a constant roar came to his attention, almost unnoticeable for its consistency, but rising with each passing heartbeat. He craned his neck to peer over his shoulder; his feet tangled, throwing him to the ground.

Teryk extended his hands, ready for the impact, to disappear into this foreign land or for the sea to sweep him away, but neither happened. His palms hit soft, dry sand, sank in up to his wrists. He struggled to right himself, return to his flight from death brought on by the gigantic wave rushing toward him, return to trying to reach the comfort of at least dying at the side of his companion, but the ground undulated beneath him. It counteracted his balance, kept him prone while propelling him forward.

It carried him fast enough for the wind to stir his hair. He shifted, heart beating hard in his chest, but every time he did, the grains manipulated him, carrying him on and up, until the mound deposited him beside his companion. Teryk grabbed Rilum's shoulder and gave the still-sleeping man a shake.

"Wake up." The prince scrambled to face the beach as the sailor groaned but didn't stir.

The gigantic wave towered so high it devoured the sky, roaring as it did like an enraged beast. To his right, a double column of black sand swirled up in the air, the two twisting round each other and reaching skyward. He cowered from it. The urge to crawl away from this new threat overtook him, and he'd have done so if the mesa on which he stood didn't end immediately behind him. It rose to a greater height than Teryk realized making any backward movement a danger to send him plummeting to the ground below, a distance beyond his guess.

The twisting sand rose high above him in a black pillar flowing like liquid. It bulged in places, the bottom of it splitting into two narrower stanchions holding up the rest. Another pair split off higher up, these defying nature by hanging downward without detaching. It resembled a tree, twisted by time and weather, but then the trunk changed, assuming an hourglass shape. At the top, the column first thinned, then widened again, ending in an oval. Teryk gaped as it whirled and swirled, rectifying itself into a nose, cheek bones, a mouth—the dark visage of a female face.

As awe and wonder consumed the prince, panic leeched its way into his chest and the roaring of water filled his ears. The sand woman blocked his view of the sea, but the earsplitting sound left no doubt the huge wave bore down upon them.

In the space between her arm and body, he glimpsed the water wall. It towered higher than the top of the swirling pillar, its apex curving downward, ready to wash Teryk and his still-sleeping companion from the world.

At least he won't know what happened.

He imagined he saw driftwood and seaweed carried inside the wave, and fish and sea creatures of many kinds. He tensed, imagining for an instant he might have the strength to resist the sea's power. As it lurched toward him, the sand woman collapsed.

Teryk threw his arm in front of his face and screamed as blackness surrounded him.

XII - Danya - Juddah's

*T*HEY SAT IN THE wagon, none of them moving, Fellick and Ive in the front, Danya and Evalal behind them, as though part of their wares. They stared across the overgrown yard toward the one-level house and the barn leaning like a thing long ago run out of energy and in need of a rest. The princess didn't know what to do; she'd found no opportunity to tell her companion of the barkeep's warning, and her sword belt with the pouch-bound Seed of Life remained lying on the wagon's floorboards. Without guidance, she settled for stretching her neck to peek past Fellick's wide back.

The long grass lay beaten, patches of the yellowed blades tinted with what resembled rust. Even the princess' untrained eye understood the severity of the struggle necessary to cause it, as well as what discolored it in uneven strips. A heap of earth beside a deep hole caught her attention, the spade used to dig it sticking out of the mound of dirt.

A grave?

Her normal curiosity would have prompted her to peer into its depths to see what it held, but she possessed no such desire this time. The conflict suggested by the broken grass gave her a good idea of what she'd most likely find: the man Krin referred to as Juddah.

Danya shivered. Beside her, Evalal sat unmoving. If the princess wasn't sitting close enough to sense her heat, to hear her occasional deep breath, she might have worried someone cast a curse to transform her into a statue. She resisted the urge to reach out, lay her hand on the girl's arm or shoulder to make sure she yet lived.

A gust of wind wafted through the clearing, rustling the still-standing blades of grass, coaxing an eerie moan from them and blowing Danya's hair into her eyes. She shivered and brushed it aside, shifted her gaze to the pouch tied to the discarded sword belt. It lay less than two hand-widths from her boot; no way to reach it without being seen. Her logical side argued against the need to—it contained naught but an over-sized seed. But she knew that wasn't quite true.

She slid her foot toward the bag, grimacing at the sound of leather sole scraping wooden floorboard. Breath held, she raised her eyes to find out if either of the men noticed; they continued staring across the yard as if trying hard might allow them to peer through the walls. Their trepidation sent a sliver of panic through her chest—what caused hesitation with a man of Fellick's repute at your side? She did her best to ignore the discomfort and eased the air out of her lungs, concentrated on moving her foot closer until the edge of her footwear rested against the pouch.

The seed didn't react.

Did I expect it to?

Her gaze returned to the floor of the wagon and the doeskin purse resting against the side of her boot. No wonder she sensed nothing with two layers of dead animal flesh between them. She shifted again, pushing her foot harder against it, the sack kept from moving by the weight of the sword belt. No movement. She placed her sole on top of the bag, searching for the seed it contained. She touched it and imagined she perceived a tremble.

The wagon shook and bounced as one of the men seated in front of her stood.

"What are you doing?" Fellick intoned.

Danya gasped, heartbeat speeding. She jerked her foot away from the pouch and raised her head toward her captors, lips trembling, searching for an excuse and coming up with none.

Instead of finding the weapons merchants glaring at her, ready to punish her for the attempt, their backs remained toward her. Ive stood.

"We can guess what happened here, don't you agree, Mr. Fellick?"

The stout fellow nodded. "Think so."

"Perhaps you might make a search for anything else we should know."

He showed the briefest of hesitations before lowering himself off the wagon, setting it bouncing once more. Danya grabbed the edge of the bench to steady herself, but Ive didn't appear to notice the disturbance it caused. The smaller, powerful man stroked the horse nearest him as he passed, then bulled his way across the yard, tramping yellowed grass beneath his boot soles. Ive returned to his seat, watching his companion.

Danya cleared her throat, leaned forward. "Excuse me."

The slender merchant tilted his head toward her but kept his eyes on Fellick, tension clear in his shoulders. She wondered what made the men nervous. He said nothing, but she took the gesture as an invitation to continue with her question.

"Why are we here?"

"We are meant to meet an associate." His voice came out flat and she detected a hint of distaste.

Danya thought back to the hushed conversation she'd overheard the weapons merchant share with the barkeep.

Birk.

"It doesn't appear as though your friend is here."

"No, it does not."

"Does he live here?" She knew the answer, only asked to see how he'd reply. The act of speaking helped quell the sparks of fear kindled in her by the nervousness she felt coming from the normally unflappable merchants.

"No. A fellow named Juddah does. He is not a good man, and I'm worried what might have happened to my compatriot."

Though his response smacked of truth, she suspected more in his words than what they appeared.

Fellick stopped partway across the yard and knelt to inspect something hidden in the tall grass. She stretched her neck farther, attempting to lay eyes on it, but with no success. A moment later, the stocky man rose again and continued his path toward the shack. He mounted the stair to the porch then disappeared inside. Danya turned to her companion; the girl noticed and returned her gaze.

Neither spoke; they didn't need to. Both their expressions communicated concern and reticence. Danya raised her eyebrows, Evalal answered with a shrug.

The door slammed shut, startling them as Fellick exited the shack. He hopped off the stair and walked straight for the lopsided outbuilding. The barn door stood open and askew, leaning farther than the building itself. Though age or inadequate upkeep might have caused the door's disrepair, to the princess it looked as if someone had ripped it from its anchors in anger.

Fellick disappeared into the barn and noises spilled out—creaking wood, the rattle of metal, the dull thump of pottery breaking. To Danya's surprise, a cow lowed in an unhappy tone. Everything went silent for the space of fifteen heartbeats before he called out.

"Ive!"

The slender man's straight back went straighter still and Danya clamped her teeth together, knotting the muscles in her jaw. Whatever the squat fellow found to cause him to beckon his partner could not be good. She heard Ive inhale a breath, hold it, let it trickle out through his nostrils, then he stood and climbed from his seat. When his feet touched the ground, he turned toward her and Evalal.

"For your safety, it's best if you ladies come with me."

Danya swallowed hard. He thought in his presence a safer place than in a wagon full of weapons? He couldn't believe they'd try to escape with unknown forest surrounding them. She hesitated, and he locked eyes with her, did nothing more than tilt his chin toward the ground to encourage her to do as he said.

With nerves vibrating beneath her flesh and no other choice before her, the princess acquiesced. He offered his help; she reached out but stopped. When he didn't waver, she slid her hand into his. It surprised her to find his skin soft and smooth as though he knew no manual labor. Her feet touched the ground, and she jerked it away. If he took offense, he showed no indication, instead turning his attention to aiding Evalal from the wagon.

Despite the time that passed with Ive's hesitation and helping the two of them down, Fellick did not call for his partner again. Either he trusted the man that much or something terrible had happened.

Ive waved his arm, ushering them across the space ahead of him. Danya looked at Evalal, noticed her own worry reflected in the girl's face, and a new thought struck her.

What if they mean to kill us?

Her mouth filled with sour saliva, and she swallowed hard around a lump grown out of nowhere in her throat. She glanced back toward the wagon where her sword belt lay hidden from her on the floorboards. She curled her hands into fists, touched sweat on her palm.

"Please, princess," he urged.

Danya pressed her lips together. What choice did she have but follow instructions and hope for the best?

What would Trenan do?

A simple answer: he wouldn't have allowed himself to end up in this situation. She chastised herself under her breath for allowing the weapons merchants the upper hand and started out toward the tilting barn. Evalal fell into step beside her in silence, but the princess sensed apprehension radiating from her—perhaps she'd formed the same suspicion about their captors' intent.

The yellowed grass crunched beneath their feet as they strode across the yard. Ive slowed to keep his two guests half a pace ahead of him. Partway to the barn, they encountered what had given the stocky man pause.

The dog's death hadn't been an easy one. What remained of its tongue not picked apart by carrion eaters lolled out of the side of its mouth. The animal's bottom half lay twisted at an unnatural angle; wounds peppered its body, but Danya assumed they'd likely occurred after it died. When Evalal saw the poor beast, she gasped and turned her head away. The princess put her arm around the girl's shoulder and guided her past the carcass. Ive didn't react.

They strode past the partially completed hole, dirt mounded beside it, the tip of a spade buried in the heap of soil. An uncompleted grave? If so, for whom? Not the dog; it was far too large even for that sizable beast. For her? She shivered and forced her gaze away from the pit, toward the listing outbuilding.

They finished the short journey across the sad yard and stopped at the entrance to the barn. Ive stood so close behind them, Danya imagined his breath caressing the back of her neck. She stared into the barn's darkness, seeing nothing but black shapes and bits of straw where thin streams of light found their way in through cracks between the boards.

"What did you find, Mr. Fellick?"

"Not Birk." His voice swam out of the blackness, identifying him as a dark shape to their right.

"I guessed it the case. He's been here, though, yes?"

"Yeah. And five or six with him."

"Now why would that be?"

Ive ushered them forward, out of the sunlight and into the dim barn. Danya's eyes began to adjust, and the shapes rectified themselves into Fellick, and a series of barrels, shelves packed full, and the sad cow which had gone silent. The interior proved as much a mess as the exterior's disrepair might suggest it to be. She watched the silhouette of the big man's shoulders rise and fall in a shrug.

"He kept prisoners in here. Two of them." He raised his arm, pointed to one spot on the floor then another.

Danya squinted, trying to see what he saw. The straw seemed as though it had been disturbed, but she'd say the same about every piece of the tinder-dry material covering the ground. At the far end of the barn—the first place he'd indicated—she spied what appeared to be an iron ring protruding from the floor. But what did that prove?

"Do tell," Ive prompted.

"They were all over the inside," he moved his arm side to side, gesturing toward the dishevelment of the straw, "but it don't appear a struggle. No blood. A man and a woman."

At the mention of the captives, Evalal reached out and grasped Danya's wrist, fingers digging in deep enough to hurt. She stifled a surprised gasp lest she gain their captors' attention.

"Eight or nine people here at once, now none."

"Plus the Juddah fella. Looks like he's in rough shape." Fellick paused and rubbed his chin. "Not as bad as his dog though. Poor love is lying dead in the field, his back broke. The carrion eaters have been at him."

Ive nodded. "We saw the beast. And the blood." He prompted the girls deeper into the barn, guiding them more than halfway so they stood a few a paces from his partner and the array of barrels and shelves. When they stopped, he laid his hands on their shoulders, left them there. Danya clenched her teeth, hoping he'd move away. "And what's this?"

"The Juddah fella collected some odd things." Fellick lowered his arm and moved the two steps to the nearest shelf. He reached out and picked up a clay pot. "Broken weapons, tools, jars, sundries. Nothing of concern to us. I daresay the law might have interest in the contents of a few of his barrels, though."

"And what do these casks contain?"

Instead of answering, the stocky man put the sole of his boot to the closest barrel and toppled it over. It struck the floor and threw up a puff of dust, the particles seeming to sparkle in the line of sunlight squeezing its way between the gaps in the wall boards. The cask's dry wood split and splintered as it hit, revealing the contents. Ive pushed on their shoulders and they moved forward, within a pace of Juddah's spilled collection. Whatever it contained gleamed a dull white, but Danya remained unsure what she looked at until Fellick stirred his toe amongst them, flicked some aside, clattering.

Bones.

Despite her best effort to control herself, a shiver rattled up Danya's spine. Evalal gripped her wrist tighter.

"What...?" Danya started but stopped, swallowed the overabundance of saliva filling her mouth. "What kind of bones?"

"Animal mostly," Fellick replied. He toed the collection again, the empty rattle enough to make the princess' gorge rise into the back of her throat.

"Mostly?"

He nodded. "Some come from men, too."

Before she reacted, Ive leaned forward, inserting his head between her and Evalal. His hands remained on their shoulders. She tensed. This was the time they'd reveal their intent. Would they end up in one of Juddah's barrels? The grave in the yard?

"See?" he said, voice quiet. "It's because of men like Juddah I insisted you travel with Mr. Fellick and me."

He straightened without awaiting a response, used his grip on their shoulders to guide them back toward the door. The nervous worry in Danya didn't subside. Was lingering in a pot, waiting for it to boil better than being put to the flames? They walked out of the outbuilding and the princess raised her arm in front of her eyes to keep from being blinded by the sun. Evalal released her hold on her companion's forearm.

"Where did they go?"

Fellick appeared beside them, tilted his head away from the barn and toward the house. "Sunset."

Ive nodded. "They're headed for the Green."

"Seems so."

The Green. The home of the Small Gods.

He pushed them back toward the wagon, removed his hands from their shoulders. Danya was thankful he did, otherwise he'd have noticed her tension return full-force. Evalal reached out and grabbed the princess' hand this time, her grip hard enough to be on the edge of painful.

"No surprise, eh, Mr. Fellick?"

He didn't answer. Ive looked back over his shoulder, searching for his partner, and Danya couldn't help but do the same. He'd taken a different route than them, following the beaten path they'd made on their way to the barn while Ive guided them an alternate course. The big man had stopped and peered at his feet.

"What are you doing, Mr. Fellick?"

"Burying the poor dog." He bent at the waist, then stood, the dog's stiff carcass cradled in his arms, treating the corpse like a delicate thing, as though it might break if he wasn't careful.

A frustrated sigh escaped Ive's lips, and he stooped close to Danya's ear. "I'm going to help Mr. Fellick. Go get in the wagon." He looked around, shrugged. "Nowhere else for you to go."

He sauntered toward his companion as the stout man carried the dead animal to the inexplicable hole already dug in the field. He climbed in to place the beast to rest at the bottom. Danya watched for a second before turning toward the wagon. She scanned the area beyond it—nothing but the thick forest with the one narrow track they'd followed for a day after leaving Krin's tavern. Any notion of flight and escape drained out of her. Ive was right, nowhere for them to go. If they tried, they'd end up lost, or worse. Whether truly the case or not, they were prisoners of the weapons merchants.

With realization, Danya's thoughts flashed to her brother, the prophecy. Where was he? She was convinced he yet lived, but what would happen to the world if the firstborn of the rightful king was lost?

Evalal's grip on her hand tightened. She pulled the princess closer. Danya leaned in.

"It's her," the girl whispered.

Confused, Danya looked at her companion. "Who's her? What are you talking about?"

They reached the wagon, and she glanced over her shoulder at the weapons merchants. Fellick busied himself filling in the hole, laying the dog to rest, but Ive's gaze lay upon them. Instead of awaiting her companion's reply, she gave the girl a boost into the wain, then climbed in behind her. They each sat back where they'd been before, and Evalal leaned close.

"The woman in the barn. Did you hear him speak of her?"

Danya nodded, unsure what her companion meant. She must have read the princess' confusion on her face because she didn't wait for any further response.

"It's the barren mother."

Danya's eyes widened. On the wagon floor beside her foot, the Seed of Life vibrated.

XIII - Teryk - Sand and Sky

*T*HE IMPACT *TERYK* EXPECTED and prepared for never came.

He continued holding his arm over his head until the muscles in his shoulder knotted with the unneeded effort, leaving him no choice but to relax and lower it. Perfect darkness surrounded him, but not perfect silence. A muted roar thrummed in his ears—not loud, but his forehead pulsed with the pressure, his eyeballs threatening to bulge out of their sockets. He swallowed hard, the wan saliva clicking in his throat.

"Rilum?"

He'd spoken the word aloud—his lips moving in concert with his tongue to do so—but the sound of his companion's name died as it left his mouth. He sensed nothing but a desperate rumble and bluster he realized must be the raging of the angry sea outside wherever he found himself.

"Rilum?"

He spoke louder this time, loud enough to hear his own voice. No reply.

A knot formed in his chest. He didn't know the sailor well—wasn't sure he liked the man after seeing the way he treated his son—but he might be the last person he'd ever see. Now he was gone, too.

Teryk allowed himself to slump until his ass hit soft sand. He took comfort from the silky consistency as his hands settled on the beach, sensed coolness between his fingers. Not for the first time, his heart yearned for the softness of the silk sheets adorning his bed at home. The silt flowed fine and sugary between his digits, but his bedding suffered no comparison.

If I touched those sheets, I'd be with mother and father, Danya and Trenan.

As much as memories of the piece of furniture itself warmed him, thinking of being at Draekfarren again brought an emptiness to his gut. Did the path laid out for him by the ancient scroll mean more to him than his own safety? He drew a deep breath and let it seep out between his parted lips.

It has been more important since the day I left the castle.

Teryk shifted, moving his hand to the right, fingers touching a hard surface. He snatched them back, worried whatever he'd encountered might be less than friendly, but no response to his touch came. Despising the tremor shaking his arm, he reached out again, cautious as he crossed the dark space.

His fingertips brushed it again, and he jerked away, but the distance of half a hand's breadth this time. With no reaction again, he moved back, traced the pads of his fingers along its shape until he recognized a boot's leather sole.

"Rilum!"

Teryk changed position, grasping the man's ankle to give him a shake, but he stopped as he sensed a presence near his own head. Had it been there before? If so, he hadn't realized it, but now he felt it with certainty, an energy pulsing and reaching out toward him.

At first, he sought to cower from it, to get as far from it as possible, but he doubted he'd find anywhere in the darkness to avoid it.

Instead of shying away, he reached his free hand up beside his head. His fingers met a cool flowing substance not quite fluid enough to be water, but which he knew to be black sand.

His contact with it lasted for the briefest of moments before the surrounding space changed. The blackness disappeared, replaced by bright light enveloping him. The mound fell out from beneath him, Rilum along with it, and the prince experienced a sensation of falling.

Not falling—floating.

For all he might guess, he dangled from unseen strands pulling him up and away from the world, air rushing around him as he rose. Teryk blinked hard to clear his sight but resisted the urge to rub a knuckle against each eye for fear of the precariousness of his position. The brightness soon dimmed; the light remained, but not enough to blind him. Blue surrounded him. It filled his peripheral vision, seeming to stretch on forever. He tilted his head back and found it above him as well but, in the distance, it darkened until it became black. He bent forward until his chin touched his chest, looked past his feet hanging in nothingness, and his breath caught in his throat.

At first, he didn't understand what he saw.

Most of it shimmered with a dark blue-green hue, large patches of green and brown breaking its consistency. Realization crept into him, and with it, fear.

He recognized the shape of the Windward Kingdom and the Leeward Kingdom, the Inland Sea separating them. He floated above the world, seeing it in a way no one had ever seen it. Its beauty might have taken his breath away if panic hadn't already done so.

A blue swath stretched between his home and the land across the sea, where he'd come to shore after the God of the Deep destroyed the Whalebone. The size of the new territory surprised him though he knew of no reason to think it small; he'd seen but a tiny sliver of the beach.

To his greater surprise, other landmasses dotted the ocean, a few so tiny as to appear no more than pinpricks from his vantage point, others larger than his homeland. In their fear of the God of the Deep, his people never strayed far enough from shore to discover the world was much more than they imagined.

How did we not realize?

He rose ever higher until the earth shrank to a blue, green, and brown disk surrounded by darkness on every side. The swaddling sky disappeared, replaced by inky blackness; the lone source of light shone from the glow of his world far below him. Teryk didn't want to stop looking, but a compulsion to turn his head—to view anything else to see—overwhelmed him. He wished he hadn't.

A man hung in the nothing beside him, a distance equivalent to the height of twenty men separating them. The stranger pivoted to face the prince, his visage appearing both full of rage and glee at the same time. A glow began around him, brightening until he plummeted earthward, a fiery tail streaking out behind.

The Small Gods are real.

And then Teryk fell, hurtling toward the world at a speed enough to prevent him from drawing breath into his lungs.

He closed his eyes and waited to die.

XIV - Danya - Vibrations

*D*ESPITE THE DIRT TRACK ending two sunrises past, Fellick guided the horses and wagon around obstacles and over hills. A few times, steeper grades necessitated they get out and pull on their harnesses, helping the animals. Not long before sunset on the second day, the trees grew nearer together, the trunks too tight to allow them passage.

Ive sighed and looked at his companion.

"No other path, Mr. Fellick?"

"Your eyes work as well as mine."

Despite the exhaustion and worry weighing on her, Danya fought back a grin at the stout man's comment. He didn't speak much but, when he did, he packed a huge dose of sarcasm into few words.

"What's your opinion on leaving the wagon behind?" Ive asked.

"You know how I feel. I don't give a tinker's damn about the cart, it's the wares I hate being unattended."

The tall man straightened in his seat, one hand held up to his forehead as he surveyed the area with an unhidden display of mockery. "Can't see many thieves hiding among the brush here, Mr. Fellick. Few others are so vain as to venture so near the Green."

"Vanity ain't why I'm here," Fellick grumbled as he lay the reins on the floorboards by his feet. He sighed and climbed out of his seat.

Why are we here?

The Seed of Life trembled beneath the princess' foot, its movement enough for her to notice, but not so much as to attract attention. Evalal's declaration of the woman who'd been at Juddah's homestead being the barren mother from the prophecy had started the vibrations, and they'd continued off and on since. Danya remained unsure whether it encouraged them to continue, telling her they pursued the right path, or if it meant to warn them.

The girl's Goddess should have chosen a more precise method of communication.

Ive followed his partner to the forest floor, then turned toward them.

"Ladies, we go from here on foot. My apologies you have to leave behind the comfort and luxury of the Fellick and Ive wain but, as you can see, we have no opportunity to continue with it."

"Where are we going?" Danya asked as she stood. Beside her, Evalal scrambled over the side of the wagon, an unexpected enthusiasm in her movements.

"It's imperative we find our friend, Mr. Birk. It appears he has come this way, doesn't it, Mr. Fellick?"

He grunted in response, but said nothing else. The princess shifted toward the wagon's edge, hesitant to remove her foot from the doeskin pouch and its contents. Her thighs ached, and she suspected the ride had pressed her behind flat, proving the sarcasm seated in Ive's description of his wagon. She feigned a stretch which became real and necessary, but she didn't move away from her sword belt. How to take the Seed of Life with her?

"I thought you intended to help Evalal and I on our journey. Instead, you've waylaid us into joining yours."

Ive tilted his head at her, half-scowled. "I believe our search for Mr. Birk and where you intend to go will end up being the same place. Funny how things work out, eh?"

She stared at him as though doing so might uncover the meaning of his words. He no more knew where they intended to go—Danya didn't know herself—than she knew their intent. Or did he? So many unanswerable questions came to mind. If the woman from the barn was the barren mother, who'd accompanied her? And who were Juddah and Birk? Where did Fellick and Ive fit in with the prophecy? Did they mean harm to either of them? Would they offer help?

He spoke again, pulling the princess from her thoughts. He awaited her response, but she hadn't heard what he said, so she waited for him to repeat himself. After a moment, he nodded toward her feet.

"The sword belt, lass. Leave the weapon it holds behind, but bring the rest with you. I suspect we might want the contents of your pouch with us."

Danya struggled to keep from reacting, hoped she kept the shock of surprise from her expression. She bent at the waist, reaching for the belt, but holding her eyes on his, waiting for him to divert his gaze. His half-scowl transformed into a grin. Did he guess what the bag contained? Had he from the start?

She glanced away for an instant to find the hilt of her sword and pull the weapon from its scabbard. It clunked against the wood floor boards as she laid it at her feet and straightened, the belt dangling from her hand. Ive smiled more fully and nodded, satisfied, before leaving his spot at the side of the wagon to help his partner with the horses. As soon as his gaze left her, Danya pivoted toward Evalal, allowing her face to register the surprise and concern bolting through her at Ive's mention of the pouch. The younger girl stared back at her, eyes wide but flickering with the confidence of her beliefs. As unsure as she was of continuing with the weapons merchants being the right thing to do, Evalal remained convinced the Goddess walked beside them, guiding their actions through means they'd never realize or understand. A sliver of the princess wished she possessed the same blind faith; seemed life would be so much easier.

With a shake of her head, she put the belt around her waist and buckled it. The pouch and the seed hidden within bounced against her thigh, its touch transferring a gentle vibration through her muscle. Though she didn't understand its meaning, it lent her a measure of relief. Deserved or not, she felt thankful for it.

Evalal helped her from the wagon until she got both feet planted on the ground. She held the wooden edge for a few heartbeats, legs wobbly from sitting on the uncomfortable bench for so long. The girl allowed her a short time to recover before touching her shoulder, requesting her attention.

The princess faced her companion. Despite the shadows of the forest falling across her face in the approaching twilight, Evalal's features glowed with an expression resembling joy, or perhaps reverence. Danya raised an eyebrow, wondering what should bring such an aspect to the girl when their situation may be dire. Evalal responded by raising her arm, pointing past her head.

Leery, Danya pivoted.

Fellick and Ive remained by the horses, sorting out harnesses and setting them up to be on their own. Beyond them lay the darkening forest of cool shadows and twisted limbs. But she hadn't been gesturing toward either the men or the trees, she'd raised her arm farther. Danya tilted her head back, scanning tree trunks. She saw nothing amongst them other than green needles and gray and brown wood. Above the treetops, the sky stretched out and away, but it wasn't all the indigo of creeping twilight.

Straight ahead, the heavens glowed emerald.

XV - Teryk - Meadow

*D*ARKNESS RETURNED.

At first, Teryk suspected he'd forgotten to open his eyes. He considered the possibility he might yet be falling out of the sky, but no air rushed around him or whistled in his ears. He blinked, sensed his lashes flutter—he lived, but the world no longer existed.

"Nghn."

The groan came from his right, startling him; the lone sound in an otherwise complete silence.

"Rilum?"

Another moan followed by the scrape of movement as the sailor repositioned himself. Teryk put his hand down to settle himself, touched cool, fine powder.

I'm back under the dome of black sand.

His chest swelled with relief while disappointment insinuated itself in his mind. Did this mean he'd experienced a false vision of the world? An illusion created by his panic or that he'd dreamed when he slipped into sleep without realizing?

It appeared so real.

He recalled the cool air on his face as he fell, the overwhelming awe. Could those excitements visit him during dream or illusion? He'd awoken from dreams before with feelings of loss or concern, but did he ever experience them in the midst of the vision?

Rilum shifted again, the crunch of his boots in the sand highlighting the lack of other sounds—no crash of waves, no swirling of surf or howl of wind. It brought Teryk back from his memories to the present.

"Rilum," he said, relieved the man lived.

"Where are we?" the sailor asked, voice hoarse and scratchy.

"Safe. I think."

"Safe where? Where be the stars?"

The prince sighed. "What do you last remember?"

A moment of near-silence passed, then the whisper of cloth scratching against cloth. He imagined his companion rubbing his eyes, attempting to vanquish the cobwebs of sleep from his head. A deep sigh followed.

"The thing eatin' the cap'n. Not much after."

"We abandoned the raft and made it to shore. While you slept, stars fell from the sky. One hit the sea and created a huge wave, but the beach came to life." He hesitated, swallowed. "To protect us. A dome formed of black silt enshrouds us now."

Teryk finished speaking and shook his head. It sounded so unreal when he spoke it aloud. The doubt he'd allowed to creep in about the veracity of his view of the world solidified. None of this could happen. Stars didn't plummet from the sky. Sand didn't move in the manner of a living thing, nor did it take the form of a woman. He didn't tell his companion the most unbelievable part.

"It—" Rilum interrupted himself to swallow hard, his throat clicking. "It don't make sense."

Teryk's head sank until his chin touched his chest. "No, it doesn't. I have no idea where we are."

As the last word left his mouth, the sand over their heads parted, letting in a shaft of what might have been sunlight, but the prince couldn't be sure. He threw his forearm up in front of his eyes to keep it from blinding him. Rilum groaned as though the brightness hurt.

With the light came warmth. It began from above, beating down on them with the intensity of the hottest day of third season, then it spread around them. Teryk glanced to his left and saw the wall of sand falling away, folding upon itself and opening on a meadow. The prince lowered his arm, his eyes becoming accustomed to what he now knew to be sunlight. Had they been under the black sand's protection long enough for night to become daytime? It didn't seem possible, but the triviality of time meant little in the face of another question.

Where did the beach go?

"I thought you said we'd swam to shore."

"I..." Any explanation Teryk might give escaped him.

The last of the sandy dome fell away. Instead of creating a swath of darkness on the emerald grass, it disappeared as though either the earth or the air swallowed it. One more mystery to which he'd never find an answer.

His gaze wandered across the meadow and found it dotted with wildflowers of many colors: red, yellow, orange, purple, blue. In the distance, the ground rose into hills and trees sprouted, small at first, then farther away reaching high toward the sky. No matter which direction he surveyed, the view remained unchanged.

"We're in a valley," Teryk said finally. He shifted to face Rilum. "Is it familiar to you?"

The sailor's eyes darted, taking in the landscape. His expression gave the prince the answer before he parted his lips to speak.

"I spent near my entire life walking the decks of the ships of merchants and kings. The land I've seen is whatever be at the ports I visited."

Teryk thought he detected a note of regret in his companion's voice, but he chose not to mention it. Sitting in the middle of an unknown meadow didn't seem the time nor the place to delve into what made Rilum Seaman sad. Not when a prophecy threatened the fall of man.

The prince stood. The ground beneath them remained a disk of black sand laced with gold, as soft and sugary as when they'd found their way to the shore. Two strides separated him from the edge of the misplaced piece of beach; he took those steps, stopping before his feet left the circle.

"Where do you think you're going?"

Teryk didn't bother looking back. The sound of Rilum's words made him realize he heard no other noises—not a sigh of wind, a chirp of birds, or the buzz of insects. A chill ran along his arms, covering the flesh with bumps.

"I'm not sure, but what's the point in staying here?"

"How do you know? We got here without intending. Maybe if we stay, we'll get somewhere else we don't mean to go."

"What if the place we end up isn't a pleasant grassy field? What if it's the top of a snowy mountain? The middle of the ocean?" He recalled his vision as he floated high above the world and the vast blue-green sea covering the majority of its surface.

It wasn't real.

He returned his attention to the meadow stretching out toward him. What happened to the sounds? Did nature ever sit so still and silent? If he concentrated enough, he thought he might pick out Rilum's heartbeat competing with his own.

Teryk diverted his gaze to his feet. The width of a finger separated the toes of the boots they'd provided him on the Whalebone from the perfect line where the sand ended and the grass began. Stepping off one onto the other shouldn't have been any different from any other step he'd taken in his life, yet his heartbeat sped, his breath shallowed. A thin band of sweat formed on his brow; if asked, he'd have blamed it on the sun but knew trepidation to be its cause.

He inhaled through his nose, filling his lungs with air smelling of sand and seaweed and wood bleached white by sunshine, not of grass and wildflowers and pollen. The breath shuddered out of his chest; he licked his lips, raised his foot, and stepped off.

"Tery—"

Rilum's word cut off the instant Teryk crossed the border between beach and meadow. The silence disappeared, its dominance usurped by the calls of birds and the buzz of insects he'd expected. Amongst them lurked an odd, unidentifiable hiss. His reticence waned, allowing space for the peace brought by a glorious day such as the one he now enjoyed. The air held the perfume of flowers and meadow; they tickled his nose, threatening to bring on a sneeze, but he fought it off and pivoted back toward his companion. The source of the out-of-place sound became clear: the sandy patch where he'd been sitting was vanishing, sifting into the earth and leaving grass behind as it shrunk around Rilum Seaman.

His companion's lips moved, but Teryk heard nothing other than the sounds of the heath. Rilum scrambled to his feet, and the sand shrank closer until the disk became just big enough for him to stand upon.

"Step off. It's okay."

The sailor shook his head, pointed at his ear.

"Step off," he repeated, this time waving his hands, gesturing for his companion to come toward him.

Rilum's eyes widened, and he shook his head again. Teryk gritted his teeth in frustration. What did he plan to do? Live the rest of his life on a sliver of beach hardly big enough to stand on? A little more of the sand fell away, the edge of the disk creeping closer to his feet. The prince wondered if it might disappear if he waited too long. A second thought occurred: if he delayed, would Rilum vanish along with it?

He gestured again, with more urgency this time, but his companion remained resolute in his refusal.

Another sound joined the meadow's melodic dissonance. Quiet and far away to start, so muted by distance he might have confused it with the buzzing of flies and bees, but it contained a different quality. The noise grew with each passing heartbeat. He pivoted, surveying the meadow, searching for the source.

At first, he saw nothing but grass and flowers and trees stretching to the tree line. None of these appeared to make the sound growing in his ears; he continued scanning. The forest at the far end of the field swayed as though touched by wind, which Teryk found odd; he sensed no hint of a breeze where he stood, and the meadow between himself and the woods did not ripple.

After a short time staring at the unusual movement of the trees, the prince realized only one patch of saplings moved. On either side, the thin trunks remained straight and true, unmoving. He squinted, attempting to figure out what caused such behavior, but it helped him see nothing more.

The first creature broke through the edge of the woods a few heartbeats later.

It must have been huge for Teryk to discern it from such a distance, but it remained too far away to recognize what type of animal it might be. It explained the shaking of the trees.

"Rilum..."

The prince stepped back as another beast emerged, then another. The space separating them made their rate of movement impossible to estimate, but a haze rose above them—dust from trampled ground—as more and more appeared. He spun toward his companion, found the sailor standing atop the small disk of sand staring past him, mouth agape. He didn't move.

Teryk rushed by, reaching for the sailor's arm as he went, unsure if he'd be able to touch him through whatever kept out the sounds of the meadow. His fingers grasped the still-damp sleeve of Rilum's tunic, and his momentum pulled the sailor from his tiny, beach-like haven. Rilum stumbled after him, feet catching and throwing him to the ground with a grunt as the wind left his chest.

Teryk stopped, boots skidding in the grass, and returned to the other man. He put his hand under the sailor's armpit and yanked him up, helping him find his footing. The sailor rose grudgingly, gaze fixed on the far end of the meadow. The prince halted and glanced back, too.

The haze of dust and pollen kicked up by the creatures grew wider and taller, obscuring the line of trees. At the bottom of the cloud, many shapes moved, and he made out several colors of... fur? Flesh? Impossible to be sure but, as he watched, his heart beat faster and a sheen of sweat dampened his palms. Though he couldn't identify what kinds of beasts these might be, one thing became clear: they headed straight for them.

The prince snatched his companion's arm and pulled hard.

"Run," he said, feet slipping in the grass as Rilum resisted. He turned and grabbed on with the other hand, wrenching the man toward him until he gave in and followed. "Run!"

XVI - Trenan - rture

*T*RENAN STOOD WITH HIS legs at shoulder-width, his one hand resting on his hip. Of the many times he longed for his missing arm, no instance proved as frustrating or unnecessary as the wish to cross his arms or stand with both hands on his hips. With a limb gone, half of a man's body language went along with it.

Practice weapons impacted wooden shields with muted *thunks*, the two dozen women paired up around the yard perspiring in the midday heat. He'd watched the sun rise and set but a handful of times since his arrival, yet every warrior showed marked improvement, even from the impressive skill levels they already exhibited.

If only the kingdom's soldiers learned their skills with such ease and speed.

Truthfully, he'd have put any of the twenty-four women handpicked to prepare for a mysterious mission up against any man in the king's legion. And many of the dozens of other Goddess warriors, too. With the army of the king made up of these fighters, he'd worry little of wars being lost. How and why this battalion existed troubled him almost as much as the fact they'd kept it a secret.

Trenan didn't move when he detected the sound of loose dirt crunching beneath boot soles. But one person dared interrupt during training.

"They only wear their armor after dusk, Yoli. I can't talk them into wearing it while the sun is out."

"And they will not while they are readying." A measure of the derision and annoyance present in her tone when they first met had disappeared, but not all of it. "Goddess wants them to be familiar with wielding their weapons under any circumstance."

He'd already known her response—they'd discussed this more than once. The concept made good sense, and he wondered if he fought against it the way he did because he never considered training his own soldiers in the same manner. Differences existed between swinging a sword in full armor or in none.

"How is Dansil?" he asked out of duty rather than concern.

"Your man will live if Goddess desires it."

He nodded, part of him wanting to ask for more detail. Many, including himself, might find the world a better place if the Goddess decided she desired his death. He opened his mouth to say this, then closed it again, choosing to keep his disdain to himself.

"You have no love for this fellow," Yoli said as if he'd spoken his thoughts.

"We have never been friends."

She snorted a laugh. "Is this what you men call it when another plots your death?"

"How did you—?"

"Goddess has told us much about you, but no matter. How are the warriors faring under your guidance?"

"They're coming along." He stole a glance her direction, awaiting her reaction to his statement, but her expression betrayed nothing. "They will be ready if this war you talk of comes."

"When it comes," she corrected. "But it's time for them to be ready now."

Trenan cocked an eyebrow at her but, as usual, she didn't direct her gaze toward him. She acted as though looking upon him caused her pain, so she avoided it. He realized he reacted to Ishla in a similar fashion, because seeing her bred distress in him, but he suspected Yoli guilty of it no matter what man stood beside her.

"The war hasn't come, but it's time to fight?"

"It is time for your part in this to begin."

The master swordsman clamped his jaw tight and breathed out through his nose. "I've spent too many sunrises and sunsets here. The princess' path grows colder with each morning and night the sun touches the horizon."

"Did I not say you will see Princess Danya again soon? Do you doubt the Mother of Death through whom Goddess speaks?"

"I don't know who this Mother of Death is. What I know is I must find the princess and return her to the king."

Yoli scuffed her feet in the dirt, impatient with the conversation. "You will find Danya—your role involves her."

"What role?" he demanded, his hand curling into a fist. "What is this you keep speaking of? And how does it involve her?"

She didn't respond at once, and he knew she meant this to torture him. Given her way, they'd never have admitted him beyond the walls, but the decision wasn't hers. The fact didn't require her to act as though she enjoyed his company, however. He resisted the urge to ask again.

"You leave in the morning," she said, pivoting on the heels of her boots. "Make sure your chosen warriors are ready."

He waited as she strode toward the door at the side of the training yard, allowing her a few steps before he spoke again.

"Leave? For where?" he called after her. "What if I refuse to go?"

She stopped, paused, then faced him.

"You won't. In the morning, your journey continues as you desire. With the rising of the sun, you depart for the Green."

⸻

Although nothing but the sun's leading edge peeked above the horizon and the City of the Sick yet lay in darkness, Trenan found his warriors already assembled when he arrived. Each of them sat their horses with the confidence bred of repetition, equipment and supplies lashed to their saddles. It pleased the master swordsman to find them clad in the armor they'd worn during their evening training rather than bare-chested.

The two dozen warriors didn't mill about. They engaged in no conversation, and none of them fidgeted with their gear or allowed their steeds to dance nervously. Trenan doubted he'd ever seen a more precise and controlled line of fighters in all his time. Despite the effort they'd put in, the fighter in him wondered how the untested soldiers might fare on the battlefield. Wooden swords and a practice yard were one thing, but the chaos of actual battle was something different. Nothing truly prepared a soldier for fight-to-the-death combat. And would it make any difference they were women? With no precedent, he possessed no way to know.

He led his horse to stand in front of them, visible to every rider.

"Is everyone ready?"

They nodded in unison, but no one spoke. Other than grunts of strain and the very occasional cry of pain, he'd not yet heard any of them utter a word. He didn't know whether they lacked the capability of speaking or chose not to do so. Either way, he expected their silence to make for a quiet and lonely ride.

Before mounting his steed, his gaze trailed up and down the avenue, expecting to spy Yoli approaching with instructions, perhaps to join them. The boulevard lay as empty as when he'd first arrived at Ikkundana. He didn't understand why she—or the Goddess—wanted him to go to the Green, but at least doing so allowed him to continue his search for the princess. What else did they mean for him to find? What did this Mother of Death see?

He raised his foot to the stirrup, grasped the saddle horn, and hauled himself up onto his steed. The horse accepted his weight with a gentle whinny, the same way it greeted him every time he'd mounted it since procuring it from the outpost. It wasn't as comfortable beneath him as the horses of the women appeared with their loads; mounts and riders had been together for a while, growing accustomed, trusting.

A helpful trait if war comes as she says.

He reined his mount around and put his heels to its flanks, prompting the animal toward the gate. The others fell in behind him before he opened his mouth to direct them to do so. Dozens of hooves clicked and clattered on the street, their harsh impacts echoing off the walls on both sides of them. Trenan raised his eyes to the buildings lining the avenue. As he'd seen no one peering from windows to document his arrival, neither did anyone watch in the dim of morning to mark their departure. No candles lit, no sleep disturbed, no sounds other than the warriors' passing.

Perhaps not the City of the Sick but the City of the Dead.

The thought brought to mind Yoli's proclamation of the Goddess predicting his coming while speaking through the Mother of Death. It wasn't the first time he'd heard of the mysterious woman. He'd never believed her more than rumor and stories, a frightful tale to keep outsiders away. This mention of her didn't prove her real, though it gave him reason to wonder.

He escorted the riders around a corner onto the avenue leading in a straight line to the wall. A lone figure stood beside the hidden portal, one elbow resting on the complicated machinations used to lay it open. Trenan recognized Yoli and raised a hand to her. She didn't so much as nod in response. Instead, she leaned against the gate-opening contraption. Unseen gears and cogs groaned, chains clanked, and the two halves of the gateway pulled first inward and then to the sides. The master swordsman had seen nothing like it.

As always, Yoli wore armor, sword dangling at her side. Seeing her made Trenan think she meant to join them on their trek, but he didn't see her horse nearby. A sliver of disappointment inserted itself in his chest, and he wondered why. Surely because, as well-trained as the warriors following him proved to be, she appeared the most proficient of them. As they neared the gate, he reined his steed to a stop and looked down at her stony face.

"You are not coming with us?"

"Of course I am." She whistled between her teeth and the clop of hooves on flagstone echoed against the walls as her mount emerged from a hidden alley partway up the lane.

The master swordsman snorted a laugh even as his heartbeat gained in pace in his chest. "Tried to keep it a secret, though."

Yoli stared up at him, her expression blank of any emotion. He couldn't tell if his words had offended her or if she possessed no smiles to spare. Either way, he shifted in his seat to avoid her gaze until the horse arrived at her side. She grasped the saddle's pommel and swung herself up with the ease born of repetition.

"We'll be glad to have you along," he said.

She nodded—the most reaction he'd gotten from her during his stay in Ikkundana. She guided her steed around, pointing it toward the open gate, then waited—her method of telling him it was time for them to go. The disgust she must feel at having to defer to a man to lead them.

Trenan sighed and put heel to horse flesh. As soon as he set out, Yoli did, too, keeping pace half a stride behind him and to his left, and the others fell in behind them. Once they passed through the gate, the gate's contraption creaked and groaned again as if tripped by unseen hands. The two pieces of stone ground back into place, any demarcation of the opening nearly invisible. As they moved away, Yoli spoke.

"Mortal threats are not just around us, sword master. Keep one eye on the sky."

XVII - Teryk - Forest

*T*HE *RUMBLE OF* MANY feet—hooves? Paws? —chased them across the meadow.

Once Rilum got going, he proved faster than Teryk, but the prince's youth gave him more stamina. The sailor pulled ahead for a while, but it wasn't long before Teryk caught up. In fact, he'd have passed his companion and left him behind the way Rilum did to him at the start, but he worried for his safety. He knew this one person in an unfamiliar place. With no idea where they might be, he didn't wish to face what may come alone.

He fought the urge to look back; the earth trembling beneath their feet told him the creatures behind grew closer with every step. The knowledge boosted his adrenalin enough to push him on without the need to add more fear by seeing what nipped at their heels.

The sailor didn't have the same self-control.

"Gods," he cursed between panted breaths.

Teryk glanced over and saw him craning his neck to look back. The action not only caused dismay, but slowed him. He grabbed the sailor's shoulder, coaxed him to increase his pace.

"Come on, Rilum."

In his attempt to goad his companion into going faster, the prince glimpsed the group coming up behind them.

They'd drawn close enough for him to make out colors, shapes, sizes. The biggest of the creatures resembled nothing he'd seen; thick legs, wide heads, green-tinted flesh or fur. Some moved upright, but most ran on four feet. Amongst them scampered smaller animals, many unfamiliar, others he recognized from drawings, and a few he'd encountered before: deer, bear, big cats. Several of the beasts appeared as though they should be predator and prey, yet they traveled together, stampeding across the meadow, bent on running down the prince and his companion.

The last thing Teryk noticed before panic and self-preservation took over and made him drag Rilum onward were the small men. Gray-skinned and unclothed, most of them ran with the animals while others rode atop creatures. He gasped and turned his gaze away, looking forward to the forest bordering the meadow ahead of them.

If we make it, we can find somewhere to hide.

It might not mean their safety, but maybe their survival.

The tramp of the sailor's footsteps behind him found his ears, but he didn't wait to see how close he followed to help him. He may be the only other person in this land, but a scroll written by an ancient hand mentioned one savior, not more.

I have to survive.

Teryk pushed himself harder and found himself thankful for the training Trenan had forced upon him throughout his youth. Many times he'd hated it and most often thought the running he made him do pointless. Now, for the first time in his life—and most likely the last—his throbbing thighs and burning lungs appreciated the relentless coaching and drilling.

The forest ahead drew closer as the rumble grew around them. They'd come near enough for Teryk to identify individual tree trunks, discern the leafy ones from the evergreens, but close enough they'd make it before the behemoths trod them into the ground? Tall grass whispered against his legs, coaxed him on. Teeth clamped, he pushed himself harder, willing himself to move faster.

The shadows of the first trees fell on Teryk, cooling him, though he suspected it might be mere perception rather than reality. Two rapid heartbeats later, he found himself amongst the narrow trunks of the leafy saplings leading to the forest proper. He weaved his way through them, aware of Rilum's presence close behind him. The sailor—used to shipboard duties, not sprinting across fields—huffed labored breaths, heavy feet beat the ground, but he maintained his pace at the prince's back.

The grass between the trunks grew sparse, replaced by low shrubs and tangled brambles as the forest itself became more dense. Wider-trunked evergreens took up space between the smaller trees, forcing them out and turning the woods into a labyrinth of brush and tree. Fallen limbs scattered around the ground further impeded their progress, and Teryk paused long enough to peek back behind them.

No animals followed them—big ones, small ones, furred, fleshed, and every color no longer appeared in the meadow. Nothing but the gray men remained, but neither did they chase Teryk and Rilum. They'd stopped at the edge of the smaller trees where the grassland ended and the forest began.

Teryk slowed, then halted. Rilum avoided running into him by dodging at the last second, twisting his body to avoid colliding with his companion. He skidded to a halt beside the prince and spun around to see what gripped his attention. The sailor's breath clicked in his throat.

"Where...?" He trailed off, the question left incomplete.

The small gray men ran back and forth along the boundary of grass and forest, arraying themselves in a line. A few remained separate from the others, and the prince heard their voices carried on the still air. Their individual words dissipated, bleeding together and making it impossible to tell if they spoke the same tongue as him.

"What's happening?" Rilum found his voice again.

Teryk waved a hand to quiet him. "I don't know," he whispered.

Thoughts and feelings, sense and emotion battled within the prince. The sensible part of him begged for them to flee, disappear into the forest and get as far away from these unusual men as possible. But the emotional side refused to let his legs retreat from the threat. He sensed an import to the happenings here, an event of unimaginable significance, though he hadn't a clue what or why he should think it the case. Rilum tugged on his sleeve, not feeling the same thing.

"Let's get our asses away from here," he said, his tone a forceful whisper.

"We don't know what happened to the animals."

"So? If they're not bein' here, then they ain't no danger to us."

Teryk faced the sailor. "What if they are circling around behind?"

Rilum's expression turned slack and frightened. "More reason to get the hell outta this place."

"It's too late." He shook his head and took a tentative step back toward the meadow and the lengthening line of gray men; they numbered far more than he'd thought.

"Where are you going?"

The prince didn't answer, instead taking two more steps away from Rilum, choosing his footing to avoid making noise. His companion huffed an exasperated sigh loud enough to negate Teryk's care if anyone listened, but no one did. The small gray men continued forming their line with no pause or hesitation.

Battle line?

Their behavior suggested they readied themselves, but for what? The animals appeared to have vanished into empty air, but they'd posed no threat to these unusual fellows. No, they prepared for something else.

Teryk crept closer, slinking around a bush with wide, bronze-tinted leaves, stepping over a branch fallen from a nearby tree, pale green lichen covering its bark. As he neared them, he realized the gray people stood no taller than half the height of an average man, with little variation in size from one to the next. Some broader and more stout, others so skinny they resembled the thin-trunked leafy trees, but their heights appeared within the width of three fingers of each other. All were hairless and unclothed, but none exhibited shame at being so any more than an animal caught without breeches.

The gray man closest to Teryk—stockier and more heavily muscled than the others—called out clear enough for the prince to catch his words. Though he didn't understand the language he spoke, his voice held a tone he recognized from the commands Trenan had barked at him countless times during their training sessions. This fellow appeared in charge.

Teryk wiped sweat from his palms on his breeches. His sun-dried clothes gave off a tangy scent of perspiration and the sea. Smelling himself thus made his belly roil; he gulped a mouthful of fresh air into his lungs, attempting to calm his nausea as he crept closer. With ten paces between him and the closest of the men, he stopped, though now he saw they weren't all male.

He crouched, hiding himself behind a bush dotted with plump red berries. Their sweet aroma penetrated his own stink, and his belly growled with hunger. He shrank back lest any of the small gray people notice his stomach's lament; finding Rilum at his side startled him. The sailor moved with such stealth, Teryk hadn't realized he'd followed.

His companion opened his mouth to speak, but the prince silenced him with a gesture. They didn't know what these things were—though his suspicions increased with each passing heartbeat—nor their intent or demeanor. No telling what they might do to the two men should they discover them watching.

Yet I find myself drawn toward them.

Teryk returned his attention to the gray figures strung out at regular intervals along the border between forest and meadow, this time looking past them at the grassy expanse beyond. The tall blades stirred with a wan breeze wafting across the field. It should have appeared peaceful, serene, but a heaviness in the air stole the inherent tranquility from the scene. Though the little people—what he suspected to be Small Gods based on the vague descriptions related in legend and lore—showed no sign of panic, urgency informed their actions.

If it's true, then Small Gods fill the land across the sea.

This thought cast the scroll and its prophecy in a whole new glow, opened it to further interpretation and made its meaning uncertain rather than more clear.

A flash at the far end of the meadow caught Teryk's attention. He shook his head, clearing thoughts he had no chance of untangling, and squinted. The light shimmered, joined by another and another, then others. It wasn't firelight—midday didn't require torchlight. It lacked the flickering of torches or lanterns.

No, the scintillating glimmers possessed the quality of starlight.

Like the stars I saw fall from the sky.

The muscles in Teryk's body tightened, his limbs preparing for fight or flight, whichever he demanded of them, but he held his place.

The shimmering glow expanded until a line of silver light emblazoned the entire far end of the meadow. Not a solid boundary, but one made of many shining pinpricks, each bobbing and fluctuating. Soon after it formed, a rumbling in the earth vibrated against Teryk's feet. The gray figures not yet set in place hurried to their positions, the stocky fellow hollering orders others passed along their ranks. Did he stand on the verge of witnessing a fight between the Small Gods of forest and sky?

"What's happening?" Rilum whispered; his words startled Teryk despite their quietness.

"I'm not sure," he replied against his best judgment, but the gray figures proved too involved in their own doings to notice them speaking. "Did you see that?"

He raised his hand, pointed at the line of dancing light and sensed his companion lean forward as though doing so enabled him to get a better view. Teryk held his breath, listening to his heart beating in his ears and noticing the vibration growing stronger. His lips parted, ready to speak of fallen stars and Small Gods, tempted to blurt nonsensical words concerning an ancient scroll and his part in a vague prophecy, but the sailor spoke first.

"Sun on steel," Rilum said. "Swords, shields, armor. Them be riders."

His observation explained both the weird light and the growing rumble far better than Teryk's flight of fancy.

A lot of horses, judging by the shaking of the earth. *Why didn't I recognize it?*

The vibration in the ground grew to become a sound—hundreds of hooves beating the turf. Amongst their deep-toned thrum, other sounds became plain: steel clashing against steel, men yelling and hollering.

Teryk knew not who these soldiers might be or their intent toward him, but fear clawed its way into his gullet. The onrushing army did not appear to have a similar effect on the gray figures.

The last of them settled into their positions, the heavily muscled male the lone one not taking up position in the line. On a shouted command from him, the others raised their arms, holding them straight out to the sides. Far too much space lay between them for their hands to touch—the result if they'd been a few steps closer to each other.

The drone of hoof beats grew louder, the clamor of struck metal and threatening voices growing along with it. The riders advanced close enough the prince recognized the colors and breeds of individual horses. Above them, a movement caught the prince's eye. The sky darkened, but not because of clouds crossing the sun.

Birds!

More wildfowl than Teryk had seen in his entire life, more than he'd have guessed existed. The men on horseback didn't falter as the multitude of winged and feathered bodies blotted out sunlight and sky. A heartbeat later, the enormous flock caught up to the horses, passed them. Their flight path headed toward the woods where the gray figures waited and he and his companion hid. A huge raven led the throng, its wide wings and sleek body so black, night might have gotten lost in it.

The flock pulled away from the horsemen, the sky opening again behind them as they went. Colors flashed amongst the birds—greens, reds, blues, yellows, and so many others. Another time, the variety would have astounded the prince, stolen his breath and left him in awe. Not now. Not with armed men bearing down on them, not when they knew not where they'd ended up or what may happen.

The raven passed over the tree line, its shadow falling across Teryk, then the darkness expanding as the other birds followed. The gray figures let out a cheer as the throng flew over them. It lasted for the length of five heartbeats before the stocky fellow issued another command and they fell into silence; the same wasn't true of the world around them.

Wings beat the air, hooves pounded the ground, swords and spears hammered against shields and men yelled. The cacophony assaulted Teryk, rattled his teeth. He put his hands up to block it out as though doing so might keep the outside pressure from expanding his head until it exploded like an overfilled water bladder. Even with his palms pressed hard against his ears, he heard a new sound joining the others.

Indistinguishable at first, as the last of the birds passed overhead and the flapping of their wings dissipated, the resonance expanded, became more noticeable. Nothing more than a hum to begin with, it turned into a rhythmic chant as its volume grew.

The sounds of the riders made the sounds indistinct to Teryk, but he assumed he lacked the ability to understand them if they'd been intelligible. He moved his hands away, the racket assaulting his ears and pounding into his head, but he wanted to find out if he comprehended any word the gray people intoned. They verbalized as one, their many small voices joining into a single great note. It grew louder, and he identified a cadence within it repeated over and over; eight or ten words they chanted again and again. This time, the stocky male who'd barked commands joined them, his arms held out to the sides like the others.

Rilum grabbed Teryk's arm, pulled at him and spoke a plea lost amongst the tumult of voices and other noises. The prince might have guessed what his companion said, but he resisted answering or succumbing to his prompting. He sensed something important happening here, an event to set him upon the proper path to fulfill his destiny.

The distance between riders and forest closed, the gleam of metal rectifying itself into rectangular shields, helmets of several shapes and styles. The men atop the horses waved swords and axes, spears and maces above their heads, threatening pain and death to any who got in their way. In response, the gray figures kept their ground, their mesmerizing chant's intonation unflinching, its measure unbroken, tempo unchanged. Teryk clamped his jaw tight enough he worried his teeth might bend and break; breath held, he awaited an explosion of warriors and steeds meeting and trampling their much smaller opponents.

It will not happen. It can't happen this way.

The space of a heartbeat after the thought completed itself in his head, the chanting changed. The cadence sped up, the tone climbing an octave. Each of the small gray figures raised their hands toward the sky in perfect unison. The trees and brush around Teryk and Rilum shivered, then shook, as though a windstorm arose from nowhere, but the prince felt no gusts against his cheek. The foliage whipped into a frenzy and he raised his arm to protect his face, but stopped halfway when he saw the small creatures lifting their arms, their wrists touching above their heads.

And a green glow rose in front of them, expanding toward the sky.

XVIII - Dansil - Conscious

DANSIL STIRRED, ROLLED ONTO his back and regretted it as pain shot through his body. He groaned, reached for his spine, and touched the bandage wrapped around him. His brows furrowed; he possessed no recollection of anyone treating his injury other than Trenan. Everything after came to him hazy and indistinct. He recalled snatches of a journey on a horse, the master swordsman seated in front of him, but didn't trust his memories as anything other than fevered illusions.

More than once, he'd thought he spied the fellow who stabbed him keeping pace with them, a robed figure at his side. Even feverish and in pain, he'd realized the impossibility of his assailant following them. The last time he'd seen Stirk, the man possessed no legs, one arm, and he suspected Trenan of killing him, but his memory grew foggy on the point.

The distant clatter of hooves on flagstone broke the silence of the dark room. Dansil raised his head, looked around. He first thought the chamber lightless, then spied a lighter square to his right—a window. He struggled himself upright, his back hurting as his hands pressed against loose straw strewn across the floor beneath him as a makeshift mattress. After a rest to allow the pain to subside, he gathered himself and got to his feet. The action left him winded. He inhaled, listening to the hoofbeats approaching as he brushed his palms on the front of his breeches, knocking off bits of dirt stuck to his skin. With small, deliberate steps, he made his way to the window, dragging the soles of his boots to avoid tripping over unseen obstacles.

The morning-cool air wafting through the opening touched his face, chilling the sweat he hadn't noticed settling upon his brow. It sent a shiver along his neck but refreshed him all the same. He sucked a lungful through his nose, recognized his own body's odor mixed in with it, and wondered where he was and how long he'd been there.

He tried to push the thought from his mind, but it nagged at him. His hazy memory failed in its attempt. Where were they going when Stirk proposed his plan? He stood close enough to the window his knees touched the wall, but didn't lean out as he glanced along the empty avenue running below his room. Though the sound of riders grew in volume, he spied no one.

Ikkundana.

The word came to him out of nowhere, and he expelled the filth from his lungs with force, spit its taste out of his mouth. Who knew what terrible disease the wind in the City of the Sick might carry? He held his breath, but his body's need to breathe betrayed him. Instead of gulping air into his chest, he sipped it like a beverage too hot to drink.

Hoof beats rattled against the buildings and the first rider coming into view caught his eye. He leaned forward, the act stretching the scab over his healing stab wounds and causing fresh pain. Breath hissed between his clenched teeth.

As the abundant clatter of hooves on stone suggested, more riders followed. A line of them came, two abreast, twelve rows, twenty-five in total, each of them armor-clad and carrying weapons. They neared, and Dansil faded back from the window to survey them from a position where he'd escape notice.

The first rider pulled level with the opening and the queen's guard recognized him at once. Few men with one arm sat horses in plate with a sword at their side. In fact, he doubted he knew the name of anyone else who fit the description besides Trenan. The queen's guard's teeth grated together at the sight of the swordsman, the muscles in his jaw bunching and knotting. He forgot the specter of disease and inhaled fresh morning air and the stink of his own sweat through his nose. Anger brewed in his gut until something occurred to him.

He kept me alive.

Trenan rode by without a glimpse in Dansil's direction, and the tension drained from the queen's guard as a question formed in place of the thought.

Why did he save me? He must realize my role in Stirk's attempt to kill him.

His mind reeled as the line of warriors continued riding by. His eyes observed their smooth young faces, their lithe limbs, but he did not register what he saw. They filed past in the brightening dawn, heard but barely seen.

He knows my part in the failed assassination. He kept me alive to make sure I'm punished.

Dansil stepped back from the window, the sounds of the warriors' passage echoing in his dark room. It didn't occur to him to wonder why a squad of well-equipped soldiers rode through the City of the Sick, or why Trenan led them. One line of thought suffocated any others, squashing details which might have appeared unusual or out of the ordinary.

He knows.

Did he tell anyone?

He wants to punish me.

He left me here. Left me to a horrible death.

His jaw clamped tight again, hands curling into fists. His entire life, he'd lived by one credo which always served him well, keeping him alive and advancing his position:

Do it to them before they do it to you.

I have to get out of here. Trenan has to die.

Dansil backed away from the window, a sudden bout of vertigo seizing him. The chamber spun; he stumbled, caught himself. A wave of nausea followed, throwing his belly into turmoil and his throat into convulsions. He reached an arm out, searching for anything to use to steady himself, but found nothing. The dark room went darker, an unsettling haze at the edge of his vision. He shuffled his feet, hoping he'd chosen the right direction to take him to the makeshift straw mattress. He inched forward, groping blindly, until his legs refused to carry him any farther. His knees buckled and the queen's guard toppled to the floor, exhaustion stealing his consciousness.

Before he opened his eyes, Dansil knew light filled the room. How much time had passed since he clambered to the window, he didn't know. Might be the same day as when he watched Trenan lead his squad past, merely later, when the sun placed itself to shine into his chamber. It could as easily have been any other day.

The queen's guard inhaled a deep breath, eyes remaining closed, and took stock of his body: manageable pain in the wound in his back, straw beneath his torso but not his legs—he'd dragged himself most of the way on to the mattress, at least enough to soften his fall. Thankful for that, if for nothing else about his situation, he shifted, hand sliding on the loose bedding, the sound of it loud in his ears, seeming to echo in the empty room.

He held himself rigid, breath captive in his lungs. The space he'd traversed on his way to peer out the window wasn't large enough to create a reverberation. Was he not alone?

Dansil recalled vague memories of someone tending to him during his recovery—a clay cup pressed to his lips and water trickling as much down his chin as his throat, soft food forced into his mouth, bandages being changed. He resisted the temptation to reach around and touch the spot where Stirk's knife had punctured him, see if his fingers came away bloody or if they'd find an expertly applied bandage covering the outline of sutures holding his skin together beneath.

He waited but no further sound found his ears, so released his breath in a wooshing sigh, the noise echoing again when he stopped. In his mind, he pictured an old hag bending over him as he sweat and gibbered in the throes of fever and infection. He saw her in a red cowl hiding boils and warts of sickness on her cheeks while age and pain warped and crooked the fingers she used to guide the needle and thread. Could this be her sitting by his sickbed, watching over his recovery and mimicking the sounds he made to pass the time? Not likely. Surely, in the City of the Sick, many needed tending.

The queen's guard forced one eyelid open a crack. At first, he saw nothing but blurs of gray and white and black past the brightness of the day and the wetness of his freshly opened eye. He blinked, dared to force it wider.

A shape reconciled itself into a robed person, as he'd expected, but not in the red cowls worn by the Goddess' sisters to warn of their sickness. Instead, this robe appeared dark as soot, its hood pulled forward to hide the wearer's face in the shadow beneath. Hands so white they practically glowed protruded from the long and wide sleeves, the fingers unnaturally long and thin. The figure's right hand lay on the pate of another shape crouched on the floor beside him.

Dansil opened his other eye, turned his head toward the unexpected visitors.

With the two of them in view, he saw the second wasn't actually crouching. Instead, he lacked both legs. And an arm.

"Stirk?" The word came out of his mouth as a rasping croak, his throat unused to producing sound since this man's knife had sliced through his flesh.

The legless fellow moved as though he might shuffle toward the straw bed, his stumps rubbing against the stone floor and explaining sounds Dansil had heard. The robe wearer's hand kept him from doing so. He stared at the queen's guard without blinking, his eyes wide. His tongue snaked out, licked his lips like a hungry animal.

"Ignore my pet." The words must have come from the robed man—Stirk's mouth hadn't moved—but it sounded to Dansil as though they came from many places.

The queen's guard's saliva dried up and the urge to urinate sprang into his lower belly. He realized that, if he thought himself able to accomplish it, he'd have jumped to his feet and rushed out the door, taking his chances with whatever the City of the Sick might hold rather than stay and deal with this mysterious being. Dansil twisted to do so, but pain shot from his wound, reminding him of the tottering steps from the window to passed out on the straw mattress.

"You need not fear." The robed figure lifted its hand from Stirk's pate, threw back the cowl to reveal a head and face devoid of hair, delicate features as likely belonging to either man or woman. "You see, you and my pet seek the same result."

Dansil looked from the smooth, sexless visage to Stirk. He leaned forward, propped on his one remaining limb like a crutch. His eyes bore into the queen's guard as though he worried he might disappear should he divert his gaze. Sweat stained his shirt and dirt streaked his face—a far cry from the hulking, formidable fellow who escaped the edge of Dansil's ax not so long ago.

"What result, stranger?"

Words scraped across his throat and tumbled from his lips without the confidence and strength he'd intended.

"The death of the one-armed man, of course." The mouth on the smooth head turned up at the corners, a ghastly slash threatening Dansil's gorge.

He shivered, the unintentional action shooting further pain from the not-quite-healed wound. His muscles tightened and strained; he wanted to leave, get as far from these two as possible, feeling that, if he stayed, things would go very wrong.

"And what's in it for you?"

"Oh, there's a small cost." The ambiguous being put its hand on Stirk's head. The legless man nuzzled against it like a cat needing attention. "But don't worry, it's not too steep."

Dansil inhaled through his nose, held it for a few heartbeats, then let it leak out between his teeth. "And Trenan will die?"

The ghastly smile again. "Indeed."

Before he intended to, the queen's guard nodded his agreement and couldn't stop. As his chin rose and fell, his stomach tied itself in a knot, his throat tightened in realization the master swordsman may not be the only one who died because of his deal. He stopped nodding and his eyes slid closed, his head throbbing, hoping against hope that, when he opened them again, the two figures would be gone.

When he did, they remained.

XIX - Teryk - Somewhere in Time

*S*WORDS, SPEARS, AND AXES hammered against the translucent green wall, each impact sending verdant lightning scintillating across its surface. The men on the outside—most of them now dismounted and wearing rage on their faces—howled and shouted, shook their fists and brandished their weapons.

On the near side, the silvery creatures—Small Gods, he'd become sure—danced.

If the magical barrier didn't separate them, the distance between gray gods and enraged men was short enough to reach out and touch each other, dance together, kill one another. But the blockade held, as the Small Gods appeared to expect, and their knowledge of the wall's impenetrability angered the warriors further.

They watched for a while, Rilum at Teryk's side, the sailor's breath shallow and quick, fearful. In his mind, the prince realized he should fear, too; they bore no weapons to defend themselves, nor possessed any idea how the Small Gods might react if they found them. But these thoughts held no sway with his body. Calm and relaxed, intuition suggested he found himself in the right place, seeing and doing the necessary things without understanding how or why he understood this. For the first time in longer than he recalled, he felt on the path meant for him.

"Gotta get out before it's too late."

Rilum tugged at his arm, trying again to coax the prince into moving. He pivoted to face his companion.

Sweat sparkled on the man's furrowed brow; his widened eyes darted from Teryk to the Small Gods, the men beyond them, and back. His expression softened the prince's heart, and he nodded. They faded behind the brush they'd used to hide them while the gray warriors raised the mystical veil, then stood. Teryk's knees creaked after having remained crouching for so long, but they loosened. As they crept away from the raging soldiers and dancing folk, he noticed the same wasn't true of Rilum; his companion hobbled for several paces before his gait evened out.

They picked their way deeper into the forest in silence, choosing their footing to keep noise of their passing to a minimum. Teryk considered it unnecessary. He assumed the small ones intended to dance before the wall as long as the men continued their anger, but he did it to help Rilum overcome his fear. They crept from tree trunk to tree trunk, hiding wherever the opportunity afforded itself until the men's fury and the gods' delight faded to a distant hum and disappeared. The prince wondered if it meant they'd gone far enough to distance themselves from it or if the sounds had ceased. He didn't voice this thought—one possibility might disperse the sailor's anxiety, but the other refresh it.

Birds chirped and sang in the branches high above them. Teryk tilted his head back, looking for a glimpse of the colored feathers they'd seen as they fled into the forest, but they eluded him. He spied the occasional bounce of a branch or rustle of needles as an unseen bird flitted from one place to another. Searching for them but not finding them, he recalled the creatures great and tiny accompanying the Small Gods in their flight. Where did they go? Did they hide somewhere amongst the trees with them?

Teryk returned his attention to picking his way through the underbrush. He hauled a deep breath into his lungs through his nose; the scents of wood and needles, of loamy earth, energized him, filled him with hope despite their situation.

"Do you know where we are?" He didn't look at his companion as he asked.

"Lost," Rilum replied and spit, his saliva spattering on a wide, green leaf. "Lost be where we are. In a land that shouldn't exist."

"What if we're not?"

"What are you talking of? We're wandering a place where no man's ever been."

"I thought the same at first. But you saw what happened: the horsemen, the Small Gods."

"Aye, I did. But if you think those be Small Gods, then you must've bonked your noggin."

Teryk frowned. He didn't recall knocking his head, but might it be possible?

"But what if they were? What if it isn't an undiscovered land, but a different time long ago?"

As soon as the words left his mouth, he realized how outlandish they sounded. Difficult enough thinking something transported them from the beach to the relative safety of the forest, but to an alternate age?

Rilum halted, grabbed Teryk's arm to pull him to a stop. He squinted at his companion, tilted his head. "You must have hit your noggin plenty hard."

"Look around. Does this not resemble our home? After seeing what happened, do you not recognize the Meadow of Exile?" Teryk swallowed as he said the words; the more he spoke, the more ridiculous the idea sounded. And he'd never seen the fabled place where the Small Gods' banishment from the Windward Kingdom occurred, merely been told of it in stories. But Rilum couldn't realize he but guessed, and the need to defend his statement compelled him to continue doing so now he'd started.

The sailor glanced around them, paused before answering. "I ain't heard of no Meadow of Exile."

"Legend says thousands of turns of the seasons ago, the men of what became the Windward Kingdom feared the Small Gods. They banished them to the Green to protect their families."

"If that's what we saw, it didn't appear no banishment to me. The gray fellers built a wall to defend themselves."

Teryk opened his mouth and inhaled, but stopped before speaking. Many turns of the seasons had passed since their nanny recited the tale—another one for their father to disapprove of if he'd known—but he recognized the discrepancy. In her story, the Goddess erected the green divide to protect her subjects, and she'd banished the other Small Gods to the sky for their actions. What they'd seen did not align with the myth.

Am I wrong?

"Ain't no way to move through time," Rilum grumbled and began walking again. "The more we stay here, the more likely we're discovered. If not by the wee gray ones, then by a hungry beast."

Teryk waited a heartbeat before following, staring back the direction they'd come. He saw nothing but trees and brush. His ears detected birds singing and fluttering amongst the branches, insects buzzing in patches of sunlight. The urge to retrace their steps, to make sure the wee folk survived the soldiers' attack threatened to overtake him, but he resisted.

I can't leave Rilum on his own.

The justification rang false. He turned his back on the forest separating him from the green wall and the gray men and followed his companion deeper into the unknown, hoping to find the truth of where they'd ended up.

—ᴇᴌᴌ—

They stood at the top of the bluff, staring at the rocky beach below. The long downward slope appeared treacherous, and he hoped the sailor wouldn't suggest traversing it. One of them might lose their footing and die broken on the boulders at its terminus. The prince glanced at Rilum, hoping to read intent on his face. His companion continued looking away, glaring along the finger of land protruding into the water.

Waves hurled themselves against it as if they did so to end their lives. The force with which they struck the rocky outcropping sent spray shooting straight up in the air, turned the surf to foam. Teryk had never seen anything like this; it exemplified the power of the sea he'd experienced when the storm ravaged the Whalebone, but this demonstration differed, inspired awe. Did Rilum stare at it for the same reason? Out of reverence?

"What are you looking at?"

He didn't answer, continued staring as though enthralled, nor did he move in the slightest. The prince worried he might be ill, or worse. After everything they'd been through, his companion falling into a trance did not stretch his imagining. A heartbeat away from grabbing Rilum's arm and giving him a shake, the sailor spoke.

"The Devil's Cock."

Teryk inhaled a sharp breath, but neither at the sailor's choice of words nor any recognition of what he meant. The disconnectedness of his response gave the prince fearful pause.

"What? What are you talking about?" He returned his gaze to his companion's face, prepared for a nonsensical answer, sure an unseen, malicious force had usurped his tongue, if not his entire being.

Rilum raised his arm and extended his finger toward the natural jetty.

"The Devil's Cock," he repeated, making no more sense than the first time. "On a map, it's called the Finger of the Goddess. Them who've sailed for any bit of their lives know it a thing of the devil. It marks the start of the turn."

Teryk stared out at the waves crashing against the rocks. Rilum may have continued speaking but, if he did, the prince didn't hear what he said. He knew nothing of Devil's Cocks and Goddess' Fingers, but he knew of the turn and what it meant. Somehow, they'd been transported from the land across the sea to their own Windward Kingdom.

They'd returned home, to another time, trapped in the Green.

—ele—

Night fell faster than it should have. The sky went from bright blue to indigo, gray, then black in the time it took the companions to find a sheltered place to lay for much-needed sleep. The sunset horizon didn't shift color except to darken; no pinks or purples or reds, simply light, then not. A half-moon hung listless, surrounded by far fewer twinkling stars than Teryk expected. He blamed his imagination; doing so proved easier than accepting they'd traveled to an age before the banishment of the Small Gods. The thought made it difficult to trust anything his eyes surveyed, anything his mind believed, anything he perceived to happen.

Perhaps I'm asleep and dreaming.

But did muscles ache in a dream? His stomach gurgle and complain? He didn't recall either happening in his sleep before, but strange things can occur while one sleeps.

Teryk watched Rilum curl into the crevice under the fallen log they'd chosen for shelter. He settled in on top of the bed fashioned of moss and leaves, making himself comfortable in the way of a man used to discomfort. Since identifying the landmark recognized from so many of his journeys, he'd said little; it confirmed an impossibility he wanted to believe less than did Teryk. The realization reduced him to grunts and single-word responses.

Fatigue burdened the prince, too, settling into his limbs and threatening to drag his lids closed, but he resisted the urge to crawl under the log with his companion. Their proximity and the shelter itself would provide him warmth from air cooled by the fall of night, but the prospect of insects, spiders, and vermin hiding beneath the tree deterred him. He crossed his arms, hugging himself against the chill, and leaned against it instead. His plan: when the weight of sleep became too much, he'd succumb, too tired to care if a mouse crawled over his shoe or a spider across his hand.

Despite his exhaustion, slumber refused to calm his mind and relieve him of his worry. His eyes darted toward every sound hidden in darkness and thick brush. The wind in the trees or the movements of small animals explained them away, but the rationale didn't pacify him.

Soon after Rilum disappeared beneath the fallen log, the soft rumble of his snores disguised any other sounds. Teryk inhaled; the forest smelled different at night and held more dampness in the air. The sharp tang of cedar softened, the earthy scent of loam becoming more prevalent. He concentrated on these things and the sound of his companion's slumber to distract himself from place and predicament, and how they'd arrived at the Green, in this time.

Memories of the gray figures dancing before the eerie wall they'd created came to him. He saw jagged lightning shoot across it with each strike of sword and axe, recalled the enraged expressions of the men on the other side. But for the colors they wore and the style of armor and weapon, they looked no different from himself, his father, Trenan. If not for the strange magic they'd seen, he and Rilum might have been home.

But how do you travel through time?

An impossible question without a likely answer, leaving one explanation: it wasn't real. Teryk determined he must be dreaming, or drugged and hallucinating.

Maybe I'm dead.

If so, death differed little from living.

He pushed himself up from the log, wiped the ass of his breeches to knock away dirt and moss and slivers. He took a pace back from his sleeping companion and the vibration of his snoring grown so much in volume it threatened to shake the fallen tree. Two more paces and it faded; the relative silence of the night overcame Rilum's dissonant breath. With teeth clenched tight enough to knot the muscles in his jaw, Teryk moved farther from the makeshift shelter. The woods drew him as though he sought an answer amongst the trunks of trees and green foliage of brush.

No chance of finding any there.

Another pace and exhaustion filled his body, weighed on him like it touched his soul. His already slow gait faltered and halted, thighs aching as if full of wet sand, and his knees trembled, then folded. He collapsed to sit on the bare patch of earth beneath his feet. His eyelids slid closed, snapped open, slid closed, snapped open. The brush and trees around him blurred into unnatural shapes, creating the illusion they gestured and swayed. Outlines scampered amongst the woods, muddied and gray, dancing, darting.

Teryk shook his head, slapped his cheek with a flat palm. The world reconciled itself into focus and he sighed, moved to stand and head back to the fallen log and the uncomfortable but relative safety beneath it. His arms and legs refused to obey. He pushed against the ground with flattened palms, grunted with the effort, but neither achieved the desired effect, instead making his brain hurt, his vision blur again.

Leaves rustled, and he jerked his chin up.

The wind?

Shapes danced and darted, moving from shrub to tree, coming closer. Teryk scrambled back, fingernails digging into the loamy ground beneath him, heels kicking up swaths of moss.

The gray forms swirled about him, noiseless but for the whisper of foliage. His own breath and the hammering of his pulse in his ears nearly drowned them out. His hand hit a root, jamming his finger, and Teryk fell backward, his head knocking against the trunk of a tree hard enough for light to flash before his eyes.

When his sight returned, the gray shapes surrounded him, faceless, converging.

The prince threw his arms up in front of his face and screamed.

XX - Ishla - Denial

THE QUEEN STOPPED, BREATHED a lungful of air, then raised her hand to grasp the door handle. She knew she'd find her husband within the chamber, alone but for his guards. The rest of the council responsible for overseeing city affairs wouldn't convene until after midday meal, but Erral took his food in the meeting room, preparing to meet the others. Ishla might not always consider him a good ruler, but she couldn't ever fault his preparation.

She released her breath and pushed against the wide wooden portal.

"Wait here," she said over her shoulder.

No need to raise her voice for Strylor to hear her. In the three sunrises since the king gave him the queen's guard post, he'd proven himself dedicated beyond expectation. So much so, she often found him standing far too close for her comfort. The previous day, she'd exited the commode and walked right into him; he'd positioned himself in the middle of the doorway, leaving her no way around him, near enough he'd likely been touching the door.

Strylor grunted his agreement from where he stood behind her. She sensed that, were it deemed proper, he'd find any opportunity to put his hands on her in the interests of—and the convenient excuse of—keeping her safe. At another time, she'd have been entering the chamber to discuss finding a new queen's guard with her husband, but other intent drove her this day. Far more important things needed their attention.

She stepped over the threshold and the king's guards turned toward her at once, weapons leveled. When they saw who'd entered, they relented, returning to their ready positions. Erral looked up from the parchment spread across the table, a half-eaten chicken leg dangling between his fingers. His gaze held hers for an instant before his eyes returned to the document before him.

"What is it, woman? I'm preparing for council. The Horseshoe doesn't tend itself, you know."

For a moment before she responded, her mind flashed to the state of the city. She rarely found occasion to venture outside Draekfarren's walls but, when she did, she wasn't oblivious to the Horseshoe's slums, the poverty and crime, the grime and filth. The city did not take care of itself, but she didn't feel certain her husband did, either.

"The sun has risen three times since you sent Osis and his men, my Lord." She cringed at using a title but his guards in the room made it a necessity. "Our children haven't returned."

"I am aware."

He set the chicken leg back on the plate, continuing to scan the parchment. Ishla took a step toward the table, moving her lower jaw side to side, grinding her teeth.

"And what will you do?"

He ceased reading, rested his finger upon the document to keep from losing his place, and raised his eyes. "Await his return. Likely he'll arrive with the prince and princess in tow, both of them ready for the punishment they are due."

"And if he doesn't?"

The king pursed his lips, leaned forward. She saw his anger brewing below the surface, his grip on it tenuous. If his guards weren't in the room, he'd not bother concealing it, but appearances continued to be important to him.

"What should I do, my queen? Should I release the full strength of the army on our Windward Kingdom, sacking every house, overturning each rock and log until we find them?"

She cringed and bit down on her back teeth. He hadn't referred to her as 'my queen' out of respect or tradition but annoyance. The words themselves didn't betray his feelings—his tone did.

"No need for sacking and overturning, but yes. Send out the army. Empty the barracks. This is our children who are missing. Leave not a single man in the city until we find the prince and princess."

Errol shook his head, let his chin droop before pushing his chair away from the table, its legs scraping on the floor.

"If it was your job to rule, the kingdom would lie in ruins."

"It's not. It is my job to take care of our children."

"Then you haven't done your job."

His words penetrated her heart like a needle forced between her ribs. Angry tears threatened, but she fought them. If she let them go, instead of emerging as sorrow and anguish, they'd bring with them shouting and ire, a torrent of unexpressed feelings and frustration. She realized revealing what brewed within her would harden the king's demeanor rather than convince him to increase his efforts, so she blinked away the tears, bit back the stinging comments desperate to find her lips. Perhaps Erral read this in her face, for the tension in his own expression eased and he sat again.

"Troops are on the move in the Leeward Kingdom and aught is amiss in the Kingdom of Water, not to mention the troubles within our own borders." His eyes fell from hers at the allusion to internal strife. He'd mentioned no such thing to her before, though she'd heard of unrest from Trenan. "I cannot spare more soldiers. You'd have me leave the city, the entire realm, unguarded in the service of finding your children. That might be what they want."

"They?"

He cleared his throat. "Our enemies. It may be foreign agents took them to lure us into a mistake."

"But what about the truce?"

"Don't concern yourself with the politics of war and peace, Ishla."

The king went back to scanning the parchment on the table before him, unwilling to meet her gaze. He said no more; he didn't need to.

"What have you done?"

He ignored her, choosing to pick up the chicken leg instead of answering his wife. His finger traced words on the paper, and he tore a chunk of meat from the bone with his teeth. Ishla watched him, her anger rising into her throat. No tears accompanied it this time as she let it spill out.

"What have you done?"

Errol slammed the drumstick down, the clay plate cracking as it split in two beneath the force. He glared at her for the space of five heartbeats before speaking.

"That you are the queen doesn't give you the right to speak to me in this manner. Be gone from my sight before I recall Osis and his men and leave the children to find their own way home."

Ishla bit so hard her teeth hurt and her jaw knotted. Her fingers curled into fists but she held her ground, silent, glaring at her husband. The king glared back for an instant before waving a hand in the air and returning to the parchment.

"Dar, remove the queen from this chamber."

The guard to her right stood at attention, heels clicking together, before leaving his post and crossing the room toward her. He stopped in front of her, blocking her view of the king. She diverted her gaze to his face, saw he didn't relish carrying out the regent's command but his position left him no choice. He swallowed hard.

"M'lady."

Dar swept his arm toward the door, waited for her to follow instructions, but he did not lay his touch upon her. If he did, the fury and rage within her might have burst forth, directed first at him and then at her husband. Instead, she spun around and stomped away. The guard followed and, when he reached out to grasp the handle, she swatted his hand aside.

"I can let myself out."

She jerked the door open, left it ajar as she stepped over the threshold into the hall. Her action caught Strylor, who leaned against the wall opposite the chamber, by surprise. He stood straight, a look of guilt spreading across his face she may have wondered at another time. Instead, she spun on her heel and headed along the corridor, leaving her husband's guard to shut the portal while her own protector hurried after her.

"My queen. Is everything all right?"

His words registered but her anger continued pressing her lips too tightly together for her to respond. Her teeth remained clenched as her mind worked. How could her husband be so nonchalant about finding their children?

It's not your husband who refuses to search harder, it is the king.

She wanted to believe it, but the words rang with untruth. The monarch should express concern for the heir to the throne, at the very least, even if he considered the princess expendable. If Teryk didn't return, what did it mean to the future of the kingdom?

A thought struck her so suddenly, she stopped dead in her tracks. The queen's guard clattered to a halt behind her, near enough he'd come close to running into her.

"He knows," she whispered.

"Who knows?" Strylor scratched his ear. "Knows what?"

She turned, not wanting to engage the man, but she needed to release her thoughts.

"The king won't do anything else to find my children," she said between clenched teeth. She didn't look the queen's guard in the eye, choosing to direct her gaze toward the red carpet lining the hall floor. "I must take matters into my own hands."

XXI - Teryk - Goddess

TERYK INHALED A SHARP breath as though he'd been underwater too long. His eyelids jerked open and daylight blinded him; he threw an arm across his face to block it out until his eyes adjusted.

His shoulder ached, his finger throbbed, the pain reminding him of the forest, the gray shapes. He wasn't in the woods anymore, he understood without seeing. Acrid smoke replaced the scent of loam and cedar. Instead of the chirp of birds and buzz of insects, fires crackled.

Panic formed in Teryk's gut, swirling and expanding until it tingled along his limbs and threatened to choke his breath. He moved his arm away, forced his eyes open and stared up at a firmament marred by smudges of gray and black. Amongst it, the bright yellow sun glowed, its light perverted by the wafting smoke. It took a heartbeat for the prince to realize this wasn't sunlight—its glow flickered, its size grew. His memory skipped back to the black and white beach of the land across the sea, the balls of fire falling out of the sky. He leapt to his feet, every muscle and joint in his body protesting as though he'd been lying in a single position as the seasons turned repeatedly around him.

A quick scan of the area revealed his location, yet it took longer for him to recognize it. This wasn't the courtyard he'd grown up with, full of gardens and lush grass, statues and the lone base of one ruined Pillar of Life. In this courtyard, two of the fabled monuments still stood while the others lay in ruins. Deep scars cut into the ground, churned the earth leaving no grass or gardens discernible, fires burned and smoke billowed. Amongst the crackle of wood consumed by fire, a screech filled the prince's ears, distracting him as it grew louder until he realized it was the fireball hurtling toward him making the sound.

His legs sprang to action before his mind thought to tell them to do so. Two paces and his feet caught. He stumbled, shuffled forward three more steps on hands and knees before finding his footing again, rushed headlong only to skid to a halt six more farther, his escape cut off by the river.

Steam rose from the rushing water and he noticed the heat surrounding him, pressing on his flesh. Sweat sprang to his forehead, dampened his clothes. Bits of debris floated past—chunks of wood, pieces of cloth, what might have been a detached limb. Teryk tore his gaze away, directed it back toward the fireball hurtling groundward, its swirling glow now too close and too bright for him to look at directly. He raised his arm, closed his eyes, and clamped his jaw tight, awaiting the impact meant to take his life and end the quest to fulfill his destiny.

It hit with a thump severe enough to shake the ground beneath his feet and fill his head with a roar. A wave of heat washed over him, threatening to push him back, send him over the edge of the bank into the near-boiling river, but he held his place. The sound of fire increased until another noise added to the tumult, one Teryk recognized as the scrape of rock rubbing against rock. He lowered his arm, lifted his chin.

The fireball had struck the base of a pillar, knocking a chunk free and impinging the integrity of the massive column. The remaining marble wasn't enough to hold the weight and it crumbled beneath the monument's mass. It tilted toward the river, falling like a tree, and Teryk followed its path, watching with an interest he couldn't have explained. Not until it neared hitting the ground did he notice the figure standing near it. He stared up at the chunks tumbling his way but made no move to avoid them, as though frozen in place. The prince opened his mouth to holler a warning but the crunch of the collapsing stone drowned him out, if his throat formed a sound.

At the last second, the man raised his arms in defense—a useless gesture under the weight of the marble pillar. He folded beneath it like paper. Teryk attempted to leave his place and run toward him, though he realized he'd be beyond help, but he couldn't move. The steam rolling off the river and smoke from the multitude of fires burning across the courtyard swirled around him, held him back.

A shape formed, the arms, legs, and torso appearing vaporous, and Teryk gasped.

How did he get out from under the pillar?

He held his breath, waiting for the man to come into view, expecting to find him hobbling, twisted, broken. His hands curled into fists, tightened until his fingernails dug into his palm.

But no figure emerged. The steam and smoke continued swirling together, taking the vague outline of a woman's silhouette striding toward him. Teryk blinked hard, licked his lips and tasted the salt of his perspiration on them. Might this be a waking dream of his mother or Danya? No, not a dream—an energy he'd never experienced emanated from the shape, pressing against him like a physical thing demanding his attention. Sweat rolled down his forehead, collected on his brow, perspiration dampening flesh and clothing alike. He blinked again, wiped his arm across his head to remove the moisture and hoped for the vision to disappear along with it.

It didn't.

Instead, the silhouette moved closer, floating above the charred ground of the courtyard until a woman stepped out of the smoke as though she'd been present the entire time.

Her hair fell past her shoulders, disappearing down her back. One heartbeat it appeared black as the night itself, the next a flash hinted at a flaxen hue. Her skin first shone smooth and pale, then became the color of singed sugar. As the prince watched, her features skipped from one appearance to another until he understood he didn't look upon a single woman, but all women.

"What are you doing here?"

He heard her words, understood their meaning, but it didn't seem she'd direct them at him.

"Who... who are you? Are you real?"

"Nothing is real and everything is." She stared at him, her gaze so penetrating it nudged the back of his skull. "There is what you perceive and what you believe. How did you get here?"

"I... I don't know."

Her face, hair, height, and body shape continued to shift as she stood before him. One moment short, pale, round, the next tall, dark, slender. Mane brushing her shoulder tops, hanging down her back, then her scalp shimmered smooth and bald before locks returned. Sometimes a countenance he recognized flashed by—his nanny, or a servant he'd seen in the halls of Draekfarren—but each disappeared before he knew for sure.

Without appearing to take a step, she stood in front of him, standing too close. She raised her arm, laid a hand no him that at first had short, stubby fingers, then long narrow ones against his cheek. Instinct told him to pull away, but he couldn't. Didn't want to.

"The beach," she said, eyelids sliding closed. "The meadow. The forest."

She inhaled, and he involuntarily breathed with her. Acrid smoke singed his nostrils, burning wood and charred flesh. His stomach lurched.

"They sent you."

Her eyes snapped open and her hand dropped from his cheek and a piece wrenched inside him, as though she took a chunk of him along with it. He drew a shuddering breath, hoping to fill the unexpected emptiness, and tasted the same sickening smoke. Unable to stop himself, he turned his head and vomited on the charred grass at the edge of the river. Tears streamed down his cheeks as he retched again and again with nothing in his gut to expel.

He remained bent at the waist for a time, awaiting another bout of sickness, but his gorge settled. Like an old man not used to standing, he straightened, wiped wetness away on his sleeve. She stood staring at him, eyes blue, brown, hazel, green. Waiting for him.

"Who are they?" he asked, finally.

"You know who they are. Their legend was born that day. And today," she gestured over her shoulder, toward the wreckage at her back, "because of that day, the others are born."

She stepped aside for him to see past her. Fireballs had ceased falling from the sky, but flames continued raging in the courtyard, blocking much of his view behind flickering tongues of fire and billowing smoke. As it drifted, he caught site of the fallen Pillar and a thought struck him.

No living person in my time has seen the Pillars of Life.

A shiver rattled up his spine, and he stared at the column, searching for the figure trapped beneath it until the drifting haze obscured it again. His gaze followed the break in the gray, shifting curtain until his eyes fell on another silhouette. He was certain it hadn't been there before.

Twenty paces away, the thing was barely recognizable as a human. The figure's reddened skin shone with wetness; no clothing, no hair, nothing but crimson flesh pulled too tight over bone, features and distinctions smeared and gleaming.

Burned.

Teryk shuddered. What pain this person—male or female, the damage done made it too difficult to tell—must be in. The shape tottered its way across the courtyard, extending first one shaking foot, then another. The smoky veil parted before each step, allowing him to keep visual contact with his or her precarious journey. With each step, the prince expected the figure to tumble, dead or close to, but he or she pressed on, amended their path to avoid stumbling in a blackened indentation. Once past it, the burnt shape stopped beside the huge chunks of shattered stone he'd seen fall, smashed on the ground and across the bank of the river.

Over dozens of seasons after the pillars fell, workers cleared the rubble from Draekfarren, save one piece, which remained in Teryk's time as a reminder. Many considered it a tribute to the Goddess and her strength, others a warning about the fragility of life. King after king promised to rebuild them—including his own father—but other things always stood in the way: war, money, a lack of skilled labor. Work to return them to their former glory never began.

The figure dropped to its knees by the fractured pillar—beside the piece that survived in Teryk's life—shoulders hunched in defeat. Its body shook, sobbing, and the prince watched this once-human deformity lean forward, place its hand on the spot where the marble toppled on the first person he'd spied. Only then did he realize the ever-changing woman no longer stood before him. Here he remained, in a long-ago time, alone but for a body burned beyond recognition.

His heart sped in his chest.

Without knowing why he should, the compulsion to rush to the figure's aid overcame Teryk. He hurried from his spot by the river, weaving his way between smoldering bodies and chunks of rubble as he crossed toward the destroyed pillar. His soles thunked against the dead earth, scorched grass crunching beneath his heels as the stench of charred things invaded his nose. Debris forced him to watch his footing as he navigated what, in his memory, should have been gardens and lawns, not a burned space littered with detritus and devastation. But not just broken rock and shattered trees, many shallow indentations pockmarked the ground, each of them scarred to the dirt.

He skidded to a halt a few paces before he reached the disfigured shape kneeling by the fallen Pillar. The person laid a red hand on the other pinned beneath the cracked marble—a pair of charred legs protruding from under tons of stone. No more recognizable than the tight-skinned being of weeping sores before him. He stood watching, hesitant to interrupt despite the urge to rush over that brought him here, and one of Nanny's stories returned to his memory. Given the time and place he found himself, he realized who the two people ruined before him must be: the priest and priestess.

Rak'bana and Ine'vesi.

She threw her head back and cried out toward the sky, startling him, the sound emanating from her burnt and dry esophagus more croak than scream. He reached out a tentative hand, as though it might offer comfort to her ravaged flesh and tortured soul.

"Are you all right?"

The ridiculousness of his question struck him as soon as the words left his lips. He thought to apologize for his lack of compassion, but the priestess stopped screaming and jerked her gaze from the sky, turned it toward him.

"G... Goddess?"

Teryk gaped at her, then glanced down at himself. To his own eye, his grubby clothes looked no different, made him look no more like a Goddess than ever. He opened his mouth to say so, but she spoke again, interrupting him.

"I failed you, Goddess. See what my failure forced you to do."

Tears rimmed her eyes, and he realized she wasn't looking at him, but past him—no, through him. He pivoted, the heel of his boot crunching on the charred dirt. Chill sweat prickled on his brow in stark contrast to the fires burning around the courtyard; a shiver found its way up his spine.

"The scroll..." the priestess whispered from behind him.

When he saw the mist forming on the far riverbank, he forgot she'd spoken.

White as summer cloud, the fog roiled and moved in and around itself without progressing or receding, the billows of gray smoke nearby staying clear of it as though repelled by fear or some other unseen force. Teryk took two steps away from the kneeling priestess, his ears noticing she'd uttered more words, but his brain didn't perceive what she said. A rustle of sound behind him made him think Rak'bana may have found her way to her feet.

As if responding to his movement, the mist expanded along the river's edge, moving and twisting, taking shapes only to dissipate as fast as they formed.

Teryk continued toward it, the world around him forgotten. The crunch of his footsteps on burnt grass came to his ears from a long distance. The charred remains of the courtyard became nothing but blurs of darkness to either side of him. The mist mimicked him, moving closer. The prince hurried his pace, driven by a need to get nearer the fog, to see what hid within it.

The vapor boiled to a stop, several tendrils of white swirling together at the front of it, forming shapes. They became arms, legs, torsos—two wispy forms materializing out of nothing. Teryk gasped and went faster. One shape would rectify itself into the woman he'd seen before, with the ever-changing face. But what of the other? The Priestess Rak'bana taken from this world to the next?

A form solidified as the prince expected; he was too far away to see the woman's features, but it didn't remain static. He turned his gaze to the second misty silhouette, the swirls of vapor beginning to solidify like the first. Arms formed, flesh the color of the inside of a seashell, not the red, peeling skin he'd seen on the priestess. Legs came into view next, then a torso encased in leather armor. Finally, the mist forming the head began to darken.

Though they remained too far away, Teryk reached out toward the shapes, as if being closer to them would... what?

The thought fled him as his foot went over the edge of the riverbank. He plummeted into the steaming river he'd forgotten lay between him and the misty figures. The water scalded his skin. He thrashed and struggled, panic filling him, and his mind recalled his time in the sea, the monsters lurking within it.

And then he sank.

XXII - Rilum - A Long Time Ago

S UNLIGHT FORCED ITS WAY through the crack between the fallen log and the ground on which it lay, found Rilum's face like a thief creeping into his space.

The sailor groaned, rolled onto his back. His joints creaked and protested. His clothes stuck to him, pasted to his skin by moisture as easily his own sweat as it might have been dew. He inhaled through his nose, scenting the half-rotten odor of the log he slept under, the staleness of his own body. None of it made him want to open his eyes or climb out from beneath his hiding place, but he knew he couldn't avoid it for long. He felt a sense of duty toward the lad, prince or not.

As the sleep cleared from his head and the reality—or unreality—of where he was and what had happened returned, Rilum Seaman noticed the dryness of his throat. He attempted to part his lips, found them gummed together, tried to use his tongue to force them apart, except it was glued to the roof of his mouth. Next, he went to crack open his lids but they were stuck, too.

A bolt of panic lanced through his chest.

What has this gods-forsaken place done to me?

Forgetting himself, he jerked his upper torso forward and cracked his head against the log's rough bark. He groaned from behind his affixed lips, raised his hand to his forehead. His fingertips found the scrape with ease, but he couldn't tell if blood welled up within it or not as a sheen of moisture covered his entire body. He lowered his hands to his eyes, dug a knuckle into each to coax his eyelids open.

A sliver of light squeezed its way through and he almost cried out, in both pain and relief. He resolved to prise them free a little at a time to keep from being blinded. When he regained the ability to see, he levered himself out from under the fallen tree.

His spine protested as he stood, his knees popped, his shoulders ached. The thing he despised most about getting older was the way his body betrayed him bit by bit, each joint and muscle reminding him of his youth gradually left behind.

He stretched, raised his eyes skyward, regarded the limbs and branches hanging over him. Most belonged to conifers with their various verdant needles, but a few leafy trees stood amongst them, the broad flat leaves shades of red and yellow. Rilum frowned—with it being second season, why wouldn't their foliage be green as well?

The sailor lowered his chin, setting the mystery aside in favor of ungumming his lip. His first try, he used only the muscles of his jaw. When that proved unsuccessful, he jammed his fingers between his lips the way one might force a board beneath a rock and use it as a lever. They came apart bit by bit. Part of him expected to hear a sound like tearing parchment, experience pain as though someone ripped flesh from his body, but neither happened. Instead, his mouth opened, and he sucked a breath tasting of dirt and loam. His throat rattled with the passing air.

I have to find me some water.

With the orifices in his face properly dealt with, he remembered his predicament. He pivoted on his heels, observing his surroundings, a crick in his neck shooting pain along his spine. As expected, trees and brush clogged the surrounding area. They appeared fuller and more leaf-covered than he recalled them being the day before when he crawled beneath the log for some much-needed sleep.

Where is the lad?

He drew his stone-dry tongue across his cracked lips.

"Teryk?"

The prince's name was his intended pronouncement, but nothing issued from his throat but a dilapidated croak suitable for making proud the hardiest of bullfrogs.

He swallowed the nothingness left in his mouth and stepped away from the mossy log, determined to find water or the prince, preferably both.

XXIII - Teryk - Battlefield

S TALE AIR BURNING IN his chest, Teryk put all his strength into a final push, one more stroke toward the surface. He knew if he didn't make it, this would be his last attempt. No more breaths, no life, no prophecy or saving the world. Of them all, this last thought most galvanized him. He pulled with his arms, kicked with his legs until his head broke through and he gasped a ragged breath to fill his desperate, thankful lungs.

He opened his eyes to muted sunlight, but no gray smoke, no vaporous white mist.

And no water.

Instead of the river, the prince sat on grass. Not the charred black stuff of the courtyard, but lush turf with hard earth beneath him. He unfolded himself and stood, noting his clothing wasn't wet, and peered from atop a hill facing downslope to a shallow, grassy valley beyond. Pregnant clouds filled the sky, running together into a blanket of many shades of gray hiding both sun and firmament. They also hid the time of day and an estimation of the season from Teryk's ability. The lushness of the meadow suggested it might be late second season.

In the middle of the lowland, armored men clashed. A few sat horses but most fought on foot. The clank of weapons and armor floated through the air, its sharpness diffused by distance. Banners flew near groups of tents at either side, but too far away for the prince to recognize them. Considering how many turns of the seasons he'd traveled backward in time—a hundred hundred, if he believed his nanny's tales—this might be any era and anyone fighting before him.

Teryk took a step toward one camp but stopped, glanced at himself. He wore a leather breast piece over a thick red jersey and rough-spun breeches.

A sword hung at his side, a shield strapped to his back pressed against him, and a helmet sat upon his head. At other times, in other situations, he'd have wondered where these items came from but, once transported to places and ages he couldn't possibly travel to, such mysteries carried little importance. A fat drop of rain struck the rim of his helm, spattered water on his nose.

"Great," he muttered as he broke into a trot.

The scabbard of the short sword dangling at his waist, much smaller than the size and weight of Godsbane, bounced against his thigh. What'd happened to the weapon? He tried not to think about what his father might do when he discovered he'd lost the Crown Sword. But if he didn't fulfill his part of the prophecy, Crown Swords and everything they represented meant nothing.

As he approached the fray, the cries and yells of men added to the clamor of weapon and shield. No one voice distinct, no words intelligible, but the cacophony rose toward the high clouds unable to hold back the increasing frequency of raindrops. The ground beneath his feet changed, the grass beaten flat by the passing of boot and hoof, dirt churned, ready to become mud at the coming storm's behest.

The banner flying over the camp nearest him snapped in the rising wind, its red fabric with gold markings rippling. It pricked a sense of familiarity in his mind, but its significance eluded him. From what he saw at this distance, few men milled around the tents; the battle engaged most of them.

Teryk stopped. The impulse to continue to the camp nagged at him, urged him to go on like someone stood at his back, pushing him. He looked from encampment to fight, rain now falling heavier and blurring the proceedings with a gray hue. When he returned his attention to the gathering of tents, it surprised him to spy a horseman galloping toward him.

The prince debated what to do. Draw his blade? What if the rider intended friendship? Then again, what if he didn't, and he didn't unsheathe his weapon?

A man in leather armor with naught but a short sword stands little chance against a mounted warrior.

He searched his memory for one of Trenan's lessons to guide him but found none. When most needed, those endless days of practice and teaching deserted him, leaving him with an empty sensation in his chest and a knot in his gut. He caught himself inhaling and exhaling short breaths through his nose, forced himself to return his breathing to normal. He swallowed the bitter saliva his mouth produced at the sight of the rider's bared steel, moved his own hand closer to the hilt of his sword. If he meant to draw it, he'd wait until the last instant, seeking to avoid inciting the horseman to violence.

If I had my armor, and Godsbane, then I'd give him a fight.

"Oy," the soldier called, his tone unfriendly. "Get back over there before I lop off your head and make you carry it with you!"

A sliver of red on the man's breast plate flashed. Teryk glanced from it to the banner, then his own jersey, finally understanding. Wherever and whenever he found himself, he appeared to be in alignment with this man and must trust the force controlling things put him here for his best interests.

The beating of hooves vibrated against his soles, the rumble seeming to loosen his feet from their place on the ground. He raised his hand toward the horseman, then did the one thing he remembered Trenan teaching him never to do: he turned his back on a man with a drawn weapon.

The rain soaked into dirt churned up through the grass, and Teryk's boots sank in shallow mud as he hurried off to the fight. He considered looking over his shoulder to see if the rider followed, but decided against it; he no longer sensed the hoof beats beneath his feet, and glancing back might betray his hesitancy.

His focus narrowed to the men engaged in combat ahead of him. He spied flashes of red amongst the foot soldiers and on the horses, but it left him no closer to knowing who they were or the army they battled than before. Soon, he'd be part of the fray.

What will I do when I arrive?

It appeared unlikely he'd get to decide for himself. The color of his jersey marked him a target for the other fighters, sure to force his hand when he reached the fighting. Still, he'd do his best to avoid combat.

His heart beat hard in his chest, though not from the exertion of running across the field. He held the short sword's scabbard with his left fist, preventing it from banging against his thigh while his right grasped the hilt, ready to free the steel. His throat clenched tight, constricting his breath, and his mind flashed to another time, another place. He remembered a darkened street, a group of men, and the pain of the beating he'd taken, the agony of a blade sliding into his flesh. Physical torment, mental anguish, fever, delusion; it returned, slamming into his consciousness like the waves breaking against the Finger of the Goddess. The blank spot in his memory filled, and he wished it hadn't.

His mind told his legs to cease their forward motion, but the directive proved ineffective. Instead, his hand gripped the sword hilt tighter, his arm moved to draw the weapon.

The image of a robed figure came to him. He saw it move close to him, open its robe, but it revealed no body beneath, exposed no limbs or torso. Under the cloth lay a space, a void, and Teryk recalled being drawn into it, unable to resist. At first, terror gripped him. Was this the end of his life? The reaper come to steal him from the world of the living?

Ahead on the battlefield, a man spied him and broke away from the fight, charging toward him. The prince raised his sword, and the two came together, their steel clashing. The impact sent a vibration up Teryk's arm to his shoulder, a sensation he'd experienced often during his training with Trenan, but few times in an actual clash. His mind reeled, sorting through lesson after lesson, searching for how to proceed, but his body responded without conscious prompting.

He pushed his attacker back and swung his own blow. The other man caught it against his blade, but at the wrong angle. It glanced off and the edge of Teryk's steel sliced his arm. Surprised, he jumped away, inhaling a sharp, pained breath. The prince took advantage, lunging forward and placing his short sword to find the space between the man's chin and the top of this breast piece. He gasped again, the inhalation gurgling with blood around the sword point. He gave it a twist before pulling it free. Blood spurted after it, spraying across his front, adding its liquid to the mud squelching beneath their feet. The soldier's knees buckled, and he folded, sinking to the ground. His weapon fell from his hand as the other clawed at his throat, attempting to keep his life from emptying itself in the grass. Teryk loomed over him, watching him die as the memories swirling in his head continued.

The void wasn't empty. A man occupied it, or what he thought might be a man. Though the figure before him stood naked, the body possessed no sex organs to guide his opinion. Smooth, featureless flesh covered the entire human shape; no hair, no nipples or navel. Lashless eyes, lipless mouth, nose, arms, legs. The fingers and toes lacked nails—more like a poorly rendered clay representation of a person than anything.

Teryk remembered being prone and immobile as the ghastly figure leaned over him, laid its hands upon him. A charge flowed through him, increasing his pain to a level he'd never experienced. It thrummed through his bones, twisted his muscles into knots, but he lacked any way to react. He couldn't cry out or pull away. He screamed inside his head, no one hearing his suffering but himself.

The man at his feet went limp, his eyes wide and shocked, hand resting on his throat. Rain fell on him, diluting the blood to a shade of pink belying the severity of its presence.

The prince's boots moved again, carrying him around the fallen soldier and toward the fight. He didn't ask them to any more than he'd intended to engage the fellow he left behind, no more than he'd wanted to end the man's life. Rain ran from his forehead into his eyes, and he desired to wipe it away with his forearm, but his arm refused to act as his own.

I am but a pawn with a role to play. But what role?

Two men appeared in front of him and he cut his way through them without hesitation. The battle raged around him, its angry sounds assaulting his ears, but his mind wandered to the other place and time as his legs carried him forward.

The torture racking him eased, replaced by a burning sensation. His throat attempted to scream but failed as the fire sank deep within him, penetrating his heart and everything inside him, filling him until nothing else remained. A heartbeat later, the wraith disappeared, the void filled back up with nothingness, and then he'd returned to his body, staring at the darkness behind his closed lids. Voices penetrated the veil, unrecognizable, their words meaningless. The tones suggested a female and one male, maybe more. In his mind, they belonged to his sister calling for him, Trenan admonishing his carelessness. Then they became the utterances of his worried mother and his angry father. She implored him to be careful, to come home; he berated his son, called him stupid and useless.

Teryk bulled his way through the fray, slashing and hacking, his legs carrying him forward with purpose, though what purpose, he didn't know. Blood spattered his forearm, covered his sword. The little resistance he encountered withered before his onslaught, and pride swelled his chest. If his father saw him now, he'd no longer think him stupid and useless, scroll or no.

He gritted his teeth at the thought of the king and lost focus for an instant. A soldier to his right caught him with a surprise blow and the short sword flew out of his hand, but Teryk recovered. He launched himself at the man without giving him the opportunity to ready for another swing.

The prince hit him in the midsection, dislodging his breath from his chest and carrying him to the muddy ground. With a quick motion, he pinned the fellow's sword arm with a knee and extracted the soldier's own dagger from his belt. The tip sank into the man's eye with little resistance; his body stiffened, convulsed, fell limp.

Teryk knelt by the corpse, staring at his pained expression—the final contortion of his features. A pang of guilt stabbed through him. This man might have had a lover, children, people who cared for him and whom he loved. Did he deserve to die?

A body tumbled beside him and the prince gave his head a shake, forcing the shame deep inside with the other dishonors and disgraces he carried. He didn't know if the soldier deserved death or not, but he knew he didn't; important things lay ahead for him, events bound to change the world for everyone, so he couldn't afford to dally here, inviting his own death.

The rain fell harder, pattering on the armor and bodies of fallen men, and Teryk jumped to his feet. Before pushing on, he cast around the ground near him, searching for his weapon. When he didn't locate it, he snatched the closest thing from the hand of a corpse.

The axe proved heavy and unwieldy, its weight and balance so different from the swords to which he'd grown accustomed. Trenan had trained him with weapons like this, but not as in depth as he'd done with the sword. He didn't have to wait long to test his ability.

A monster of a man came at him, a roar of a battle cry echoing behind his visor as he brandished a mace. Teryk ducked under his first swing and hit him on the back with the flat of the axe head. The impact sent him reeling forward, but he kept his balance and regained his equilibrium. The two faced each other, both glowering, searching for an opening. Teryk's gaze trailed across the man's shoulders and arms, his hips and chest, watching for the slightest movement to show his intent. In his avoidance of eye contact, he spotted an insignia on the fellow's breast plate, visible beneath smears of blood and dirt.

Once again, he lost his focus upon recognizing the crest.

My father's mark.

The man howled and charged, swinging the mace at the prince in a wide loop intended to separate his head from his shoulders. Teryk raised the axe and caught the blow, hooked the club with the bottom curve of the blade. With a twist of his wrists and taking advantage of the momentum of the swing, he pulled the weapon from the soldier's hands, sent it tumbling to the mud. The fellow overbalanced and went to one knee. Teryk didn't give him the opportunity to recover, holding the point of the spike protruding from the top of the axe handle to the man's throat.

"Open your visor," he growled.

The prince's heart hammered in his chest while waiting for the warrior to comply. It took a moment, but he did.

The opened helm revealed a face familiar to Teryk. Despite no lines beside his eyes or gray showing in his short-trimmed beard, this was the man who would give over his rearing to nannies and soldiers. Here knelt the king who'd one day call him stupid, useless. The prince snarled, his upper lip pulling back to show his teeth.

"Father." He spat the word, clearing the foul taste of it from his mouth, and watched the king's expression tilt with confusion.

"I am no one's father."

"Not yet."

Teryk didn't know why he'd come to this place, this time, but with the man he'd disappointed so often kneeling in front of him at the mercy of his axe, realization dawned.

But what will happen to me if I kill my father?

The answer to such a riddle lay far beyond his comprehension. Whatever force possessed the power to transport him through the ages must also have planned for this. Killing his sire might be the key to saving the world. Phrases from the scroll rattled through his mind, each of them spoken in his sister's voice. None of them suggested the death of the king, yet here he was.

The memory of the words brought up another recollection: the regent ordering the parchment burned, punishing him and Danya.

Rage consumed Teryk, flooding out of his chest and through his limbs, energizing his muscles. He jerked the axe away from his father's throat, raised it toward the overcast sky. Droplets of rain rolled off the steel, spattering on his nose and cheeks as he enjoyed the fear crossing the king's face. He brought his hands up, turned his head.

Teryk swung the weapon, closing his eyes with effort as he did. The blade bit into flesh and a man cried out in pain.

XXIV - Rilum - A Long Time Ago

A BREEZE STIRRED THE foliage hanging in front of Rilum Seaman's face, some of them brushing his cheek and nose. He held his place, motionless, watching the little gray people as they scuttled back and forth.

He'd seen them before, more than once. In his wanderings to find sustenance—leaves and berries and the odd slow-moving insect he got his hands on—he'd come across them on three or four occasions. He lacked the ability to remember how many times, but he'd turned tail and fled when he did. This time, it occurred to him they may lead him to food or water.

A vague memory tickled the back of his mind, a recollection of many of the gray-skinned fellows gathered together, of men on horses, and of a green wall, but a haze obscured the remembrance. He failed to place when or where it happened, if it did at all. As he observed them going with their business, the vision of the past faded, forgotten moments later.

They wore no clothes, their hairless bodies lithe and sinewy. To Rilum, they appeared threatening and dangerous. If they produced a lamb shank and a wine skin brimming full, he doubted he'd leave his covering of brush to partake if they invited him. He remained unmoving, watchful, tensed to flee.

The point of a leaf rubbed against his cheek, the sensation a mix of tickle and itch. He raised a hand to sweep it away. As he did, his elbow contacted a heavily laden branch, the impact shaking it outside the cadence and rhythm of the breeze. The group of the gray skins closest to him halted their seemingly pointless meanderings and diverted their gazes in his direction. Rilum froze, breath caught in his throat, fingertips resting on his face.

They stared at his patch of brush for what seemed an eternity. A drop of sweat rolled from his forehead and into his eye, its saltiness stinging, but he fought the urge to wipe it. Tension knotted his muscles. The small men continued their long-distance scrutiny but made no move toward him. His always-dry mouth became arid, and any attempt to swallow proved fruitless.

Finally, the closest gray skin looked away, returned to the activities with which they occupied themselves. The sailor parted his lips and allowed the air to escape from his lungs a bit at a time, controlled so as not to make any sound. When he'd begun breathing again and the odd creatures re-engaged in their own doings, he inched backward from his brush cover. He cringed with each movement, progressing with such care and delicateness he expected his tendons might snap with the effort and leave him writhing on the ground at the mercy of the little ones.

Will they eat me?

A pathetic drop of saliva squirted into his mouth at the thought of food and eating. He swallowed it as quickly as it appeared, his throat thankful for the tiny watery respite. When he cleared himself of the hanging branches and fluttering leaves, he stood, knees creaking, backed away a few more steps, then turned and ran.

He didn't remember seeing animals before his latest encounter with the gray skins, but now they appeared to be everywhere.

Somehow, his nose recognized their proximity to the beasts before he came upon them and he avoided direct contact. He'd amend his course, choosing another direction to take him away from them. One time, their odors surrounded him. Not knowing what else to do, he scaled a wide-trunked tree with low-hanging branches. It occurred to him that, if his aching and atrophied muscles could help him make his way into the higher limbs, then he wouldn't find safety up high from any creature possessed with the ability to climb.

He settled onto a limb, back leaning against the tree's trunk as a knot pressed into him. Not much time passed before satisfaction for his decision to force his poor self to scale the heights of the tree swept into him.

The first animal sauntered into view a few moments later. It walked on four feet, its body squat and wide, coarse hair bristling along its spine. Two chipped tusks protruded from its short, flat snout, and each breath came out a snort.

As it approached the base of Rilum's hiding place, more of its scent wafted up to the sailor. It reeked of dirt and feces, but he detected another odor beneath he realized was the animal's flesh. His stomach rumbled.

The next beast made a much more dramatic entrance to the scene below him. Its long, sleek body shot out of the brush, startling the first creature. It turned to escape, but the new arrival pounced before it got three strides as its hoofed feet slipped in the blanket of needles on the forest floor. The second beast's sharp claws sank into the first's flesh, pulling itself up its back to plunge pointed incisors into its victim's neck.

The squat animal squealed and Rilum pressed his hands to his ears to block out the sound, but he didn't stop watching.

An instant later, the fight ended. The tusked creature thrashed and struggled, but the larger, stronger beast prevailed. The skirmish finished and the pungent aroma of blood blossomed in the air.

Rilum's mouth watered.

—ele—

Darkness fell by the time the long and sleek animal satisfied its appetite. It ate until its stomach refused more, then laid down to sleep and allow its meal to settle. The sailor squatted on the wide limb, licking his lips and swallowing the saliva flooding his gob whenever he inhaled the coppery scent of the animal's blood.

After the predator took its leave, Rilum knew to resist the urge to rush to the carcass, take some time before descending from his sanctuary. The beast may come back itself, or the whiff of freshly killed flesh might attract other hungry denizens. So he waited, shifting from foot to foot to keep his legs from going to sleep, to occupy himself until he could wait no more.

When the time came, he shifted on the branch to lower himself from the tree. Despite his best efforts, his numb limbs failed him. With his first step, his boot slipped, and he tumbled from his perch. He bounced limb to limb, bashing his arms and legs, his head and back as he caromed his way to the ground.

He landed with a dull thump hard enough to force the breath from his lungs with a grunt. For a while, he lay waiting to recover, staring up at the branches above, the slivers of night sky and twinkling stars peek-a-booing through the spaces between. When a pinch of air trickled into his chest, Rilum rolled onto his front and crawled toward the animal's remains. Shards of sticks pressed into his palms, ignored, decaying needles stuck to his hands, his knee struck a protruding root shooting pain along his leg.

The pungent bouquet of spilled blood drove him.

When he reached the carcass, the sailor leaned forward, buried his face in the gaping hole left when the beast of prey made its meal. He sank his teeth into cold flesh, shook his head side to side the way he'd seen the other animal do as it feasted. A strip came away from the bone and Rilum lifted his hands to stuff it into his mouth.

He chewed with vigor and relief, forgetting the potential dangers of the surrounding forest. The stink of meat and blood filled his nose, seeming to adhere to the inside of his nostrils as he inhaled it. He gobbled it, the sinew snaking down his throat.

The instant it reached his belly, his body revolted.

He turned and retched, vomiting the freshly swallowed meat in long strings to hang from his lips until he grabbed them and yanked them from his esophagus. He freed it, then returned it to his mouth, chewed again, devoured it a second time. This time it stayed put.

Rilum lowered his head and ate.

XXV - Teryk – Truth Be Told

*T*ERYK'S *EYES SNAPPED* OPEN, and he gasped a breath into his lungs as he sat up. The softness of a mattress supported him and he gazed at the dull gray of a stone wall. Neither registered because, once again, he knew not where he was or how he got there. This time, though, it mattered less. How he came to be anywhere or anytime seemed impossible.

I killed my father.

He covered his eyes with one hand, did his best to calm his breathing. Logic said, if he'd killed the king, then he himself should be no more. The thought made his head light, and he swallowed around a lump developing in his throat. After everything he'd seen, all that appeared to have happened, should anything surprise him? Since finding the scroll, the world had become unrecognizable in so many ways.

A deep inhalation filled his lungs but did nothing to calm the trepidation creeping along his limbs. He threw off the blanket covering him and draped his legs over the side of the bed. His feet came to rest in the fur of an animal turned into a rug. The sensation on his bare soles reminded him of his youth—similar shags covered parts of the floor in his chamber at Draekfarren. Many a morn he'd sat on the edge of his mattress wiggling his toes to enjoy the luxurious experience as long as possible before beginning his day. Another time, another place.

He pushed himself to stand, the movement making vertigo spin his head, so he reached back, rested his hand on the thick bed to keep his balance. As he waited for it to pass, he looked down and surveyed himself. The white chemise he wore fit as if it was made for him. He didn't recall ever having a top in this style. The plain, dark gray breeches rested comfortably on his hips, their quality high.

Teryk inhaled through his nose, his sense of equilibrium returning. Somewhere nearby, sandalwood incense burned, though he spied no burner anywhere, nor the telltale ribbon of smoke carrying the aroma to his nostrils. The rest of the chamber appeared unremarkable—small, with the bed, a desk and chair, a chest, and no more. Little to see, all of it high quality. A carving of a ship at sea decorated the trunk's lid, highlighted by an outline of gleaming brass. The same metal formed the hinges and hasp, polished with care. A darker wood composed the sitting furniture, so dark as to straddle a line between deep red and night black. An intricate design of painted flowers and ivy wound its way around the legs from floor to desktop and seat.

Teryk stepped away from the bed, dragging his feet through the rug's thick, soft fur. He considered crossing the short space to the chest, opening it to search for clues of his whereabouts, but veered toward the door instead.

He stood in front of it, staring at the handle set in an iron plate, the keyhole beneath. Locked or not? Who or what might lurk behind it?

Not only do I not recognize where I am, I don't know when, either.

A tiredness settled into the prince. How long since this began? The making of the Green, the Small Gods' fall, the battle. Did it happen in the blink of an eye or, as his body now suggested, had the sun risen and set multiple times since his last opportunity for rest?

He sighed and extended his arm, grasped the handle but paused before testing it. If it opened, where should he go? If it didn't, what then? He recalled the way an unseen hand drew him across the battlefield, directing him to where he needed to be. If it happened thus before, he must trust it to be the same again.

His fingers tightened, and he tugged it with a solid yank. The door swung open, smooth and silent on well-oiled hinges, and Teryk peered into the wide hall beyond. Thick carpet, ornate wall sconces, and meticulous portraits the prince recognized, though he'd never known the people they depicted.

"I'm in Draekfarren."

He spoke the words aloud without thinking, clamped his palm over his mouth as he did and faded back into the chamber. After a few breathless moments passed, he lowered his hand and peeked around the jamb. The hall lay empty in both directions, so he stepped out, bare soles padding soft carpet.

He'd been to this part of the castle, though rarely—the guest wing. Visiting nobles and their attendants laid their heads here during their visits and, judging by the size of the chamber and the style of his clothes, he must be here as the latter, not the former.

He stood in the hall for a dozen heartbeats, glancing one way then the other. To the right led deeper into the castle while the other route headed outside. He waited, expecting the guiding hand as before, and it took but the space of ten more beats of his heart before he strode to the left, not knowing if he'd chosen it himself or if another force decided for him.

A huge stained-glass window interrupted the line of portraits hanging on the wall to his right, the pattern symmetrical but nonsensical. Sun shone through, casting colored puddles of light onto the hall carpet, each of them creeping across Teryk's limbs and body as he walked. He passed three more chamber doors to his left before reaching the end of the hallway where a staircase led to the lower floor. He paused again, listened for footsteps on the stairs or the metallic rattle of an armed guard, but heard nothing. Satisfied, he descended the steps, the stone risers cool on the soles of his feet.

The stairway curved, following the inside rounded wall of a corner tower. As a child, he loved these staircases. They afforded one the ability to creep along, hidden by the wall's contour to avoid notice by someone else—a sister, for instance. Today, the same bend, the same possibility of a person hiding beyond his vision slowed his step, made him cautious. He might find an armed man a few steps farther on, or run into a noble returning to their room. Likely no matter if he did, for it seemed whoever guided him also disguised him, evidenced on his father's field of battle.

The stairway ended at an iron door, as every portal to the outside did in Draekfarren. He wondered again whether he'd find himself locked in or free to roam. He didn't hesitate this time, grasping the handle and leaning his shoulder against the metal. It swung open with ease, flooding the landing with sunlight bright enough to blind the prince while his eyes grew accustomed. Teryk squinted, filtering out the brightness while his vision returned. When it did, he gazed out on a courtyard of trimmed grass and hedges pruned into shapes with not a single a leaf out of place. Without exception, it appeared as he remembered it from his visits. He'd spent most of his life in the main gardens, but liked this terrace near as much. It possessed an air of being hidden away from the rest of the castle, a private oasis to take refuge with little fear of discovery.

The prince stepped out into the light and pushed the door closed behind him. It clanked against the stone jamb; since he'd encountered nobody thus far, he doubted anyone lurked within earshot. Outside, a flagstone path led straight away into the yard; he followed it but did so to one side, choosing to walk in the grass instead. The short lawn tickled his feet, sent a refreshing sensation up his lower legs and brought a smile to his lips. The warmth of the sun on his face and the green blades on his soles seemed so long ago, so distant. Did it delight him so other times in his life? He didn't think so, because he'd never imagined it not being a part of his world.

When you perceive no risk of losing a thing, it's more difficult to appreciate it.

The thought drove the smile from his mouth; it wasn't just sunlight and grass he'd taken for granted, but also Trenan's guidance, Danya's laughter, his mother's love. His heart ached over them; he didn't see a future in which he'd ever walk beside any of them again.

Ahead, the tumbling gurgle of a fountain reached his ears. The larger hedges of the topiary hid it from him, but having seen it before, he pictured in his mind what they concealed. His feet carried him toward it, each step silent in the grass. As he neared, the quiet murmur of a woman's voice came to him on the still air. He stopped, listened, but it sounded as though she spoke a different language. If so, it meant he remained sometime far in the past; the ancient languages had died along with the banishment of the Small Gods, spoken in secret circles, if at all.

The prince crept farther from the path, avoiding the space between hedges where one entered the topiary's cool interior to sit by the fountain and enjoy the water's music. He circled around the outside of the hedge fortress; in his memory, he'd find another small opening near the base of the largest bush. He hadn't decided if the gap occurred naturally or if his father or a previous king commanded it created on purpose—a hole through which someone might spy on their visitors. The latter, most likely.

He arrived at the spot, happy to discover it opposite the entrance to the enclave where he remembered it. Here, the hedges grew closest to the castle wall, this stretch of it blank and windowless—another hint toward the opening being man-made. Teryk checked over his shoulder to make sure no one saw him. Confident of being alone, he squatted, bent closer to the hole. Here, naught but the length of two horses separated him from the woman sitting near the fountain, and her words floated to him through the warm air.

She's singing.

Though the lyrics remained indistinct, both the melody and her voice proved familiar.

"Mother?"

He whispered the word then felt compelled to glance around, be sure no one heard. He continued to be alone. Teryk lay flat on the grass, but wriggled forward, bringing his face to the opening in the hedge.

She sat on a marble bench to the left of the fountain, her profile visible as she gazed into her crossed arms. A blissful expression perched upon her visage as she cooed and sang and rocked back and forth. It took the prince a moment to realize she wasn't hugging herself and singing to her forearms. She held a bundled blanket, its contents hidden from him, but he realized what it contained.

It's me.

Teryk's heart swelled with equal parts joy and hurt. How peaceful and happy she appeared away from his father and the crown which weighed heavy on her head in his time. Here, now, the contented smile refused to leave her face, giving her a glow. How he wished to be the babe in her arms again, without a care or the fate of its people hanging on his shoulders like the yoke on an ox. With it to do over, would he follow Danya into the river under the castle? Insist on heeding the words of a prophecy written so many turns of the seasons ago? He didn't have answers to those questions and, truly, they made no matter. Here he was instead of his own era, with no way to change his circumstances.

His mother stopped singing and rocking, looked up from the bundle gathered against her, gazing toward the entrance to the topiary hideaway. Teryk followed her gaze, his eyes finding the man lingering beneath the green and leafy arch. He'd entered in silence, might have been watching for a few moments before she'd noticed him. He leaned against the hedge with arms crossed, a grin on his face. The prince didn't recognize him, though he thought he should.

Seeing him, his mother stood, her joyous expression expanding further. The new visitor strode toward her, his smile matching hers. As he approached and Teryk saw him more clearly, he realized who he gazed upon.

Trenan.

His gait gobbled up the ground between them and he put his arms around her in an embrace like he'd never seen the two of them share.

Both arms. He has both arms.

Blood rushed away from his face, his cheeks went chill. Trenan with both arms meant his father was dead, killed by his son. Thoughts swirled in his head, none of them landing long enough for him to grasp. The master swordsman bent and pressed his lips against the queen's. Teryk's eyes saw the kiss, but didn't register the act as it lingered, as Trenan's one hand cradled her head, his fingers finding their way through her hair while the other rested on her hip. She held him with her free arm, pulling him close against her as she twisted to keep the babe from being crushed between them.

My father is dead. The queen rules the kingdom in his place.

True, but he understood it wasn't the important thought he needed to pick from the morass in his head. He grasped for another as the couple before him separated, though their hands remained on each other—lovers unafraid of discovery.

How long since the battle?

Maybe it wasn't his mother, but someone who resembled her. Or perhaps he'd skipped farther forward in time than he thought and he wasn't the babe at all. The queen held Danya her arms—that must be it.

"How is the prince today?"

Trenan's question slammed into Teryk's brain like a dart into a board, pinning one of the unavoidable thoughts.

My father is dead; Danya will never be born.

His mother smiled, removed the blanket from the baby's face for the swordmaster to better see. "Happy. And hungry."

He didn't look at the baby, instead gazing into her eyes. He trailed the tips of his fingers along her cheek, over her shoulder, down her arm. "When can we tell the kingdom?"

She looked away, moving her gaze to the young prince in her arms; he did the same, but the smile disappeared from his lips as it did from hers. A weightiness filled the air between them, a palpable tension not present the instant before. The master swordsman ran a finger along the baby's cheek.

"You know we can't. The people mourn the loss of their king. The kingdom needs to believe he left an heir."

She whispered the words but, despite the gurgle and splash of the fountain, Teryk heard her as though she stood beside him, whispering in his ear. Trenan didn't respond, instead continued gazing at the babe in her arms. Teryk's teeth clamped together tight enough to hurt his jaw. His mind raced back through his life, searching for hints and signs of this between his mother and the man who trained him, raised him, for a memory of how long passed between what he recalled as Trenan losing his arm and his birth. Was she pregnant when the battle happened? He didn't recall the subject ever coming up.

The master swordsman nodded, the movement barely noticeable. He glanced up at her, forced the corners of his mouth to curve up into a strained smile. He stepped back and spread his arms.

"Can I hold the prince?"

"Yes, of course. Hold your son. The world will never find out he is yours, but their lack of knowledge doesn't change the identity of his true father."

Trenan took the babe in his arm, but Teryk didn't let his gaze follow. His mouth dried up and his forehead prickled.

Hold your son.

He blinked, pushed himself up to his knees.

Son.

Legs watery and unstable, he stood and put a hand to his forehead, lurched an unsteady pace away from the topiary.

"Trenan is my father, not Erral." He licked his lips then wiped his forearm across his mouth. "I'm not the firstborn child of the rightful king. No one is."

Another step, his body swaying atop uncertain legs.

"The world will perish."

Vertigo overtook him, and the prince stumbled back three steps, then ahead before his feet tangled and he pitched forward. He landed hard, the impact jarring his head. Things around him changed instantly. The dissonance of steel on steel replaced the soothing gurgle of the fountain; the scent of grass and brush disappeared, overpowered by the coppery reek of blood and muddy ground. He put his gauntleted hands under himself, pressed against soggy, churned turf and pushed himself up to observe his surroundings.

Men swirled, their weapons flashing. Rain pattered against Teryk's cheek and he understood where he found himself, and when. He climbed to his feet, the ax he'd used to kill his father dangling from his right hand. Without thought to his actions, he trudged forward, moving past the fighting men as though they didn't notice his passing. A few strides ahead, he spied the man for whom he searched on one knee, visor raised. The prince stopped in front of him, lifted the ax's spike to the king's throat with no intention of doing so.

"I am no one's father."

Deja vu sent a shiver along Teryk's spine and his mouth opened, words spilling out despite his not intending them to.

"Not yet."

He pulled the ax from his father's esophagus, raised it skyward. The king lifted his arm to protect himself, turned his face away. A shout from his left gave Teryk pause, and he directed his gaze toward the soldier rushing to save his monarch. The prince amended his stance and brought the weapon down, separating the warrior's limb from his shoulder instead of splitting the king's head in two.

Trenan cried out and fell to the ground, writhing on the sopping grass as blood squirted from his wound. Teryk backed away a step, his stomach threatening to rise into his throat. The ax slipped from his grasp and he looked from the master swordsman to the man he thought of as his father.

Did I set things right?

The king leaped forward, snatching Trenan's sword from his hand as he did. The point of it entered Teryk's belly and, to his surprise, he felt the full length of it slide through him and the tip exit through his back. Pain exploded through him and he gasped, the sudden inhalation sucking droplets of rain into his mouth. He relished the refreshment of them for a moment before Erral wrenched the blade from his gut and he coughed the acidic flavor of blood onto his tongue.

He tottered in place for a few seconds, watching as the king threw aside the sword and rushed to Trenan's side, shouting for a medic as he did. Teryk hacked into his hand, viewed the red clot doing so left in his gauntlet, then fell forward. He didn't stop himself, giving into the inevitable impact of hitting the muddy ground...but he didn't.

Instead, when he hit, it wasn't grass, but water.

He went under, the chill of it shocking him. Briny fluid found its way into his mouth, stung his eyes. He kicked and thrashed until his face broke through and he emerged from the sea sputtering and coughing. But salty water was the only thing he tasted, the tang of blood gone from his tongue.

Why should I taste blood?

His heart beat fast in his chest and he gasped for air, lungs thankful to find it. The smooth surface of the ocean allowed him to keep his head above the water line with little effort. He blinked the briny sting from his eyes, the world around him blurry. Straight ahead, a hazy brown smudge dominated the horizon. He blinked again and again until his vision returned and he saw the ship, words painted on the side near the bow. He squinted until they became legible: *Devil of the Deep*. Faintly, he made out the shape of a man waving at him, pointing.

The ship's name tickled the back of his mind, teasing out a suspicion that it should hold meaning for him. The feeling remained undefined, an itch he couldn't reach. He concentrated. Why should he recognize this ship? He realized other things he didn't know: where he was, how he got here.

Who am I?

Panic clawed at his gut, but waves washing over him, splashing up into his face, made him forget it for an instant. He craned his head toward the source of the ripples, saw the bubbles rolling across the surface. A heartbeat later, a sliver of gray flashed, then broke through. A flat skull emerged atop a long, smooth neck, a wide mouth lined with pointed teeth opened, a screeching roar tore through the air.

And the God of the Deep rose from the sea.

XXVI - Rilum – Long Ago

*R*ILUM GAZED AT THE clump of hair in his hand. The tangled strands lay across his featureless palm like a small, dead animal. He exhaled, his breath stirring it back to life momentarily before it returned to its final slumber.

This wasn't the first shock of hair he'd pulled from his head. It wasn't even what currently caught and held his attention.

The sailor rotated his hand palm down, the fine strands fluttering to the ground, landing around his feet. He didn't watch their erratic fall, instead concentrating on the white skin stretched across the back of his hands.

White.

Not pink. Not scattered with dark hair. He sensed his hands once appeared thus, though he couldn't be sure. Now: white like a frost-covered rock. White like the foam atop an angry wave. White.

His shortest finger had grown to match the others, each of the digits the same length. Or were they always this way?

He reached up with his other hand, took hold of the edge of his thumbnail between his other thumb and forefinger. It rocked back and forth, moving beneath the flesh until it came free. He pulled it out, a last attached string of skin following like a bit of elastic until it snapped. Rilum held it up in front of his eyes, turned it, examined it, then let it drop to settle amongst the hair scattered around his feet.

XXVII - Trenan - Road to Draekfarren

GIHL PULLED THE WET blanket tighter around his shoulders and wiped rain away from his face.

"Why the fuck did I let Krin talk me into this?"

The horse he sat—the fastest in the kingdom, by his estimation—said nothing in response. Its hooves splashed in puddles, the dirt track turning to mud beneath them, and the speed his mount stored in its haunches didn't mean a tinker's damn for keeping him dry.

"What the fuck was with that bird? Who's ever seen a bird shittin' out storm clouds?"

He hung his head, doing his best to hide from the rain pelting against his face, lank, wet hair stuck to his cheeks. A stiff gust of wind threw a sheet of drops hard against him, each droplet a pinprick stinging his skin. The horse took exception to the extra dowsing and shook its snout, throwing more water at him from its mane.

"Damn you," Gihl sputtered. He wiped his arm across his face and thought of a hundred things he'd rather do than ride this lonely dirt road in the rain performing a task he didn't understand for a man who held no more sway in his life than serving him ale. "Fuck this."

He reined the horse to a halt and straightened in the saddle. The muscles in his legs tightened, readying to turn the speedy nag around and beat a hasty retreat to his home, but he stopped when he looked along the dirt track ahead.

More riders than he possessed fingers on his two hands sat in the middle of the road. The length of ten horses separated him from them and how he hadn't heard them approaching made little sense. Another thing to blame on the rain. He considered reaching toward the short sword dangling from his belt, but the strangers wore armor, each of them with swords more dangerous looking than his at their waists. To draw his blade meant his death, to be sure, so he kept his hand as far from the grip as possible.

He sat staring at them, and them at him, as though none of them had ever seen another rider before as cold rain ran down his back. He shivered. After an interval longer than seemed comfortable, the front two riders detached from the others and came toward him. Gihl's fingers tightened on the reins and he wondered if his horse was as fast as he thought. Maybe not the best time to find out.

"Ho, rider. What has you riding a muddy track on this dreary day?"

Gihl didn't respond. Droplets of water dripped from his ragged beard, ran down his face from the unkempt hair plastered to his head. His gaze darted from the man who'd spoken to the second person. This one wore stern features, but softer, and it took him a moment to realize it was a woman. He might have wondered about this, perhaps commented on it, if the first soldier hadn't released the reins and wrapped the fingers of his lone hand around the hilt of his sword. Gihl gulped; he knew of this fellow. The fact didn't relieve any of the stress of his situation. If anything, it produced the opposite effect.

"I know you," he said. His words came out sounding breathless, as though his horse rode him to this place rather than the other way around. He swallowed hard again, did his best to suppress the nervous quake threatening to shake his spine but met with little success.

The rider narrowed his gaze, looked him up and down. He shifted in his saddle but did not relinquish his grip on his weapon. "If we know each other, I apologize for not recalling your face."

Gihl shook his head, sending water droplets flying from his beard, his hair.

"No, we've not met, but I've heard of you." He drew a forearm across his eyes, wiping away the rain. "The one-armed swordsman, the king's man. Everyone in the kingdom with a brain in his noggin knows about you."

"We don't have time for this," the female rider said, leaning toward her companion. He released his grip on his sword long enough to gesture for her patience, then replaced it.

"I am Trenan." He nodded in a way that didn't require he take his eyes from Gihl's. "And you are?"

"Gihl. Krin sent me because I have the fastest horse."

The soldier raised an eyebrow. "Who is Krin? And where did he send you?"

"Trenan," the woman said, annoyance plain in her voice.

Gihl suddenly thought he'd be better off having to deal with the one-armed warrior than his companion. He suspected she'd prefer to kill him and finish it than anything else.

Trenan turned his head toward her and their gazes met for an instant. Gihl couldn't have said what passed back and forth in the look, but he thanked the gods he wasn't standing between them.

He let his gaze fall away, searched his lap and the ground at his steed's feet, scratched his beard. His fingers caught in a knot in his facial hair; he tugged to free it, cringing as he did. A series of heartbeats passed, and he hoped the odd and frightening pair of riders had forgotten him. When he raised his head again, he found both sets of eyes boring into him.

"Well?"

"Draekfarren," he blurted. "He sent me to Draekfarren because I have the fastest horse. Fastest in the kingdom, I'd wager. Faster'n every—"

"I don't care about the fleetness of your steed," Trenan snapped. "Why are you headed for the seat of the king?"

Gihl felt as though someone slapped him across the face. His breathing shallowed as the master swordsman pulled a finger's breadth of steel free of his scabbard. A fat drop of rain struck Gihl's eye, blinding him as he blinked it away. He was about to meet his end on a muddy road in the middle of nowhere carrying out a task in which he had no business being involved. In fact, with the feared warrior staring at him, awaiting his reply, he couldn't remember why Krin had dispatched him on this miserable journey. Because he owed too much on his tab? No, he found himself here because he owned the fastest horse in Woodsel. But why did he send him? What was the message he meant him to carry? He searched his memory for the last things he remembered before the barkeep showed up at his table and tossed the coins in front of him. He'd been enjoying a pint when something disturbed the calm in Krin's Tavern.

But what?

Not a fight—too early in the day for that. He recalled visitors, but nothing out of the ordinary. Just the weapons merchants. What were their names? Sheckle and Pive? But it wasn't them who'd so concerned Krin, but the young women with them. He hadn't seen them, but the barkeep recognized one of them, which caused his upset.

Gihl's eyes widened.

"The princess," he whispered.

Trenan yanked two more fingers of steel free of the scabbard and prompted his horse closer for Gihl to witness the day's gray light glimmer on his weapon. He contorted his face into a frown, a threat not to lie. Gihl shriveled before him, shrinking back into his saddle.

"What of Danya? Have you seen her?"

"See, Trenan? We must go," the woman said.

"Krin did," Gihl replied, voice trembling. "He told me to ride fast as the wind, but I don't think the wind can sit a horse."

The master swordsman pursed his lips. The muscles in his jaw tightened, and he urged his steed two steps closer, bringing him within arm's reach. When he spoke, he did so with precision, emphasizing each word.

Gihl shifted in his saddle, the sudden urge to urinate making it impossible for him to find a comfortable position. He glanced from Trenan to the woman, then past them to the group of riders behind them, wondered who they were, why they were there, where they might be going. The hiss of steel on leather jerked his attention back to the one-armed man. The tip of Trenan's sword hovered a hand's breadth from his neck. Gihl gulped.

"Tell me everything, simpleton, and do it now."

The bump in Gihl's throat rose and fell again, his panicked saliva clicking as he swallowed. His mouth opened, lips quivering as he attempted to wet them with his tongue with little success.

"Two men," he said, his arms crossed, hugging himself as he rocked in the saddle trying his best not to void his bladder. "They had her."

"What men?"

"Th...the weapons merchants."

"What do they look like?"

Gihl hesitated, rivulets of rain coursing down his cheek all but unnoticed with the threat of death poised in front of his eyes. Trenan moved the pointed end of the blade forward and he flinched, turned his head away.

"One tall and skinny, the other shorter, wider."

"Fellick and Ive."

He shrugged, the message the barkeep meant him to pass along flooding back to him at the last second. "Krin said to tell the king they were taking her toward sunset."

"The Green," the woman interjected, her words directed to Trenan, not to him for confirmation.

Gihl watched them stare hard at each other but didn't move, the tip of the swordsman's weapon hovering a finger's breadth from his throat. It went on long enough he worried they might have forgotten him and he'd never move again without the risk of slitting his gullet. Finally, whatever held them dissipated, and the soldier lowered his sword then slipped it into its scabbard with more ease and grace than a one-armed should be capable of. Gihl inhaled a shuddering breath, kept it for two heartbeats, and released it again, hoping this meant he might live after all.

"Can..." He stopped, swallowed hard. "Can I go home?"

The master swordsman brought his gaze to bear on him. The intensity of his expression made Gihl want to slide from his horse and run off into the forest, never to look back. His bladder failed him.

"You have a duty to the kingdom. Continue on to Draekfarren and seek a soldier called Osis. Tell him everything you've told me. And tell him I sent you."

The master swordsman put his heels to his steed, and the animal responded at once, moving past Gihl and continuing on the muddy track, hooves splashing in deepening puddles. The woman came next, fixing him with a gaze rivaling that of the king's man. He shrank away from her, happy his rain-wet pants hid his loss of bladder control.

Without a gesture from either of them, the rest of the warriors followed, twin columns of riders flowing past on either side, a stream of horse flesh and armor parting around a shaking rock. When they'd passed, he remained where he sat, neither prompting his steed to move nor turning to watch them go. Even after the sounds of hooves on wet track disappeared, he waited, shivering, wishing to be anywhere else. Raindrops beat on his head, ran down his face, threatened to choke him every time he breathed too deeply through his nose.

After a while, Gihl sat straight in his saddle. Through his soaked trousers, he felt like he noticed the difference between the rain and the cold piss trapped inside his pants. He cleared his throat, spat a wad of phlegm on the muddy ground, and pulled the horse's reins, turning her in the direction from which they'd come. He let his mount advance a step before hauling back on the lead again, stopping her.

"What if they stopped somewhere ahead and they see me not doing what the one-armed bastard told me to do?"

The rain pattered. His horse snuffled and blew water from its nostrils. Nothing and nobody else offered any advice.

"He'd kill me," he said, answering his own query.

The mare pawed the muddy ground, splashing in the rivulet flowing along the middle of the track.

"Fuck."

He turned his mount around again, pointing her toward Draekfarren. He dug his heels into her, prompting her forward with no more certainty this was the right thing to do than heading home.

At least this direction meant less chance he'd die.

"What now?"

It wasn't long after the rain stopped when Gihl spied the three figures on the road ahead. One stood straight, a robe draped from his shoulders and a cowl pulled up to hide his face. The second either knelt by the robed figure, was a child, or the smallest damned man Gihl'd ever seen. The third crouched on hands and knees, puking beside the track.

"Fucking lovely."

He reined his horse to a stop, looked side to side in search of a path which might allow his escape, but the trees and brush grew too close together. Face them or retreat? They didn't look the most dangerous of sorts, but maybe they wanted him to think they weren't. As he glanced back up the road at them in the same positions, he recalled a saying—something to do with discretion and valor. He couldn't remember it, but thought it ended with the words 'fuck valor.'

Through pulling reins and tapping heels, Gihl got the horse pointed down the narrow track away from the three strangers... or so he believed. When they faced the other direction, he found them right before him, closer, the one who'd knelt losing his lunch standing beside the others. Turned out he was a big man, imposing, and Gihl's heart sped up in his chest, knocking against his ribs as though it sought to break out. He tugged on the bridle, urging the mare to back up.

"I'm not looking for no trouble," he said, voice quivering. He considered reaching for his short sword but pulling the weapon was more likely to get him killed than if he stayed away from it and left it alone. Why did he bother carrying the damn thing?

None of the three made sound nor motion, which may have been worse than if they demanded his money or his mount. At least then he'd know where he stood. Not knowing their intent scared him.

And how'd they get behind me so quick?

He decided he didn't want to find out what they wanted or how they'd gotten around him. He dug his heels in again, yanked the reins again and jerked the horse's head around harder than he should have. The nag responded, rearing up and twisting to face the other direction, ready to launch itself down the track the second he prompted it to do so.

They never gave Gihl the chance.

The big man's arm caught him around the waist and yanked him from the saddle. His right foot snagged in the stirrup, wrenching his knee, and he cried out before it pulled free and he hit the ground with a sodden thump. The impact jarred the breath from his lungs and he gasped trying to restore it.

"Where's the one-armed man?"

The big fellow held him by the front of his shirt, the fabric bunched in his fists, and his face hung a hand's-breadth from Gihl's. With no air in his chest, he couldn't respond, so settled for widening his eyes and shaking his head, teeth gritted against the pain in his knee. The stranger shook him once, moved closer.

"Where is he?"

Spittle flew against Gihl's nose and cheeks and he recalled seeing this man vomiting at the roadside moments before. His own gorge rose, a lump in his chest making both breathing and answering the angry fellow more difficult.

Gihl lifted a shaking hand, pointed along the road the direction the master swordsman and his troop had gone. The same way led to his home. He wished he'd heeded his first instinct and abandoned Krin's stupid task the second he'd gotten clear of the tavern and the barkeep's line of sight.

"Toward sunset? The Green?"

Muddy water lapped against Gihl's ear as he nodded.

"Why?"

His lips parted and closed, his throat working to make a sound, but nothing came out. The big man shook him again, jerking him up off the ground, snapping his head forward, then dropping him again. Dirty droplets splashed onto his face.

"Why?"

Gihl opened his mouth again, forced his tongue and gullet to do the things they needed to do to produce sound, and this time they did.

"The princess," he said, the proclamation coming out more gag than actual words.

"They have the princess?"

Gihl shook his head, neck sore from the latest shaking he'd endured. "Weapon merchants. Have her. Taking to Green."

The big man's lips peeled back from his teeth in a sneer dripping with such hatred it made Gihl flinch. His limited future in the grasp of this maniac became clear to him and he deiced he needed to do anything necessary to save himself.

"The king," he gasped. "I'm to inform the king."

"Are you?" The hate-filled expression turned to an ugly smile, one lacking the smallest sliver of humor, warmth, or happiness. He leaned closer and, now Gihl had his air again, he smelled the man's sour breath when he spoke. "Tell you what: I'll pass the message along for you."

A lancet of hope poked through Gihl's fear. "So I can go home?"

The terrible smile broadened, an expression worse than the hateful sneer.

"Oh, you'll be going back where you came from."

The first blow from the big man's clenched fist sent flashes of light exploding across Gihl's vision, as if the stars in the sky sprang to life all at once. The second broke his jaw, the bright pinpricks forced away by the pain. With the third punch, he tasted blood on his tongue, then filling his cheeks and spilling from his lips. When the fourth struck, he barely noticed it through the agony consuming him; he only hoped for consciousness to leave him. He tried to move his mouth, to beg for mercy, but had no idea if he met with any success. The world grew dim, leaving him with the vague impression of the fellow's face, his horse's front leg, and then a different visage loomed over him.

A cowl concealed the figure's features. Long fingers reached out from loose sleeves and peeled the hood back to reveal a smooth pate so white it might have glowed. The dark eyes stared at him, a smile on the lips much more gentle than the one worn by the fellow who beat him. The robed figure raised his arms, stretched his hands to Gihl's face, laid his fingers on the side of his head. For an instant, the pain from the beating subsided, and Gihl thought his life saved.

Until the burning began.

The long appendages seared themselves into his flesh, sinking through his skin and into the bone beneath, pressing their way toward his brain. Agony expanded in his skull, pushing outward, bulging his eyes and popping his ears.

Gihl screamed.

———

Dansil stood back, panting from the exertion of smashing his fist into the rider's face. He drew his arm across his forehead, wiping off what might have been rain, sweat, or blood. When he'd caught his breath, he stepped away from the fellow; he still felt the pain from the stab wound given him by Stirk, but not the debilitating kind he'd experienced at Ikkundana. He watched the robed healer crouch over the fallen man, lay his hands on him. The queen's guard turned his back instead of watching what he knew came next, flexing his left hand now missing two fingers he'd possessed the day before. He reached up, grasped the saddle's pommel, and put one foot in a stirrup. Before he climbed on, fingers gripped his ankle.

He jerked his head, at first thinking it might be the healer laying hands upon him, but found Stirk holding his leg. The legless man teetered but stayed upright.

"Where do you think you're goin'?"

"The healer's method of travel don't sit well with my insides. I'll be taking the horse from here."

"But you don't—"

Dansil shook free of Stirk's grip and the one-limbed fellow toppled over into the mud with a splash that brought a smile to his lips. He threw one leg over the horse's back and guided the nag to turn toward the Green, uncaring if he should trample Stirk or the healer. He set his heel to horse flesh, and the steed bounded forward as its former rider began to scream.

Dansil thanked whatever god might bother to listen to him he was getting away from them, though he knew he'd never really get away.

Never again in his life.

XXVIII - Rilum – Long Ago

*T*HE WATER REEKED OF salt.

It attracted Rilum from a distance, drawing him through the forest of trees and brush to a rocky shore. He picked his way over stones the size of his head and around boulders too big for him to scale. The air turned cold again and his short breaths boiled out his mouth in rolling white mist, but not so colorless as the flesh on his hands and fingers. He supposed the breathy fog suggested he should notice the chill, but he did not.

When he reached the edge of the water, he stood watching as waves rolled across the smaller stones with a hiss to gather about the soles of his boots. At some point, he'd worn holes in them, and the sea touched his feet. He leaned forward, scooped water into his pasty palm, and raised his hand to his mouth.

The salt stung his tongue and set his mind reeling, though he didn't know why. He sensed he should remember this flavor, this scent; nothing came to him to explain why. It did not satiate his hunger, nor did it make him want to imbibe more of the briny fluid. He wiped his hand on the front of his pants and spat into the wash at his feet, his thick and sticky saliva floating atop the rolling waves like a thing swimming for its life.

Rilum turned and left the wad of phlegm behind, continuing along the shore at the edge of the water, his soles squelching inside his soaked boots. He'd gone fewer than ten paces when he realized he wasn't alone.

Normally, his nose warned him when other creatures lurked near, but the stink of salt in his nostrils and throat clogged his sense until he raised his gaze and saw them standing farther along the shore, staring at him.

They stood on two legs like him, had two arms as he did. Hair on their heads, clothes on their bodies. Their shoulders hunched and their eyes opened wide as they watched him. He stopped, a spark igniting in his chest.

They look like me.

Not exactly; their skin wasn't white, their hair wasn't patchy, he suspected they'd have all their teeth. But his flesh had once been pink, his hair full, his set of teeth complete. The memory of those things was hazy in his mind, separated from the present by time and distance, but the sight of them brought it back, the remembrance carrying enthusiasm and hope on its shoulders.

The sailor started out again, increasing his pace. If it hadn't been so long since he saw others like himself, he might have raised a hand in greeting. If he'd been in the habit of speaking, he'd call out a friendly hello, but his eternally parched mouth hadn't spawned words in ages.

The two men tensed at his approach and Rilum told himself they did so because it surprised them to see him here. One of them turned to the other and spoke too quietly for him to hear. When he finished, they both bent at the waist, their nervous hands working to gather items from the shore. The sailor put no thought to what they gathered until they flung the first stone at him.

It bounced off his thigh, not quite hurting him, but throwing off his gait so he nearly stumbled. The part of his face where once he'd possessed eyebrows dipped. Why did they throw rocks at him? Shouldn't it delight them to find another of their kind on these hostile shores?

A second rock flew past his ear, its odd shape causing it to whistle through the air. The sound might have delighted him if the next, larger projectile didn't hit him square in the middle of his forehead.

This time, the impact hurt. Rilum closed his eyes, shook his head. His feet tangled, and he fell, the sharp edge of a rock digging into his knee. The spark which seeing them lit in his chest extinguished like a guttering candle in a stiff breeze, replaced by explosive rage. He climbed back to standing as another stone struck him in the shoulder, a fourth in the belly.

His vision narrowed, the sea and the rocky shore all but disappearing until it appeared to him they stood at the end of a tunnel. They continued hurling stones, some striking him, most of them missing, but he no longer noticed. He increased his pace, his feet finding their way across the rugged ground as though he'd done it a thousand times before. Frantic, the two men stooped to gather more rocks, launched them without taking the time to aim; fewer and fewer of them found their target.

As the space between them diminished, they gave up beating him back with thrown stones. One turned, intending to flee, but stumbled on the closest rock and fell to the ground, flailing. The other decided on a different tack and moved toward Rilum, fists clenched.

The sailor crashed into him full-force, sending him sprawling. Before he had any opportunity to recover, Rilum fell upon him. He snagged the fellow by his wrist and yanked, rending his arm from his shoulder. Blood squirted, and he screamed as Rilum went for the man who'd tripped.

He clambered away, his face gone white, but still not as white as his attacker's. His feet churned against stones that slid out from beneath his efforts. When Rilum reached him, the stranger raised his hands in front of him, but they did him no good as the sailor clubbed him with his companion's arm.

He hit him again and again until his defensive gesture gave out, arms falling to the rocky ground at his sides. Rilum continued hitting him, the fellow's cheeks and forehead having turned shiny red, covered with his own blood and his friend's. The tang of it forced its way into Rilum's consciousness, past the reek of brine, the stench of his own body. Viscous saliva crept into his mouth and he stopped swinging the severed arm and let it fall from his tacky, blood-smeared hand.

He drew his shriveled tongue across cracked and pitted lips.

The other man's terrified screams pulled him out of his hunger-lust. Rilum turned and found the fellow had leveraged himself to his feet to stumble away toward the forest. He craned his neck to peer back at his friend's horrific death. Rilum deserted the dead man to stalk after the runner. He stooped on his way without slowing, plucked a rock from the ground twice the size of his own fist.

He caught up to the fellow in no time. The stone contacted his skull with a satisfying crunch and he crumpled as if the blow had severed every tendon in his body.

Rilum didn't bother to find out whether the man was dead or continued to live. He dropped to his knees beside him, leaned in, and tore into the soft flesh of his belly with what few teeth remained in his head. Blood splashed across his cheeks, into his mouth, down his throat. His stomach rumbled happily.

XXIX - Man from Across the Sea - Woman in the Woods

*I*T HAPPENED SO FAST. Jud-dah jerking away from his captor, the ensuing chaos, pushing the woman behind himself for protection, her touch slipping from his so words faded back to indecipherable.

Two men grabbed him by the arms as he watched the man who'd imprisoned him fold to the ground, life gone from him. Their fingers hidden in the cuffs of their robes dug into his flesh, sending pain through his biceps. He ignored it, instead surprised to find slivers of sadness and compassion at the fellow called Jud-dah's death. After being locked in a barn, forced to dig beyond exhaustion, and watching the mistreatment of the woman captive with him, he shouldn't experience anything but relief at the man's execution, yet he did. Somewhere deep inside, he sensed Jud-dah and his dog might be the lesser of evils.

The other men, including the one not dressed in black cowl and robe, turned their attention toward him. He tensed, awaiting an attack. A fat drop of rain struck his temple, rolled along his cheek as lightning cut a path across the darkened sky. In the flash of light, he realized they weren't staring at him; they gazed past him.

The leader—Jud-dah called him Birk, he recalled—pushed his way between the others to stand beside the prisoner and his captors. In response, the man twisted against the grip of the two holding him to look back over his shoulder at what usurped their attention.

The rain pelting against the glistening wall spattered bright patterns, then rolled along its surface as though it had struck a window. Behind the barrier, the woman—his companion in the barn and on their journey, the person who'd given him the ability to understand the world—knelt on hands and knees. She raised her head, cocked it to one side, listening.

"Howdshee geto verthar?" the fellow called Birk said in the gibberish the man hoped he'd never experience again.

None of the others responded. He wasn't sure Birk expected any of them to answer, but neither did Ailyssa act as though she'd heard. He leaned toward the green divide, pulling against the two robed men's grasp. They held firm, but his closer proximity to the wall allowed the nameless man to glimpse her between the spider webs of lightning cast by the rain hitting it.

It wasn't Birk she attempted to listen to, but the black-haired creature stalking toward her.

Its thick mane bristled and its yellow-white teeth stood out in stark contrast to its dark fur. The snarled mouth may have meant a growl emanated deep in its chest but, if it did, only Ailyssa and the beast's own ears detected it. It crept closer to her as she moved her head, sightlessly attempting to locate the predator.

His gut knotted, and he tugged hard against his captors' grasp, trying to free himself, though he didn't know what he'd do if he succeeded. She couldn't hear him if he yelled, couldn't see him any more than she saw the shaggy black beast. And the shimmering veil kept him from reaching her side.

How did she get over there?

The thought popped into his head, swallowed right away by swirling emotions. The two robed men held him fast, and Birk stepped up beside them, his face a hand's breadth from the wall.

"Gidub," he yelled. "Gidub anrun."

Again, Ailyssa made no sign the words found her ears. The urge to call out and warn her dropped the nameless man's mouth open, but no sound emerged. He realized the futility in trying. Despite having understood and being able to speak when in contact with the woman, his mind failed him as to what he'd say. Likely nothing more than a grunt.

The beast took one slow step after another, creeping through the brush toward its prey. She tensed, the cords in her neck prominent. It appeared the urge to flee gripped her body, hardening her muscles, but her lack of sight kept her in place like a plant rooted to the ground. Her nostrils flared as the animal moved close enough for her to detect its odor.

The nameless man imagined how it must smell: musty and musky, a mixture of damp fur and carrion breath. As much as he wished for her to run away and save herself, another part of him hoped for the beast to finish her quickly, minimize her pain. How awful for her to kneel in this strange place, helpless and awaiting her death at the fangs and claws of a fearful brute.

Less than the length of an arm separated the animal from the woman, the threat so palpable even Birk watched. The nameless man's jaw gyrated, grinding his teeth together, but he couldn't stop himself. His tongue pressed hard against the roof of his mouth, his hands curled into fists.

Ailyssa flinched with the waft of the beast's exhalation on her face. Her expression contorted, twisting with strain and fear. The nameless man held his breath, wanted to look anywhere else. Rain ran from his hair into his eyes, and he blinked it away, unable to remove his gaze from Ailyssa's impending death.

But the animal halted as though the aroma it detected did not lend itself to feeding. It got no closer, nor did it retreat. Ailyssa continued her prolonged flinch, recoiling from the hot breath on her cheek.

Time slowed. The rain grew heavier, more and more droplets pounding the green curtain until the near-constant fireworks playing across its surface hid Ailyssa and the beast from sight. He struggled to lean closer, blinked more water from his eyes.

Through the occasional break in the spidery, verdant lightning, he spied his friend raising her arm, reaching toward the animal. Its lips peeled back, exposing the sharp teeth hidden in its maw.

What is she doing?

Her hand neared the beast's mouth, its snarl appearing to continue, deepen.

"No," Birk called out. "Stawpid."

A gust of wind pushed a sheet of rain against the veil, the sudden explosion of gnarled green fingers obliterating his view of them. Raindrops slammed against his back, his captors' black robes snapping and waving. When it subsided enough to see again, it revealed Ailyssa standing, one hand on the animal's head. The beast's lips relaxed, hiding its teeth again, its demeanor noticeably different. Its hackles lay flat, the tension in its muscles diminished. Ailyssa's physical attitude mirrored the creature's, the fear and strain in her face gone.

Birk took a step toward the veil until his nose threatened to brush it. He raised his hand, slammed it against the shimmery wall. Green shot out from the impact, like cracks in thin ice, widening and lengthening as he left it resting upon the surface. Once again, the crawling light hid woman and beast from view. The nameless man wiggled and contorted, trying to peer between the arms of lightning, but to no avail. After a time creeping by at the pace of a snail working its way up a hill, Birk removed his palm, and the fissures dissipated. The visual interference eased back to the spider webs caused by the rain.

Mouth agape, he leaned forward, the two robed men allowing him the slimmest bit of movement. At first, he thought his eyes might have fooled him. He blinked hard to clear water and fear from them, but the scene before him remained unchanged.

Gone.

The bushes where Ailyssa had knelt, and then stood, lay flattened, a telltale sign of her presence. Nowhere did he see the woman who'd made the indentation in the brush, nor the animal on which she'd laid her hand.

"Dammit," Birk snarled and slammed the edge of his fist against the veil.

The long cracks shot across its surface again, as though it might break into huge, green shards. At the same instant, lightning streaked across the sky, turning twilight into day. Thunder assaulted their ears. The nameless man stared straight ahead at the spot where the woman who'd allowed him to understand had been. His heart ached at her absence, his mind reeled. Where did she go? Did she still live?

What in the name of everything holy was happening here?

XXX - Rilum - Long Ago

FOR A WHILE, HE wished he hadn't killed the men on the beach.

The sentiment lasted only a short time, then he remembered how their meat had sustained him for so long. After gnawing the last shred of flesh from their bones, he'd spent an indeterminate number of days wandering the shore, hoping to find more of their kind. Whether he'd have slaughtered them to eat or befriended them, he didn't know.

But no other men or beasts presented themselves, and hunger drove him back into the forest. The creatures of the sea stayed where they were and the animals of the woodland loathed the rocky seashore. So he came to be sitting atop a rotting log, its surface covered with moss intent on leeching every bit of moisture and nutrient from the wood before rot turned it to dust.

He raised the dead crow to his mouth. He hadn't killed it himself, though he wished he did—fresh meat dripping with warm blood always tasted so much better. He'd found the bird deceased on the forest floor. Whether it'd died because its time was up or because some predatory creature wounded it and abandoned it to die, he cared not. Either way, his grateful belly rumbled appreciation for its sacrifice.

The bird's black feathers tickled his lips. He opened them as wide as possible but couldn't spread them far enough for his three remaining teeth to tear a piece of its flesh off. He growled in the back of his throat, thick saliva sticking his tongue to the roof of his mouth, and lowered his hand. With the other, he dug a nail—when did they get so long? —into its meat, slicing downward. He repeated the action beside the first incision, pulled a strip of food and plumes away from its breast. Fat white maggots spilled out, some landing in his lap, others bouncing off his leg to disappear into a crevice in the log or lost on the loamy forest floor.

He stuffed the crow filet into his gob, feathers, grubs, and all, forcing the chunk of sustenance between his lips with two fingers. When did it become so difficult to open his mouth? So much time, so many changes.

The rotten wood pressed against his ass as he sat, his jaw the only part of him moving as his last three teeth worked to tenderize the meat. When he swallowed—the piece as whole as when it'd passed his lips—the sharp spines of the bird's feathers raked his throat, brought the flavor of blood to his tongue. He ignored it, plucked another strip from the bird, and forced it between his narrow lips.

As he chewed, he gazed out into the forest. Everything around him had taken on a gauzy, white hew in the time after he'd feasted upon the rocky shore. At first, he suspected a change with the world, but what began a mist became a fog, and now a gauze, and it stayed with him day and night, relentless.

When did it become so difficult to see?

XXXI - Danya - Reunion

*T*HEY TRUDGED OVER UNEVEN ground, the trees dense enough around them Danya no longer knew one direction from another. The odd time the heavens peeked through the canopy of limbs above, she glimpsed stars dangling in the night sky. Before she and Teryk discovered the scroll, she gave little thought to the legends of the Small Gods. Now, whenever a dot of brightness sprinkled across the darkness did so much as shimmer, she wondered what it might mean. More than once she imagined she spied light streaking through the dark, always at the edge of her vision.

Evalal gripped her hand to prevent them from becoming separated as they followed Fellick, Ive trailing behind. She didn't doubt the stout man knew where they headed, but she felt less sure she wanted to go with him.

"Worry not, princess," Ive said as though he'd listened in on her thoughts. "We won't let anything happen to you."

"We're not worried," Danya replied and squeezed Evalal's hand like the girl needed reassurance, not herself. "I don't know where we are."

"Close, yes, Mr. Fellick?"

The stocky man offered no response. The younger girl looked up from watching her footing, met the princess' eyes. They peered at each other for a few moments, Danya searching her companion's expression for any sign of her thoughts.

What did the Mother of Death say?

Whatever she may have said, it appeared to give Evalal reason for calm. The princess opened her mouth, tempted to ask it aloud, but closed it without speaking. No matter how Ive framed things, she must assume they held ill intentions in their hearts.

The Seed of Life bounced against her thigh as she walked, struggling to slow her racing heart, unknot her clenched gut. She rested her hand on the pouch, hoping for the hard seed to offer her the comfort for which she searched. It didn't. It pressed against her palm like any other inanimate object—no energy, no vibration, no relief. Danya sighed and diverted her attention to watching her footing, searching for distraction if unable to find peace.

She allowed her thoughts to drift to Teryk.

What has befallen my brother?

She found herself at a loss trying to remember their last interaction. She hadn't known at the time he planned to go off on his own to fulfill the prophecy. Did he offer subtle hints about his plan? After all those turns of the seasons as both siblings and best friends, did she miss him telling her his intent?

The forest turned to sparse saplings, and then the trees gave way to brush. The scrub thinned, disappeared, and yellowing grass brushed her calves, reached up toward her knees. Surprised at the sudden change, Danya raised her head.

Ahead of them stood a verdant wall unlike anything the princess had ever seen. It stretched from ground to sky, reaching high enough to make trying to see its top put a kink in her neck. The entirety of its surface glimmered with an ethereal light so dim it might not have glowed at all, yet so unmistakable, she didn't doubt its luminescence. On the other side lay a world painted green. Thick-trunked trees reached toward the wall's upper edge but fell well shy. Clusters of foliage clogged the space between them, and a wind she saw but which did not brush her cheek waved the branches and shook the leaves.

"What—?"

"The veil," Evalal whispered, leaning closer and gripping her hand tighter. "Beyond lies the Green, the land of the Small Gods."

"Correct," Ive confirmed. "Mr. Fellick assures me we near our goal."

Danya scowled—she hadn't heard the stocky man utter a single word. Did Ive know his partner's thoughts? It didn't seem likely, but he'd shown the apparent talent more than once in the time they'd been traveling with the pair. It made her want to shiver.

They covered half the distance from the edge of the forest to the shimmering veil before Fellick amended their course, directing them leeward, away from sunset and the wall. Despite turning from the green barrier, it held Danya's gaze. She squinted, peering through its translucence. It appeared a curtain of light, looked not solid enough to keep the wind on one side from blowing to the other, never mind imprisoning the Small Gods and preventing her world from entering.

The princess released Evalal's hand, allowed her path to drift toward the veil. The girl made a sound behind her, a sharp exhalation between her lips Danya recognized as a muted warning, but she ignored it. Her arm dropped to her side, the tips of her fingers brushing the tops of the grass. As she approached the wall, she noticed occasional jagged lightning flickering across its surface and wondered what caused it.

"Princess."

Ive's voice floated to her ears, but she paid no heed, the veil enthralling her. Three more paces carried her within arm's reach of the shimmering curtain. She raised her hand, hesitated as a butterfly with black highlights on the edge of its white wings fluttered past her face. Its erratic flight brought it closer to the wall until one wing touched and lightning crackled silently outward from the contact point. The insect dropped to the ground. Danya inhaled a surprised breath and crouched, searching amongst the tall blades to find it. She found it creeping along a broad fern and she held her palm out. It crawled onto her finger, its legs tickling her skin with surprising energy before it took to the air, choosing a path away from the veil.

Danya stood again, raised her arm, extended her fingers toward the green curtain. Her fingertip hovered the width of an eyelash from its surface.

"Princess."

Ive's voice startled her. She jerked from the shimmering barrier and spun to face him like a child caught sneaking a treat. She rubbed her hand on the front of her breeches, her finger tingling where the butterfly's tiny feet had walked upon her. Her forearm brushed against the pouch dangling at her waist and the Seed of Life shivered against her thigh.

"We should not tarry. Mr. Fellick says we have a distance to travel to reach our goal. We must make haste to arrive while the sun is high in the sky."

The thin man took her by the arm and guided her along with him. His grip wasn't tight or harsh, and she allowed him to lead.

"You will want to complete this journey, princess. I believe we'll find someone you'd like to see."

Danya glanced back at the Green, and a movement caught her attention. She squinted, attempting to make out the cause. The rustling of branches continued until a shape emerged—a large, hairy creature with pointed ears, a thing of nightmares.

It didn't notice her and the others, nor did her companions see the beast. By itself, the animal might have thrown a scare into her, but the woman walking beside it, one hand touching it, fingers gripping the fur at the scruff of its neck, caught her attention. She wore her hair cropped close to her head. Her eyes stared straight ahead as though not seeing what they gazed upon. A distinct aspect of sadness, despair, and loss marred her features.

The Barren Mother.

───···───

The nameless man sat on the log, hands in his lap, staring at Jud-dah's body twisted on the ground. Pain contorted the dead fellow's face, a reflection of the last thing he'd experienced before his life ended. For the entire morning, the men in robes milled around the corpse without moving it or covering the excruciating expression. Birk kept busy preparing a modest meal for himself and his captive, though none of the others partook.

With the sun approaching its zenith, all but three of the robe-wearers left, trudging toward the forest with not a sound from anyone. If their leaving surprised or upset Birk, he made no sign of it. As his captor continued preparing their meal, the man from across the sea watched plump flies flit around the corpse, landing in the dead man's open wounds to dine before taking drunkenly to the air again. He avoided inhaling too deeply for fear he'd smell or taste the ripening flesh wafting to him. Staring at the blind eyes and knotted beard, he recalled the prison-barn and its sundry contents—the shelves packed full, the mysterious barrels. What sort of fellow possessed such a collection?

A lonely one.

The voice in his head belonged to Ailyssa, so clear he almost looked up expecting to find she'd crept up behind him. He didn't, knowing she'd gone, led away by a ferocious-looking beast and leaving him alone in this foreign world, a place he knew neither how he'd gotten to or where he'd come from. He remembered nothing of himself before being in the sea as a monster rose to destroy a ship and then waking on the beach, Jud-dah standing over him.

The chain affixed to his ankle clanked as he shifted on the log in search of a more comfortable position. He leaned over and grasped a handful of links, picked it up and rattled it, the loose end attached to nothing. The sound attracted Birk's attention and their eyes met. The nameless man frowned, held the restraint out toward his captor and shook it again. If it served no purpose, why should it continue chafing his skin and weighing him down?

Birk crossed the space between them, crouched in front of him. His lips curled upward but lacked both humor and happiness, the angle of his mouth suggesting a crueler mindset. He reached out and grasped the chain near his ankle.

"Nod gunna cumov." The smile became a grin, like he kept a secret no one knew and he refused to tell. "Idsalok widnokee."

The nameless man tilted his head and frowned. Why did he understand the words with Ailyssa's touch on him but at no other time?

Birk let the constraint drop to the ground with a clank. "Yer daman frumac rossdasee."

A knee popped as he stood. He winced, shook the discomfort from his leg. The nameless man seized the opportunity, lunging forward and grabbing his captor's wrist. Startled, Birk jumped back, jerked his arm to get away, but the prisoner held on.

"Ledgo," he cried, his voice higher pitched than before. "Gidim offamee."

Discouraged to find grasping Birk didn't offer the same effect as did Ailyssa's touch, he let go as his captor yanked again. Momentum sent him stumbling backward. The nameless man recognized the opportunity to overpower him and escape, but more hands grabbed him, forced him back on his log.

⁓⁓⁓

They stopped once during the next leg of their journey. Fellick pulled rations out of his pack, handed out cured meat and chewy bread to everyone without a word, and they ate in silence. With no chance to relate what she'd seen to Evalal, Danya began to wonder if she might have imagined what she saw. When they finished eating, Ive produced a wine skin he passed around. She hesitated when it got to her, but thirst overcame reluctance and she felt relieved when she found it contained water instead of wine. She gulped two mouthfuls before the tall man took it back, and they set out on their way again.

Not long after they paused for the brief repast, Danya spied the first robed figure.

He stood at the edge of the forest beside the thick trunk of a massive cedar, his form near invisible in the shadows. The princess squinted at the silhouette, not sure if she should trust her eyes in the late afternoon light. Three heartbeats later, Evalal elbowed her in the side and nodded toward the shape. Their captors gave no sign they'd seen him.

The robed man did not follow them and, when Danya strained to look back over her shoulder, he'd either left or the shadows had swallowed him whole.

She wiped nervous perspiration from her palms onto the front of her breeches. The green, the woman and beast, now the watcher in the woods, all of it increased her discomfort.

"Mr. Fellick says we are getting close," Ive said, again without so much as a grunt from his stocky partner.

Danya split her efforts between looking back for the robe-wearing follower and attempting to see past their captor-guides at what lay in their path. For a while, she spied nothing but trees and brush, grass and rocks. Until a movement at the edge of the woods caught her attention. She touched Evalal's forearm and gestured at a spot ahead of them.

Another figure wearing the same garb as the first—or perhaps the same fellow—stood by a leafy bush. His black clothes made him appear a man-shaped gap in the verdant leaves. Nothing differentiated him from the original fellow. If he'd hurried, he might have gotten ahead and waited for them, but this fellow's bearing didn't suggest someone who'd rushed to his place.

Danya slowed her pace, letting her hand drop from Evalal's arm. When she reached Ive's side, the tall fellow raised one brow but said nothing.

The princess leaned toward him. "I think we're being followed."

She nodded at the man standing in front of the bush; they'd drawn even with him. Ive gazed across the grass to the edge of the forest, watched the figure for a heartbeat before returning his eyes to the path ahead.

Danya expected a response from him right away, but he made her wait. He swallowed, the prominent lump in his throat rising and falling.

"No need to worry, princess. They are here for us."

As if awaiting Ive's cue, the robed man left his place by the bush and walked a line parallel to theirs, matching their stride. A little farther along, another figure dressed the same emerged and joined the first, then a third. Despite the thin man's reassurance, a fresh sheen of perspiration coated the princess' palms.

The ground sloped upward, preventing her from seeing what lay ahead. The number of men keeping pace with them grew to five, each one identical to the next. None of them turned their cowl-hidden faces toward the group, their steps matching in the measured cadence of a death march.

"Priests," Fellick said, noticing her continued interest in the robe-wearers. "They are priests."

Danya nearly stopped. She'd heard stories of the black priests, her parents encouraging her to dismiss them as fancy, like they did the Goddess, her priestesses, and both kinds of Small Gods. Yet she walked beside the fabled veil separating the kingdom from the home of the Small Gods, her Goddess-follower companion accompanying her as a clutch of black priests stalked them. Did it leave any doubt the stars prepared to fall from the sky?

They crested the short hill, and ahead of them stood another group of robed silhouettes. Two other figures with them didn't match their garb, and a third unmatching shape lay on the ground. As they approached, one man not wearing a black robe raised his hand and started toward them.

"Fellick! Ive!"

Beside her, Ive returned the gesture of greeting. "Ho, Birk. It looks as though we have arrived in time."

Danya attempted to see the other fellow with the group, but the lanky weapons merchant stepped in front of her, blocking him from her view.

"A little too late, I'm afraid. The woman got away. Slipped through the veil."

The Barren Mother.

"But I see you have the princess."

"Aye. And you?"

Birk stopped and moved aside, waving his arm in a grand gesture as he did, a grin on his face so wide, someone else might find it humorous.

"I present to you the man from across the sea."

Danya gaped at the other fellow, halted dead in her tracks. Her eyes widened.

"Teryk?"

She broke into a run.

———

"Tare ick!"

The woman bolted from the others, but no one made any move to stop her. Tall grass bent before her, a trail of broken blades left in her wake. The nameless man tensed, unsure of her intention as she bore down on him. When she reached him, she threw her arms around his neck. He attempted to pull away, but she gripped him tight, pressing herself against him. His head spun, his gut roiled. Who was she?

"Tare ick," she repeated, breathless. "Wareuv yubin? Ayewuz so wureedbowchew. Ayethotchew werded."

She slackened her grip and leaned back, continuing to hang on to him. Now he saw her up close, he realized she was older than the other captive, but much younger than Ailyssa. A young adult, but no more. And the nagging sense of recognition nipped at his thoughts. Did he know her as it appeared she knew him?

She stared at him, eyes glistening on the edge of tears born of relief, love, happiness, judging by her expression. He answered with raised eyebrows and searching gaze, grasping for any clue to identify her and why he should recognize her. It took but an instant for her to recognize his disorientation.

"Tare ick? Izzmeed anyuh."

She released her grip from around his neck, and the man called Birk grabbed her by the arm, pulled her away like a parent with a child. She allowed him, but her gaze stayed locked on the nameless man's features, her hopeful expression melting to concern. The other men and the girl arrived as the line of black robes joined the group. Her eyes remained on him, pleading for him to respond to her, to realize her name, their relationship.

He didn't. He lowered his head, traced the curves of the chain attached to his ankle with his gaze instead of looking at her and disappointing her with his faulty memory. Her eyes stayed upon him but he didn't look up.

The men spoke to each other, their strange language falling on his ears. Through the thump of his heartbeat, he sensed what he might have interpreted as excitement and hope in Birk's words. He chattered more quickly than usual, his voice of a higher pitch as he updated the others on what had happened.

The nameless man pressed the heels of his hands against his eyes.

"Tare ick?"

A chastising tone quieted the woman and then three male voices carried on the conversation, though one of them said little. Feet shuffled in grass and the hard log pressed against his buttocks. Instinct begged him to remove his palms from his face to make sure his life wasn't in danger, but he couldn't bring himself to do so. He became acutely aware of the surrounding noises. Each foreign word bludgeoned him like a club, each trod-upon blade cracked in his ears with the volume and force of a snapping branch. He heard the veil behind him, too. It hummed, crackled as an insect buzzed against it.

Before this, he hadn't noticed the slightest sound emanating from the barrier.

It held an energy he might have guessed at, pulsing and throbbing in the air. It exerted pressure in his ears as though he'd jumped into a lake and dove too deep.

Like when the grate trapped me at the bottom of the river under the castle.

His breath caught in his throat and his body tensed. What river? What castle? He concentrated, searching for the thread of memory finding its way out of the depths of his mind and into his awareness. A vision of running water came to him, an iron grate, struggle and panic. Trapped under the lattice, convinced death awaited him until hands found him, pulled him out.

And the shred of recollection ended.

Whose hands?

He raised his head, pulling his face from his palms and opening his eyes, his surroundings blurred from holding them closed for so long. The people around him appeared faint and gauzy, the grass a streak of yellow-green. He blinked a few times to clear the gummy haze, and the world came back into view.

Birk and the black-robed men were gone, no trace of them left behind. The young woman who'd embraced him sat on a log beside her companion, their hands held in their laps, bound by lengths of rope. The tall, skinny fellow stood near them while the stocky one waited a few paces away, staring up the shallow hill. He followed his gaze, found the object of his interest.

———

When days of peace approach their end,
  And wounds inflicted are too deep to mend,
  A sign shall come, a lock with no key,
  Borne by a man from across the sea.
  A barren mother, the seed of life,
  Living statue, treacherous knife.
  To raise the Small Gods, a Small God must die,
  When stars go out, the end is nigh.
  One must die to raise them all,
  Should Small Gods rise, man will fall.
  One can stop them, on darken'd wing,
  The firstborn child of the rightful king.

The words from the scroll echoed through Danya's mind as she stared across the clearing at her brother while Fellick bound her hands.

He doesn't recognize me.

Her gaze slid to the chain attached at his ankle, its end going nowhere, as though the ability to unlock and remove it wasn't a possibility. Realization brought a pause to her breathing.

The lock with no key.

The barren mother.

The seed of life.

Facets of the scroll's prophecy materializing together? Or the results of fanciful imagination?

He isn't the man from across the sea. But he is the firstborn child of the king.

Danya shifted on the log, Evalal to her right, already bound. Fellick finished tying her wrists and stood, turned back to his partner. The princess glanced away from her brother with his hands hiding his eyes from her and focused on her traveling companion. Any concern the younger girl may have possessed before had disappeared from her face, leaving her with the same expression of unconcern with what transpired. When she saw Danya scrutinizing her, she half-smiled and leaned toward her.

"The Goddess has a plan. We don't see it, but she does."

Danya opened her mouth to respond but sighed and looked away instead. Sometimes she wished she enjoyed the same faith Evalal displayed; it seemed it might make life easier. Meeting the Mother of Death had shifted her opinion about some truth behind legends of the Goddess toward belief, but the chasm between belief and faith is wide. She'd seen more unusual—unbelievable—things since she and Teryk had found the scroll than she'd experienced in the entire rest of her days. Yet ongoing, unwavering faith eluded her.

She looked at her brother, barely recognizable with his shaggy hair and stubbled face, his clothes stiff with dirt and old sweat. He continued pressing the heels of his hands to his eyes, so she watched Fellick instead. Instead of rejoining his fellow weapons merchant, the stocky man separated himself from the others. He sauntered past to stand with his back to them, directing his gaze up the shallow hill climbing away from the green wall as though awaiting an arrival. His right hand rested on the pommel of his sword, but whether doing so meant he expected trouble, or a soldier's habit, she couldn't guess.

A vague beaten trail in the grass running toward the woods rather than up the long bank denoted the path Birk and the robed men had taken when they left. No other sign of their presence remained. No one discussed their departure; they'd wandered off as though part of a predetermined plan.

Danya tilted her head back, surveying the sky. The sun shone bright on the meadow, only a few wisps of cloud remaining from the passage of the strange bird that seemed to leave a storm in its wake. She saw no other winged creature come to bring sunshine, or wind, or fog. She shook her head—one more unbelievable detail in her once-normal existence that had become filled with the incredible.

As she lowered her gaze, she noticed a tremor in the log beneath her, slight enough it might have been her imagination. She focused her attention toward it, at first thinking it a vibration caused by the Seed of Life. She understood it wasn't the case.

Horses.

Fellick must have realized it at the same time; his sword hissed from its scabbard and Danya raised her head to stare past the squat fellow, the sun glinting on his bared steel. The tremor beneath her ceased and, though the earth's gentle shake suggested several riders, she spied a single horseman guide his horse to the brink of the hill. He paused but an instant before pulling his weapon and sliding from his saddle in a manner many horsemen would have made awkward but which was second nature for a man with one arm.

"Trenan!"

XXXII - Rilum - Not So Long Ago

*H**E DIDN'T FIND* THEM on the shore this time.

Four of them. Not so much like before. More similar to him now. They slouched around the small clearing ringed with trees, shuffling their feet, heads drooping. Searching. Looking. Hunting. Occasionally, one stopped, bent, picked an item from the ground and put it into his mouth.

Through his gauzy vision, he realized their skin wasn't pink, but not white, either. The color of weathered canvas. Two had patchy hair, another none, the fourth's hung past his shoulders with a single spot with a handful missing. They still wore their tattered clothes, clinging to the last vestiges of their former selves as though doing so might take them back to when they knew something other than the hunger. A time when their lives included wives, children, things.

Once-was-Rilum settled on his haunches. The breeze blew the right way to keep his scent from them, and theirs wafted across him, sank into his skin. They stank of salt and sweat, desperation and hopelessness. Familiar odors—he'd smelled of them himself until he took to smearing mud or feces on his bare flesh to hide his essence when he hunted. He moved in silence, but too many times his stench cost him meals.

For ages, he'd wondered what he might do if he found men again. He vaguely recalled their flavor, the way it satisfied his belly, but he'd learned to hunt in the time since. The hunger stayed with him always; perhaps if he hadn't just gorged on the two-horn his thoughts may have been different. But with its blood smeared across the indentation where once had been his mouth, curiosity got the better of him.

And so he watched, waited.

They were stupid, the same as he'd been at first. They seldom wandered from their tiny clearing and into the forest. How would they feed without hunting? How would they survive if they didn't protect themselves?

They'd do neither if it wasn't for him.

Thrice he intercepted predators determined to make them their meal. Each time, he ate most of the meat himself, but left the rest for the four during their long slumber. He didn't sleep that way anymore. Instead, the days and nights passed at an excruciating slow pace. He felt each moment it took the sun to cross the sky, counted every breath he exhaled while the moon lit the forest.

Those moments pained him, each inhalation hurt.

He no longer slept, leaving pain and hunger, waiting, despair to possess him. Though the craving drove him to feed and feed, a minute sliver remained in him that wished for the long suffering to end. Part of him wanted to die.

This time while they dozed—their sleeps became shorter during the period he watched them—he circled the clearing, found a spot which allowed the breeze of third season to waft his scent across their position. He crouched on hands and knees. Waited. The sun rose and set. The moon cast its dark shadows on the forest floor. Birds sang, animals chattered. The hunger gnawed at his gut, but he resisted its need.

And he waited.

XXXIII - Trenan – The Green

*T*RENAN SLID OUT OF the saddle, his fingers wrapped around Godsbane's grip before his feet touched the ground. He signaled to the others to stay put as he leaped over a low bush, pulling the sword free as he ran, sharp edge glinting in the sunlight. The oily scent of the well-kept blade wafted to him, reminding him of bygone fights, of battles fought long ago. How many lay dead at his hand? Impossible to count. Hundreds of blades—maybe thousands—had left notches in his own. He'd wiped so much blood away from his silver steel. Despite his lack of faith, he prayed after every time, asking whatever God or Goddess to forgive him for taking those lives, beseeching them to take mercy on the men sent on their way from this world.

The stocky man lifted his sword, ready to accept the attack. Over his shoulder, Danya watched, hands bound. To her left, across a short expanse of grass, her brother sat on a log, a confused expression on his brow. His face appeared slack enough he might soon drool on himself. Trenan's heart raced—he'd found them, the princess and his son. Before the first blow fell, he decided to offer no prayers once he dispatched these men from the world. They deserved what they got, which didn't include mercy, now or after their deaths, and taking their wretched lives required no forgiveness.

The second man, tall and slight, stood near the princess. He'd have to keep his eye on him; best to dispatch the stocky fellow as quick as possible to make sure the other one didn't harm Danya.

His gait gobbled up the last bit of ground separating them, and Trenan raised his weapon. His opponent grinned and, in the instant before steel clashed against steel, the master swordsman understood this man's experience included his share of battles and fights, too. Without a doubt, his sleeves hid a multitude of scars, but the suspicion didn't deter him—no one bore injuries as great as his.

Their weapons came together with a deafening clang, the impact sending a jolt up Trenan's arm hinting at the strength of his opponent. He drew back and struck again, and the stocky man received the blow with deft, quick moves. His breadth and thickness made his power expected, but he possessed more agility for a fighter of his girth than one might guess. Another stroke, and Trenan formed a good sense of his foe.

He took a step away, reset, and the other fellow smiled.

"An honor to meet you, swordmaster Trenan. I'm sure you've never heard of me, but they call me Fellick."

"Fellick. If you want to leave here with your life, release the prince and princess."

"Prince and princess, you say?" He tossed a casual glance over his shoulder. "These two? You must have made a mistake. You'll find the heir to the throne hidden somewhere in Draekfarren castle, playing games and learning lessons, not on a patch of grass outside the Green. This be the foretold man from across the sea."

Trenan fell on him again as he spoke the final word, but the attack didn't catch him off-guard. The blow struck the edge of his blade, slid toward the hilt. With a twist of his wrist, he guided it away. Fellick chose not to counter, instead waiting en garde for the master swordsman's next strike.

What is he up to?

He moved to circle him, gaze darting over the fellow's shoulder at Teryk and Danya and the slender man.

"Over there's Ive," Fellick said, repositioning himself to keep Trenan from slipping past. "Won't hurt them. Not unless I tell him to."

"Fellick and Ive are the foremost weapons merchants in the Windward Kingdom. You cannot be them. Why kidnap the prince and princess if you are?"

"You flatter us, sir," Ive called from his place near Danya. She appeared to cringe at the sound of his voice in her ear. "But we are the men of whom you speak. I believe we provided you a sword once. Not the one you wield today, but a lovely hunk of metal, nonetheless."

Before Trenan replied, Fellick pounced. The master swordsman raised his blade in time, catching the blow. The clang of steel rang out, but he realized his opponent held back from striking with his full force and strength. Instead, he manipulated the attack, so he ended up with his face near Trenan's ear.

"Have you not seen the fire in the night sky?" he whispered, breath hot on Trenan's neck. "More is at work here than you understand."

Trenan jerked away, pulling himself from his opponent's grasp. He glared at the man, wanting to question what he meant; he'd watched the streaks of light crossing the sky, appearing to head for the ground, but care should he have for shooting stars? His mouth opened, intending to ask for an explanation, but Fellick attacked again, interrupting his intent. Their swords clanged together again and again. Each blow sounded vicious and likely created a convincing display, but they carried far less than the stocky man's full strength. Confused, Trenan defended himself but didn't counterattack.

Fellick's advance pushed him in a semicircle, turning him so he saw the complement of warriors who'd accompanied him from Ikkundana. Sun blazed on arms and armor of the women sitting their horses. They watched, awaiting any signal he needed their assistance. They'd stay thus, holding their ranks as he'd taught them, until he told them otherwise or the enemy forced their hand.

What's that?

Movement in the bush beside them, behind. A flash of black, then Fellick's attack turned him again, faced him away from his troops. His heart jumped into his throat; the women ranked among the best warriors he'd seen, but they remained untested. In his turns of the seasons training and teaching young soldiers how to fight, how many times did he see his most promising swordsman cut down by their initial adversary? How many froze or fled at the first drop of blood? No matter how confident he felt with anyone's ability, he couldn't guess their true mettle until their weapons tasted flesh, or steel kissed their skin.

Trenan took the fight to the stocky man, pushing him back toward the others to position himself to peer up the hill. A figure emerged from the brush, features hidden beneath a black cowl. He didn't appear to hold a weapon, though Trenan couldn't see his hands; the dark robe covered him from the top of his head to his feet. None of the warriors noticed him—the master swordsman needed to warn them.

He deflected Fellick's next blow, then launched a counterattack purposely taking him near the man. He intended to plant his hand against the fellow's chest and push him away, give himself enough room to signal his troop of the impending danger. Before he did, Fellick guessed his intent, caught him and pulled him close.

"Leave it be," he said, the words carried on a harsh whisper. "Everything about to happen must transpire."

Trenan stared into his face, pushed against him to break his grip, but he proved too strong. Realizing he couldn't escape the stocky man's grasp, the master swordsman tilted his head and hollered a warning.

"Yoli! Look out."

As soon as he spoke the words, Fellick released him. Trenan stumbled away and made what should have been a fatal mistake: he turned his back on his opponent. He didn't have to put thought to it to realize what he'd done, but the need to warn his warriors, to rush to their aid, caused his choice.

Other figures emerged out of the brush and trees around the riders, all clad in the same black robes, save one. Instead of attacking, they encircled the warriors, arms raised to the sides of their bodies. The women took notice of them at Trenan's warning and faced them, weapons poised to defend. They outnumbered the men three to one, but the sense of danger hanging in the air made it seem the opposite.

Before any of them moved, the pommel of Fellick's sword contacted the back of the swordmaster's skull. An instant of agony exploded through it, then the world slipped into darkness.

—ele—

The master swordsman's eyelids fluttered open to find himself sprawled on the ground staring at blue sky. He turned his head to the left, cringed at the pain it caused. Beyond a set of legs—Ive's, he judged—grass carpeted the way to the shimmering emerald wall separating the Windward Kingdom from the wilds of the Green. He pushed himself up on his elbow, aware his sword no longer lay at hand.

The tall and spidery Ive occupied the space between him and the veil. On a log to his left sat Princess Danya and a young woman he didn't recognize, their hands bound, both of them unmoving. A short distance away, Fellick stood beside Teryk. The stocky man's own weapon rested in its scabbard but he held the crown sword loosely in his off hand. Trenan took this in briefly before redirecting his gaze.

The prince barely looked himself. In fact, if the master swordsman hadn't been with him since birth, he might not have recognized him. Fine reddish-blond whiskers well beyond being called stubble lined his jaw and upper lip, and his dirty, knotted hair hung longer than when last Trenan saw him. It suggested the passing of a much greater amount of time than had truly elapsed.

"Teryk?"

The prince's eyes flickered toward him, but the expression they bore lacked recognition. He appeared confused, distressed.

"Teryk?"

"He doesn't understand," Danya answered for him. "Or know where or who he is. Words make no sense to him."

Trenan glanced back and forth between them.

"Are you all right, princess?"

She shrugged. "They haven't harmed me or Evalal." Her eyes moved toward Ive, then crossed the space to Fellick before returning to Trenan. "But neither have they let us leave."

"My humblest apologies," Ive said, though to Trenan's ears he didn't sound either the slightest bit apologetic or humble. "But now we have your brother, our time together is drawing near its end."

Danya's face contorted as she tried to divine what the weapons merchant's words meant, but Trenan understood. Service in the king's army taught him to assume the worst. Do not expect mercy from the enemy, and give none in return. They wanted Teryk and needed Danya no more. When you're done with a thing, you get rid of it.

Ive left his place beside the princess and her companion—Evalal must have been who Trenan saw spiriting her away from the execution—and crossed the short space to Fellick and her brother. His footsteps padded in the grass, the lone sound outside the gentle waft of a breeze in the trees, the buzz of unseen insects. Trenan heard no clash of weapons, no shouts of battle. What had happened to his warriors and the men surrounding them? He thought to pivot himself around, peer back up the hill, but the scrawny man's approach to the prince might hold some threat. Although he held no weapon, Trenan readied himself to leap to Teryk's defense should the need arise.

Ive settled in beside the younger man, towering over him, a wan smile on his lips as he reached out and grabbed the lad by his shoulder. Teryk raised his gaze, his expression holding no panic or distress; Ive wasn't gripping so tight as to hurt him or cause discomfort. The weapons merchant faced him again.

"Speak to him now."

Teryk's eyes widened and he, too, looked to Trenan. The sword master hesitated, and the prince stared at him, waiting.

"Are you all right, Teryk?"

His mouth dropped open in a parody of surprise. After a few seconds, it snapped shut again, as though he realized he'd left it agape. He swallowed hard, the lump in his throat bobbing. His lips twitched.

"Teryk? Is that me?"

Trenan blinked. "You are Teryk, prince of the Windward Kingdom."
What's happened to him?

XXXIV – Rilum – Not So Long Ago

*O*NE OF THEM STIRRED with the sun risen enough in the sky to cast light upon the forest, but not so high as to melt the layer of hoarfrost whitening the green leaves of the brush.

The chill of the rime touched once-was-Rilum's spine. As he shifted for the first time in days, it crackled, a second skin splitting wide to allow his movement. Moments later, one of the used-to-be-men raised his chin. Eyes grown over by a thin, white film examined the trees at the edge of the clearing. Ears diminished to naught but pinpricks listened. A tongue protruding through a mouth too small for a finger to penetrate tasted the air. A nose that had melted into its face, the nostrils darker spots beneath ghastly pale flesh searched for and found his scent. Its head bent toward him.

Once-was-Rilum rose from his hands and knees. The hunger no longer burned in his gut alone; it flowed through his body, his arms and legs, threatening to tie his muscles in knots. If he looked down, he might find a hole in his middle.

He didn't. Nor did he pay heed to the one who'd detected his presence. He barely held the craving at bay. It drove him, heightened his senses so he felt every living thing around him: the little long-tails scuttling though the detritus scattered across the forest floor; the furry ones climbing in the trees; the fliers; the creepers. Only the small ones nearby—larger prey had scented them and given them a wide berth. He caught the odor of a sharp-tooth, but too distant for him to catch.

For the first time in many sunrises, he took a step. Time to feed.

By the time he'd collected enough of the smaller creatures, all four of them were awake and standing. They remained together in a group in the middle of the clearing, staring at him as he approached. How could they bear to be so near one another when the hunger must be on them the way the orange fungus insinuated itself in the bark of the trees? Whenever he woke from a sleep, blood lust forced him to eat any living thing close to him.

They watched him stride out of the woods, three of the furry climbers and two long-ears dangling from his blood-soaked hands. He'd resisted the hunger until it made him dig his fingernails into one of the long-ears. He'd pulled free a handful of its innards and smeared them across his face before bringing them to the huddled group. A string of intestines still hung from the eviscerated animal, a loop of wet, pink insides dragging on the ground collecting rotting needles and bits of dirt on its tacky surface.

One of the four stepped away from the others. The remaining patches of long hair on its head identified it as the fellow once-was-Rilum thought of as their leader. He ate first when he left food for them, drank water before his mates. No noticeable difference between them suggested why. Perhaps in their previous lives, he'd been in charge and it carried through to their new existence within the hunger.

The hole in the fellow's face where men had mouths stretched open and a sound like rocks rubbed together found its way out. An attempt to communicate from one without the ability directed toward another with no possibility of understanding. Once-was-Rilum continued his approach. When he came within ten paces, he tossed his spoil into their midst, including the one he'd already fed upon. Other prey skulked about the forest waiting for him.

They fell on the feast with no hesitation, growling and snarling until their sharp nails pried open the animals' bellies and they pressed the steaming flesh to their faces. The animalistic noises turned to slurping and sucking, wet sounds that brought the hunger back to once-was-Rilum.

Satisfied they'd gotten enough sustenance, he headed into the forest to find more game for himself. Once accomplished, and the craving grew quiet again, he'd return with more for them. And then he'd teach them to hunt for themselves.

XXXV - Horace - Creatures

IT WEREN'T DARK YET, but it were gettin' damn close.

Horace's boots scraped along the forest floor as he pressed on, still by himself. He'd seen no sign o' Ivy, not that a man o' the sea knew anythin' about trackin' in the woods. If a horse galloped its way through, he might've missed signs it'd passed by. Put him on the deck o' any ship and he'd taste the wind and tell you how bad the storm were goin' to be. He'd figure the direction a boat headed by the shape o' the waves. Sometimes, he claimed the ability to smell how close they was to land. In the woodland, everthin' looked, tasted, and smelled like a forest with no distinction between one thing and another.

He pressed on. What other choice did he have? Lay down on the ground and wait to be ate by animals or bugs? Didn't sound like a good time. At least this way he might find Ivy and, if he did, she'd get him the hell outta here.

He'd given up callin' out her name a while back thinkin' it more likely to attract them things he didn't want to have comin' for him than gainin' her attention. She were a creature used to the woods and this place they called the Green. When she wanted to find him, she'd do so. In the meantime, he just had to stay alive.

With great care where he placed his feet, Horace walked beside the translucent veil. While he found himself navigatin' the tangle o' forest on this side, it looked like grass on the other; not that he trusted his eyes 'cause the nature o' the shimmerin' curtain kinda turned everythin' to smudges. He wondered if he'd ever find himself on the other side again. But wonderin' wouldn't get him anywhere, nor keep him from becomin' some beast's meal.

The ol' sailor shuddered and directed his attention back to his forested bit o' the veil, searchin' between trees for signs o' his friend's sister, watchin' for a creature comin' to eat him. Weren't long before he caught a glimpse o' movement between trunks ahead.

Horace stopped dead in his tracks, his breath turnin' shallow. For a bunch o' beats from his speedin' heart, he saw nothin' else. The biggest chunk o' him surged with hope at the possibility o' findin' Ivy again, but he weren't takin' no chances until he knew for sure what his peepers was showin' him.

A patch o' dark fur flashed between a couple more trees and Horace's rapid breath got itself caught in his throat and stopped up completely. Coldness touched his skin and prickled the hair along his arms. The thought o' turnin' tail and gettin' the hell out occurred to him but he realized thrashin' through the brush, the thing'd discover him quicker. Best to stay put and hope it didn't sniff him out.

A wide, thick bush adorned with jade leaves and ruby berries blocked the creature from his view again. He glanced side to side, prayin' for a glimpse o' Ivy comin' to his rescue the way she'd done the first time they met. He found the space around him empty o' any sign o' the gray lady and his chest threatened to buckle 'round his heart. Energy rushed into his limbs, the fight-or-flight part o' him gettin' ready, but he struggled against the urge. Start backin' away made more sense.

He eased his right foot back, movin' it with slowness and care to avoid attractin' the beast's attention. It were goin' the same direction he'd been headin', so maybe, just maybe.

Horace wondered if the furry beast had the ability to climb trees, or if he himself'd be able to if it came down to it.

The animal's broad head and shoulder emerged from behind the brush, its gaze trained straight ahead without notice o' anythin' to either side. It loped out into the open. About then's when he saw the woman.

She walked beside the beast, dwarfed by its size, her skin shining extra white next to its blackness. Her hand rested on the scruff o' its neck, disappeared into the thick fur so it looked like she didn't have one.

Horace's mouth fell wide, an unintentional breath whistlin' its way into his chest.

He regretted doin' so and slapped his palm o'er his gob, waitin' for the beast to gaze toward him, to bare its teeth and snarl. It didn't. Turned out he stood far enough clear for it not to hear. Now all he had to do were to hope it couldn't scent him, either.

He shook his head, attemptin' to wipe away this impossible vision o' woman and animal. He blinked, rubbed his eyes, stared at them expectin' the two o' them to disappear like nothin' but a tricky shape in the mornin' mist. But it weren't mornin', and the forest didn't contain no mist. Fearful spit flooded into his mouth so much, he needed to suck it back in lest he drool down his chin. It became clear he were lookin' at somethin' real: a woman with her hair cut short walkin' alongside a hairy, sharp-toothed behemoth, the fingers o' her one hand graspin' the fur at the big critter's neck. Exactly the kinda thing he'd worried might find him and eat him if he spent too much time in one spot. The creature, not the woman.

All his thoughts about escapin' left him in a hurry. So far, it didn't hear him or catch his aroma; couldn't take a chance on it seein' him, neither. In spite o' the fear and worry about the ferocious beast, his mind wandered on back to the woman walkin' beside it.

How come it ain't eatin' her?

The first o' many questions what rattled their way into his noodle.

Who is she? How'd she get behind the green curtain? How'd she make a thing like that her pet?

They moved slow and with care, the woman and her beast, as though one or the other o' them experienced trouble with walkin'. Not unlike himself. Judgin' from how the animal looked to be leadin' her, he guessed it must be the lady havin' difficulty. He wondered if she were hurt and, if so, why the furry thing'd want to be helpin' her.

As he watched, bein' careful to control his breath and keep from shufflin' his feet and attractin' attention, another movement at the edge o' his vision caught his awareness. It flitted past like a bird on the wing, havin' disappeared by the time he got his head turned toward it. The ol' sailor frowned, concerned to find the forest suddenly so busy with people and creatures when he hadn't seen fowl nor beast since he lost track o' Ivy.

Another flash o' muted color. Gray? White? Somewhere in between? Horace squinted hard, searchin' for somethin' to tell him if this were the missin' Ivy. If so, he needed to warn her about the woman and her creature travelin' not so far ahead o' her.

A branch shook and quivered, then a second did the same, makin' him realize it weren't one thing movin' through the forest, but two or more.

Another beast with a woman clingin' to it? Hard enough to believe he'd seen one such thing. All this activity gave him more reason to appreciate the ship-bound life he'd grown to hate—weren't nobody or nothin' on the damn boat you wasn't expectin'.

Never knew what lay beneath them waves, though.

He shivered and put the thought from his head, concentratin' instead on where he'd seen the flutter o' movement. Out the corner o' his eye, he still spied the lady and the beast; he understood what he were dealin' with there more'n he did whatever hid itself amongst the brush.

Subtle motion in three different places convinced him it weren't Ivy sneakin' up on the others, least not unless she'd got some o' her friends to join her. Unlikely, but it didn't mean weren't more o' them Small Gods he'd seen before. But why would creatures like them need to sneak up on anythin'?

Whatever were hidin' came to a break in their cover. A shape flashed across the space from one bush to the next—long ganglin' arms, scrawny body, pale skin.

And no eyes or mouth.

The sight of it turned Horace's knees watery and his insides to ice. Two more similar figures darted through, keepin' pace with the first, and then them faceless hid themselves again.

The ol' sailor's gaze flashed back to woman and beast. They continued movin', pickin' their way through the forest as if afraid o' steppin' in an unseen pile o' shit. Neither person nor animal possessed the slightest inklin' o' the horrible creatures creepin' up on them.

The sudden urge to cry out and warn them parted Horace's lips, but he stopped himself before doing so. Ivy'd given him a good sense o' what them faceless things was about, but he didn't have no idea what the furry, toothful beast'd do if it caught wind o' his presence. Killed by a beast with a ferocious mouth or beings with none whatsoever—not muchuva choice.

Instead o' shoutin', Horace closed his gob and waited. He realized what he should be doin' were findin' a way to get the fuck outta the area as quick as his feet'd take him. Couldn't, though, and he weren't sure why. His brain made the suggestions to his legs and feet to start themselves movin', but they wasn't payin' attention, and his gut knotted and twisted at the idea o' runnin' away.

A drop o' nervous sweat rolled along his temple and he swallowed a lumpy wad o' saliva. Bush leaves moved again, closer to the woman and her furry escort.

Why don't the beast know they're after them?

As the three o' them crossed the space in the brush, Horace noticed their pale skin streaked with a darker color and realized they'd smeared themselves with somethin' to hide their scent. Camouflaged themselves, he thought they called it.

No need for such nonsense aboard a ship.

But he weren't ship-bound, and neither was the faceless, the furry beast, nor the woman. The rules o' the forest differed from the ones he'd spent all them turns o' the seasons adherin' to. The ol' sailor'd never imagined he'd miss ridin' them waves.

His feet finally started movin' again. He picked one up and set it down again, takin' care not to put it on top o' a branch what'd crack or a pile o' crinkly dead leaves. Strange thing: the step his foot took after all that time weren't away from creature and woman, but toward them, and he didn't know why.

The brush a mere ten paces behind them shook and the furry animal stopped its measured pace, raised its head. The sound o' a deep growl rolled across the space separatin' them from him, and the lady rotated her head on her neck. For whatever reason, she didn't appear to have any clue what direction she should be lookin'. Her unsurety didn't stop the beast, though.

The great furry thing wheeled around, pullin' itself from its companion's grasp. Panic flashed across her face, plain to Horace even o'er the distance what lay between them. The animal crept away toward where the brush hid the three faceless things and the woman's hands reached out, graspin' at the empty air. Her head turned this way and that, not settlin' on anythin'. Seein' her do so made the ol' sailor realize the truth o' her: she couldn't see.

He took another step, then a second. More sweat ran from his brow, but he weren't so worried about the furry creature becomin' aware o' him anymore. The beast seemed more concerned with the more realistic threat posed by the three faceless things.

The animal coiled itself, thick muscles bunchin' under its fur. It looked ready to launch itself toward the near thicket what hid the stalkers when they leapt out, movin' way quicker'n Horace'd ever have thought possible.

The beast sprang forward to meet them in mid-air, a half-growl, half-roar comin' outta its mouth. The woman screamed, suddenly aware somethin'd gone very wrong but not havin' any idea what it might be, or where around her, or how bad. Horace's heart sped in fear for her, again without knowin' why such a thing should be the case.

His feet picked up the pace, carryin' him toward her as the faceless three clashed with the creature of tooth and claw. The beast roared and thrashed, its cacophony shakin' saplin's and rattlin' foliage. The pasty things made not the slightest noise other'n their limbs whisperin' through the air and their taloned fingers rippin' through fur and flesh.

Horace concentrated on the woman, doin' his best to keep his attention away from the fight. Leaves and branches smacked at his face, plucked at his sleeves. Creepers caught at his boots, but he pulled himself free without breakin' stride. Amongst the usual foresty odors o' wood and moss, another scent crept its way into his nostrils, a coppery aroma what threatened to make him gag.

The stink o' blood.

He dared a glance to his right toward the clash o' furry beast and the pale o' skin and immediately wished he hadn't.

The creature what'd been leadin' the woman snapped the air with powerful jaws, swung massive paws what ended in sharp claws, but its efforts did it no good. The three faceless things darted in and out, stabbin', slicin', rendin', and movin' too quick for the poor animal to catch them. A pale skinned thing avoided one of the beast's strikes with a deftness what seemed impossible for a bein' without eyes, and made its way onto the furry back. It sank talons deep into the mighty animal's neck, reached its other hand around in front, avoidin' the gnashin' teeth.

With a flick o' its wrist, its sharp nails slit the creature's throat.

"Fuck me dead."

Horace bit his tongue and pivoted away, regrettin' the curse squeezin' its way outta his lips.

Not many strides remained between him and the woman, so he redirected his attention to her. She'd turned her head toward him, hearin' him crashin' through the brush even o'er the beast's angry roars what had now become strangled, gurglin' cries. She raised her hands in front of her face, cowered from him and the sight o' it squeezed Horace's heart. Other'n Dunal, he couldn't think o' any time he'd purposely hurt anyone, and he wished he could go back and undo what he'd done to the simple shiphand.

The ol' sailor slowed, found himself outta breath.

"I—" He stopped tryin' to speak, struggled air into his lungs and out, attempted it again. "I ain't gonna hurt you."

He held his hands out in front of himself, showin' her his empty palms before rememberin' weren't no point; if he wielded a trident right in her face, she wouldnt've known any better.

She scuffled away from him, her feet tanglin' and throwin' her to the ground. He pulled up short o' where she lay, not wantin' to make it any worse. She didn't say nothin' and, in noticin' she weren't makin' any sound, he realized there weren't many other noises, either.

He turned himself around, movin' slow as though doin' so might make seein' what'd happened easier. It didn't.

The furry beast lay on the ground, chest heavin' and the occasional breathy huff gettin' expelled through its nose, the fight gone outta it. And most of its blood, too. The three faceless things lit into it, tearin' away chunks o' fur and flesh, rubbin' the warm and bloody bits against their skin-covered maws. Seein' the ferocity with which they'd dispatched the huge predator made Horace curse himself for not runnin' the other direction.

But somethin' made him come this way against his will. Somethin' about the blind woman drew him; not sure what, but ev'ry bit o' his mind and body screamed at him about her importance.

Behind him, a noise escaped her. Not more'n a peep, probably a sound she didn't intend to make, judgin' by the size o' it. He almost pivoted to look back, but it turned out he weren't the only one what heard her.

The nearest of the faceless raised its head, stood, and took a step toward them.

XXXVI - Rilum – Now

*H*UNGER. *ALWAYS THE* HUNGER.

The sharp-tooth hadn't scented them. After so much time hunting together, he no longer needed to give the others direction. They knew how to disguise their smells for the hunt, how to determine the wind's orientation and approach from the correct path. They moved in silence, creeping toward their prey, the semicircle they formed around it tightening with each step they took.

The sharp-tooth's head jerked out of the log in which it had buried its snout to feast on the grubs within. Once-was-Rilum had fed on the same insects ages past, dissatisfying as they were, but he'd since become an expert hunter. He'd taught his companions the same skills, and all but forgotten the bitterness of the wriggling white things.

The beast moved its gaze toward him, ears standing straight, the coarse fur at the back of its neck rising, but too late. He shot forward, talons finding the animal's throat with practiced ease, and his allies joined the fray. The creature roared, lashed out with its wide paws, but its claws found empty air. Many like it had fallen to them; instinct and experience guided their attack in a manner to make short work of their prey but keep them from harm.

All but that one.

The sharp-tooth's struggles diminished from desperate flailing to limp distress as blood spurted from its throat and fingers dug into its flesh. Its knees faltered and gave way, the beast's body flopping to the ground with an expulsion of air. It continued snapping its jaws, but no longer possessed the energy to raise its head for more than a heartbeat. With little danger to them, once-was-Rilum and his companions began tearing strips of meat and fur from the animal.

The first piece touched once-was-Rilum's face and the familiar pang of frustration flooded his chest. A long time ago, he'd enjoyed a mouth filled with teeth. His body recalled the satisfaction of biting into a chunk of food, rending it to smaller pieces with incisors and molars, tasting bloody juice on his tongue. Though he no longer possessed a mouth nor the teeth once within it, the beast's energy and life-force still found its way into him. It penetrated his skin, satiating the craving, but it never satisfied the ache of disappointment.

They gorged, the sharp-tooth's fight ending along with its life. The bouquet of its bloody flesh filled his head even if its flavor could not. The hunger took over as he ripped chunk after chunk of muscle and fur, tendon and cartilage from the carcass, rubbed it against the indentation in his face to imbibe its goodness, then cast the wasted piece aside. Its essence overtook everything except the sight of his companions partaking in the bounty, the sounds of rending meat and cracking bone.

He didn't realize they weren't alone until three quiet and impossibly familiar words floated across the forest.

"Fuck me dead."

Once-was-Rilum stopped, straightened, cocked his head in the direction from which he'd heard the voice. He concentrated and identified other odors leeching past the stench of the blood smeared on his face: salt, smoke, meat, sweat.

Man.

He stared with his carapace-covered eyes at the gauzy white silhouettes of tree trunks and brush, shapes hidden amongst them. He tensed, ready to defend or attack, until another odor found its way into his head.

This one gave him pause. He'd smelled it before, many times. Once, they hunted a creature with a similar scent as this, back when they were five. It was the reason they'd become four, before a sharp-tooth had made them three. A hard lesson learned that day.

Once-was-Rilum waited a few moments longer, attempting to determine the small gray creature's intent. The faintest crunch of feet on moss suggested a retreat. Satisfied no danger threatened, he returned to his feast. The stink of a man would be easy to find.

Perhaps they'd be four again.

XXXVII - Dansil - Toward Sunset

*W*HEN THE TREES AND bushes became too dense to negotiate on horseback, Dansil guided his mount toward the track, halting before they reached it. He slid out of the saddle and picketed the horse on a handy branch, then trudged through the thicket to the edge of the road, brush and leaves damp from the previous day's rain depositing their wetness on him, extinguishing any hope of his clothes drying.

He'd drawn close enough to see the group he'd been pursuing and count the number of riders. Dansil ducked back into the foliage of a wide-leafed bush, breath held as he anticipated a sentry calling him out. His heart beat in his ears. By the time it did so twenty times, he decided he hadn't been spotted and released his air from his lungs.

It made little sense their goal turned out to be a widening of the dirt track in the middle of nowhere. He leaned out, confident none of them kept watch. His eyes darted from one rider to the next, not bothering to see their faces, instead counting their arms—the surest way to pick Trenan out in a crowd.

Each of the gathered riders possessed two.

He's separated from them, gone on ahead.

It meant they neared their goal. Dansil straightened and hurried from his hiding place, choosing a path both away from the muddy track and deeper into the woods. He passed by his picketed horse, noting the trees nearby so he might recognize this spot when he came back for his steed.

As he cut through the brush, broad leaves slapped at his face, splattered droplets of water across his cheek and forehead, against eyelids. Each unexpected contact startled him and he looked around, expecting to find the robed healer, reaching out toward him to relieve him of another piece of himself, or Stirk's deformed body grasping with his remaining hand to snag him by the ankle. No one. He flexed his three fingers and wiped the dampness away with the sleeve of his jerkin.

He moved doing his best to keep the noise to a minimum. Trenan's soldiers may not have appeared to be paying attention, but he doubted that was the case. Despite his care, his own movements grew louder in his ears, so he slowed, stopped. He listened to his heartbeat, his breathing, and the rustle of leaves, the gentle tromp of what might have been footsteps.

Dansil squatted, faded as tight into the nearest brush as he could. The forest remained dense, though thinner than where he'd left the horse. He inhaled a slow, steady breath through his nose, scenting wet moss and moist wood, then held his air.

A flash of black between tree trunks caught his attention. His heart sped, and he shuffled deeper into the damp foliage, leaves dumping cold droplets onto his neck to run down his back. Had the healer found him, come to extract more payment? He curled his left hand into a fist, scowled at the feel of the missing fingers.

Another glimpse of black accompanied the first, and another, then more, their direction taking them along an approximation of the path Dansil himself followed to get here. He watched, eyes darting from one flash of dark cloth to another, until he spied a figure bringing up the rear wearing clothes other than plain, colorless robes. If this was the healer come for him, the strange being had brought several friends, none of them Stirk.

A cramp threatened in Dansil's left calf, the muscle drawing itself into a knot, but he dared not move to relieve it. He set his jaw, clamping his teeth against the pain as the group moved past, unaware of his presence. It constricted into a ball uncomfortable enough to curl his toes. Still, he waited until the parade of strangers went by, their sounds fading until silence ruled the forest again. Only then did the queen's guard stand, the twist of sinew in his leg paining him so much he covered his mouth to keep from crying out.

He stood a moment, one hand clasping the closest branch to hold him steady while he flexed his foot, curling and uncurling his toes inside his boot. He pressed his lips tight, moaned in the back of his throat waiting for it to pass. When it did, he took a last look around, scouring the surrounding forest for any glimpse of a black robe. Without any, he set out again, pushing himself as fast as he dared, the remnants of the knot lending him a distinct limp.

The trees thinned and his progress became quicker. In the sky ahead of him, a wall of shimmering green rose, stretching from the earth up and up and up so high it appeared to grow past the sun. He tilted his head, attempting to divine its height, but found it impossible, thought it may go on forever.

Stopping at the top of a hill, grassland spreading out below, he looked first to his right at the wall continuing as far as he could see, the ground beside it cleared of trees and brush the same as in front of him. He directed his gaze to the left, saw the shapes amongst the yellowing grass.

The queen's guard crouched. Too distant to make out their faces, he faded back to the edge of the forest and hurried along the tree line, both the cramp and the spot where Stirk stabbed him pestering him with discomfort. Dim sounds crossed the space to him—the clatter of swords, he thought, but couldn't be sure.

When he got close enough, he dropped to the ground, pressed himself against the stiff grass, and waited. The noises he'd heard ceased, and no others replaced them—no one calling out, no approach of footsteps. He held his breath listening as long as his lungs allowed before releasing the air. He propped himself up on his elbows, counted six people in the clearing below.

If a fight there'd been, it was finished. Three sat; of the others, one stood as though guarding the seated trio while the other two stationed themselves apart. Dansil squinted, attempting to pick out any features that might identify the players arrayed beneath him. The first thing he noticed—what he'd been searching for—was the missing arm.

Trenan sat away from the others, or at least appeared to until the queen's guard realized he wasn't sitting, but kneeling.

Like a beaten dog.

A fight had occurred, and the other fellow bested the renowned soldier. Part of Dansil rejoiced at the defeat, but another side of him wished he'd driven the swordmaster to his knees. The man standing between the so-called master swordsman and the seated figures appeared familiar, though he couldn't recall from where he might have recognized him.

His eyes traveled to the two sitters. A moment of scrutiny revealed them as women. He suspected one to be the princess. Next, his gaze moved across the short space between them, found a tall stick of a man—also familiar. As for the last fellow, the seated one, he didn't think he knew him. Dansil crawled forward as if a third of the length of his body offered to bring him close enough to recognize him. He squinted hard, stared.

The lad's unkempt hair hung to his shoulders, draped onto the skin of his chest bronzed by the sun, whiskers dusted his cheeks. He held a chain wrapped around his forearm, the trailing end of it attached to his ankle. The distance and his appearance cast doubt, but recognition came.

"Prince Teryk."

Trenan had rescued them both. Despite his foul-ups, the kingdom would once again hail him a hero while Dansil found himself relegated back to his job babysitting the queen. Anger stirred in the queen's guard's guts, the pressure of it building, making him purse his lips. He gathered himself, ready to stand and stomp his way down the hill. What might happen once he reached them, he didn't know, for the blind engine of his rage drove him.

Before he took his first step, movement flickered amongst those in the clearing at the bottom of the slope. Dansil stopped, stared. As the action unfolded, his eyes widened, his mouth fell open. The anger in his gut melted away, replaced by surprise, shock. His mind reeled at the unexpected twist of events. No longer did he need to take care of ending Trenan's life himself.

And he'd be the kingdom's hero.

He turned his back on the people at the base of the hill and hurried toward the place where his horse awaited, uncaring if anyone heard him. If the sun remained and the dirt track dried, he'd make good time heading for Draekfarren. Once returned, he intended to report what he saw to the king and queen. Then they'd take care of the master swordsman's fate. Might anything be more satisfying to Dansil than his death?

Death and disgrace.

XXXVIII - Horace – The Mother

*A*FTER HAVIN' SEEN HOW fast they moved, Horace realized weren't no point in tryin' to run away.

He couldn't understand how the things might see, given they didn't appear to have eyes no more'n they did mouths, but the one what heard the woman make her peep stared right at him. If the pale feller possessed a real mouth, it'd likely have flicked its tongue out and licked its lips while lookin' at him. The way it leaned toward them, the white flesh on its forehead wrinklin' as it took another step, suggested it preferred the taste o' humans o'er the furry beast.

The ol' sailor stared back at the abomination. Where did a thing like that come from? Its smooth head and featureless face, and how expressions appeared to form even without eyes and mouth mesmerized him. It moved one slow pace at a time, as though sneakin' up on him, tryin' not to scare him in spite o' the fact he gawked right at it. And he might've kept on starin' until it walked up and slit his throat with them sharp talons if the woman hadn't scuffled in the brush.

The faceless thing turned its head, directin' its sightless gaze toward her and remindin' Horace o' her presence. His stomach did a flip. He needed to do everything in his power to protect her, to keep her safe.

Why?

The answer came to him as though he'd asked it out loud to a group o' academics.

She's the Barren Mother what Ivy talked about.

He pried his attention from the colorless thing and darted toward the woman, hopin' his movement didn't prompt their stalker to hurry.

She did her best to scramble away from him, heels diggin' at the ground, pushin' and pushin' to escape, but the brush surroundin' her held her back. He understood it were him she wanted to evade, because she couldn't know the other things what threatened them. Maybe lucky for her bein' blind.

Horace bent and got his arms around her, fightin' through her thrashin' and protestin'. He grasped her, speakin' in a whisper as close to her ear as possible without her scratchin' his face or punchin' him in the jaw.

"Be calm," he urged, despite himself experiencin' anythin' but calmness. "I'm not the one what's gonna hurt ya."

Her fight stopped as though he'd picked just the right words. Her eyes found his, but he recognized they didn't see him. She did what he took to be a nod and reached up to encircle his neck. Her doin' so caught him off guard, but he recovered quick, his own arms slippin' around her, fingers lockin' together behind her. He lifted her up, thankful for her ability to help. Had he needed to pick her up by himself, her weight would've caused him to tumble and given the faceless thing the choice which o' them it wanted to eat first.

When she got her feet beneath her and found her balance, he pivoted back toward their stalker.

It'd moved three more paces, closin' the space between them, movin' slow like it thought they didn't realize its presence. Not close enough to touch them, but Horace estimated two good leaps for it to get there.

The woman shivered against him, her one arm around his waist as she used him for support and guidance. Not too far gone, he needed Ivy's help to stand and move. Now he found himself the helper. But how long before his poor body refused to keep goin'?

He recalled how Ivy came to his rescue the last time he'd encountered these creatures—or others like them. If she were there, she'd find a way to protect them.

Where is the little gray girl?

Horace wanted to turn his head, scan the surroundin' forest in search o' his friend Thorn's sister, but didn't dare tear his gaze away from the horror creepin' up on them. He stared at the red smeared across its chin, noticed the skin on its cheeks tighten like it pulled back non-existent lips into an unseen snarl. He didn't have much experience with creatures found upon the land, but he thought that kinda expression suggested somethin' gettin' ready to attack.

"What is it?" the woman asked, voice quivering.

"Best you don't know," he said, surprised to find his response didn't share the same scared soundin' quake.

He tightened his hold around her shoulders and pulled her with him, the two o' them draggin' their feet along the ground as they inched away. But the pale abomination followed, takin' another step, then another. It moved faster than them, closin' the space a bit at a time. Horace wanted to run but feared doin' so because it'd give the thing their backs. And if they tried hurryin' backward, they risked gettin' tangled in creepers and branches, fallin' and makin' themselves easier prey. With no other choice, he set his jaw and continued easin' them back.

As if the creature sensed the sailor's indecision, it stopped, coiled itself, ropey muscles collectin' beneath the shiny skin. In the instant before it sprang, Horace's whole life flashed through his head. To his disillusionment, it didn't take long, and all he recognized were regret—for spendin' so many turns o' the seasons doin' what he hated, for desertin' his family to do so, for failin' Thorn, and now for not bein' able to save the woman. Remorse, disappointment, failure. What kinda life did he live?

The thing sprang at them. Horace pulled her hard against him and pivoted away from the blood-smeared horror, puttin' his body between her and it and gettin' ready to die.

XXXIX - Rilum – Now

*A*N ODOR FOUND ITS way through the sweet bouquet of juice and meat and saliva, past the fetor of wood and needles and moss. Unusual, but familiar. A scent recently detected but which also lingered from sometime long, long ago.

It stopped, surveying its surroundings with one carrion-filled hand raised halfway to its face, blood running along its stick-like fingers, pooling in its palm, dripping from its wrist. It observed the world through the usual gauze.

The hairy beast lay splayed at its feet, chunks torn away from its body, used, and cast aside in the brush. It no longer breathed, the lump of muscle in its chest ceased beating; it made sure of it by tearing it out and devouring it. One other crouched to the side, preoccupied with ripping flesh from their fallen prey, opening its abdomen and pulling out loops of entrails. The second other had strayed from the kill.

It straightened, turned its head first one way then the other until it detected a flicker. The other stood several paces from their feast, facing away. It wondered what made it leave behind such delicious fare. More movement—two figures beyond the other. One of them had been with the beast. Even with the overpowering stink of the animal's matted fur, the odor of her womanness had been clear. But why forgo tasty meat for a skinny woman?

But the second figure caught his attention. It bore the same scent he'd detected recently with a little one and was why the other had deserted their feast.

Once-was-Rilum took a step away from the fallen beast himself, wanting to get a clearer scent of the air. Two steps from the kill and the odors became more recognizable. He smelled the woman, the man, the forest more plainly. His brow wrinkled and all but what he searched for filtered through the flaps of skin long ago grown over his nostrils.

As with every part of their home, a faint whiff of a small one remained here, but its faintness suggested some time since the little creature passed. The fellow previously accompanied by a gray one wasn't so protected now.

Once-was-Rilum understood why his companion had wandered from their meal. A different quality in the flesh of a man attracted him, an enlivening it brought not found elsewhere. An energy, a flavor, a fervor. Rarity. He took two steps away from the dead beast, following along behind the other. With his brethren so fixated on its prey, it wouldn't notice him coming to partake alongside.

His feet whispered in the creepers and leaves lining the forest floor, the sound of his passing so quiet, he couldn't hear it himself. Thick, gummy saliva oozed into his mouth, held fast by sealed lips. Silent and quick, he moved closer to his companion. The odors of the man and woman grew with each step. Instead of enticing him, the man's pungent scent made him wary. During his unknown time in this place he'd found few men, either on his own or after he allowed the others to join him. But he remembered each one—their aroma, their flavor, how consuming them gave him energy. Enough for him to wonder if his companions might have the same effect, a question answered when the third other met its end.

It should fill him with expectation and excitement at what lay in his immediate future, but a quality about the odor quelled it. Instead of anticipation buoying him, anger made his bones leaden. The desire to strike out in punishment filled him, threatened to spill out.

Two more steps and not only did the man's stink fill his head, his face assumed a shape and features. Older and more wrinkled than he remembered, the cheeks weathered, the eyes sadder. He recognized the man without knowing him until one word swam out of the miasma of his mind and made itself clear.

Father.

Had once-was-Rilum heard it spoken, he wouldn't have understood its meaning. But it clarified in his head not as a sound uttered, but as a package of images, memories, feelings; things near unrecognizable to him as he'd experienced none of them in so long. The combination conjured a variety of responses within him, each of them tingling along his flesh. He knew the tightness in his chest and tension in his muscles, though he didn't know to call them anger, but the speed of his heartbeat, the rapid pulse in his ears, were foreign.

Ahead of him, the other stopped, coiled. Once-was-Rilum recognized the action; many times he'd done the same, readying himself to pounce on his prey. The way of the world. They needed nourishment, had found it together for a long time. Not now. He wanted the other to stop, for him to leave the man alone, but not to have the flavorful morsels of his flesh to himself.

Inexplicably, he wished the fellow to live.

The other leaned back, collecting energy for the leap as once-was-Rilum had taught him long ago. After the change, this one had been like a newborn, unable to hunt for himself for ages, needing constant attention and instruction, but he'd learned, and learned well. Now, as instinct and nature required, he readied for another kill in a long history of kills. The first once-was-Rilum didn't want him to make.

The last he'd ever attempt.

An instant before the other left his feet to pounce, once-was-Rilum tensed, coiled, and leapt in one smooth movement. He hit his companion in midair, catching him by surprise and throwing him off course. They flew past the man and woman, and once-was-Rilum saw the expressions on their faces through the gauze covering his vision: fear and shock. He wished to see thankfulness, appreciation, recognition, but found them absent. He suspected they'd been so before the change, but he still couldn't allow the other to end the man's life.

They crashed to the ground, and something popped—a bone, a joint. Momentum sent them rolling, and the son saving the man took advantage of catching the other off-guard. His talons found the soft flesh of his longtime companion's belly, sank in to his second knuckles. Blood spurted across his hands, combining with the congealed fluid from the fur-covered beast. With his other hand, he reached for the other's throat, but he'd lost the luxury of surprise and his adversary caught his wrist, twisted hard. Another snap and pain surged up his arm, through his shoulder and chest.

He'd felt this kind of agony before. They were efficient hunters, but sometimes their prey proved too strong. As before, he ignored it, intent on his goal, determined to save the man.

XL - Horace - Savior

*T*HE SECOND FACELESS CAME outta nowhere, pluckin' the first from the air before it had the chance to tear Horace and the woman into pieces.

She curled up against him, warm and shiverin', not seein' what went on nor makin' any kinda sound. For himself, he wished he couldn't see what were happenin', either, but when he made a try at closin' his eyes, he found himself unable to do so.

So he watched them roll across the ground. He heard a pop, a snap, but weren't sure if it came from one o' the things or if they fell on top o' branches what broke underneath them. The blood what spurted out, though, were definitely from them.

Neither o' the pale abominations made a noise as they fought other'n the sound o' their limbs thrashin'; no snarlin' or growlin', gruntin' or groanin'. They moved quicker'n Horace'd ever seen a livin' creature move. He watched mesmerized, forgettin' his life and the life o' the woman in his arms was in danger from these creatures.

But why'd one attack the other?

Made no sense, but no chance he'd figure it out any more'n divining the reason for the tides or how a fish holds its breath so long. Last two didn't matter, either, just the way things was. They was alive. Nothing else mattered.

They tore at each other with their overgrown nails, the sound o' rippin' flesh enough to make the ol' sailor's stomach do a flip. He wrenched his gaze away, and it found the third o' the creatures what'd stopped gorgin' on the furry beast to find out what its fellows got up to. When it spied them, it abandoned the carcass, beatin' a straight line through the underbrush toward the fracas. Seein' it dartin' their general direction prompted Horace into movement o' his own.

"Come on," he said close to her ear but not expectin' any o' the pale terrors'd hear amongst the ruckus o' their fight.

He tightened his grip around the woman's shoulders, turned her from the bloody skirmish, and began herdin' her away from danger. She allowed him to do so, cringin' and startin' with each sound o' talons tearin' flesh. He couldn't imagine how terrifyin' it must be for her not bein' able to spy what made them horrible noises. Plus she were lettin' a man she didn't know lead her into the woods. Horace suspected if the roles was reversed, he'd likely curl up on the ground and wait for his turn to die.

The woman were much braver than him.

As he guided her away, steerin' her around fallin' log traps and pokin' branches, he glanced back o'er his shoulder time and again, makin' sure no abomination followed. None did. Instead, the third of the creatures joined the first two in their grisly wrestlin' match.

The three o' them stayed on their feet, tangled together as they tore at each other. Blood smeared most ev'ry exposed bit o' pale flesh and they was so intertwined, it made it impossible to tell one from the next—not that Horace'd've been able to recognize any if they stood in front o' him smilin' mouthless smiles.

One o' them raised an arm what dangled in a spot where a joint shouldn't've been, but it didn't notice this inconvenience. It swung the arm, usin' the bottom part and hand like a whip to attack its compatriot. Another had a chunk torn outta its belly and a purple curve o' its insides bulged through the jagged wound. The last sported a long gash on its face, skin pulled back and away like a taut and ripped piece o' canvas. Horace thought he spied features what belonged to a man hidden behind the white flesh.

The sight o' such a thing nearly gave him pause, but by then the woman got movin' of her own accord, makin' it her turn to keep him goin'. He diverted his attention to watchin' she traveled a clear path what wouldn't trip her up. Five paces passed under their feet before he couldn't help but look back one last time.

The thing with the split in its white, fleshy mask stared right at him, the pale skin gone from the features what hid beneath. No doubt he gazed upon a face what'd belonged to a man. Despite the blood coverin' cheeks and forehead and nose, he felt a spark o' familiarity in his chest what flared enough to make its way into his noggin, too.

Before he scrutinized the blood-soaked face, the others grabbed it, pulled it down toward the ground and outta his line o' sight. Horace's heart skipped a beat or two, knowin' he should've recognized them eyes but unable to place them.

He shook his head, put the thought from mind. The things what wanted to kill and eat him had given him the opportunity to.

XLI - Rilum – Now

*T*HE SECOND OTHER SLAMMED into them and once-was-Rilum heard another snap, but recognized the sound didn't come from him. His leg made the first noise. Even now, as he stood fighting with his companions over this man his mind called 'father', the jagged ends of the broken bone grated and ground together, pain like he'd never experienced shooting along his thigh.

For the first time in forever, he sensed the specter of a life before, an age before the white gauze cowl inhibited his vision and satiating the hunger meant everything. An existence somewhere other than this forest. Visions of water washed through his mind, the sounds of waves against wood, and the screech of gulls. Heat on his face, rain on his cheeks, the pang of loss in his heart.

Heart.

The tasty muscle found in the chest, but it wasn't the tissue itself aching so, was it? A bit of flesh and sinew didn't experience such things; that came from somewhere else. How long since he'd felt any ache other than the hunger? How long since his life included the bouquet of oiled boards, the flavor of brine on his lips, the freedom of open water and endless sky?

One of his companions caught him off guard, a sharp talon finding its way along his face from forehead to chin. He jerked back, so it only grazed him, but it found him enough to split his flesh. Blood rushed into his mouth, threatening to choke him. It stung his eyes.

The sensations gave him pause. He blinked.

Blinked.

The white gauze disappeared from his vision, color returning to the trees and leaves, the glimpses of sky peeking through the boughs overhead. He spat the coppery taste from between his lips, a long string of thick, bloody saliva falling onto his chin, dangling. His eyelids flitted again; he looked past his companions trying to kill him, and his eyes met those of the man. Memories and feelings rushed into once-was-Rilum, some invigorating him, others crushing him, the sum of them so tangled and indecipherable they became nothing more than a knotted ball clogging his chest.

He saw him clearly, knew him.

He wondered if his father recognized him, too. Would he come to his rescue? Protect him from death at the hands of his former companions?

Before the father turned his back on him to flee, once-was-Rilum understood these weren't possibilities. The others would tear him to pieces in the blink of an eye. No, this was his opportunity to save the old sailor.

And so the pale abomination once and again the son of Horace Seaman didn't experience the same heartbreak as when his father left him before. This time when the man turned his back on him, he determined to ensure his survival.

The two others grabbed his shoulders, dragged him to the ground. Once-and-again Rilum let them, his mind and body set on ending their existence though it meant the end of his own.

He clamped his jaw, growled in the depths of his chest, and flashed his talons out at the throats of his companions.

XLII Teryk - Memory

*W*ITH THE TALL MAN's hand on his shoulder, the words they spoke became clear, as when Ailyssa laid her fingers on him. He hadn't expected it to be so; Juddah touched him without the same effect, but the slender man—whom the others called Ive—placed his grip as though he understood its ability to help him comprehend. As soon as the word left the one-armed fellow's lips, he realized he'd spoken his name. After not knowing it or his history, not understanding those around him, he possessed an identity, a story.

"Teryk? Is that me?"

"You are Teryk, prince of the Windward Kingdom. And I am Trenan. Do you remember?"

The Windward Kingdom.

Scraps of memory filtered through the haze clouding his mind from the moment he recalled Juddah pulling him out of the surf. He found a shred of familiarity in the face of the one-armed man, a sense of safety and warmth when he gazed upon him. Without a doubt, he knew him, and he'd been someone important in his life.

His eyes moved from the grizzled warrior to the two young women seated on the log. The younger of them didn't kindle the same feelings in him as the fellow calling himself Trenan, but then his gaze found the second woman. His heart jumped in his chest and a word struggled its way to his lips.

"Danya."

Where the name might have come from, or what it should mean, eluded him, but the woman's reaction made it plain it belonged to her. Her eyes widened, and she opened her mouth to speak. The muscles in her legs flexed as though she meant to stand but an impediment held her back from doing so.

"Teryk. Thank the gods."

"It appears the young prince lost has found his way again," Ive said, his grip on Teryk's arm tightening until it caused pain. "Does anyone care to remind him why we find ourselves in the last place we should want to be? Or will the task also fall to me?"

"The scroll, Teryk," Danya said. "Do you remember the scroll?"

He narrowed his eyes, concentrating. His mind tingled, the answers he searched for beyond his reach, taunting him. He recalled a cavernous room made of marble. Statues towered along one side, a lectern stood at the far end. The image wavered, then he saw Danya standing by the rostrum, her hands leaning on it, holding open a scroll threatening to roll itself back up if she let go. Behind her lingered the woman he'd seen in a foggy, near-forgotten vision of fire falling from the sky.

Rak'bana.

It came to him unbidden and unexpected but he realized it belonged to her, as he now understood himself to be Teryk, the prince.

"The firstborn of the rightful king," he muttered, no more understanding of where those words emerged from than about the name Rak'bana.

"Yes," Ive said. "And do you remember what it means?"

Teryk stared straight ahead, his breath shallow as he concentrated harder. His gaze crawled from Danya with her look of expectancy to Trenan, his visage unreadable. Fellick shifted, moving toward the one-armed man, positioning himself between the soldier and the princess. Beyond the unfamiliar people, at the top of a short hill, stood the men in black robes who'd killed Juddah and forced Ailyssa away. They remained motionless, arms raised to the sides to form a rough circle around a group of mounted warriors. None of them moved, but the sight of the shadowy figures tied a knot of anger in his gut. Now he recalled his name, he realized the connection he and Ailyssa shared came after everything else—she hadn't been a part of his life. But she'd been the only person to help him when he found himself lost, and she was gone.

"Teryk?" Ive prompted, pulling him out of his trance.

"I am the firstborn child of the rightful king, prophesied to save the kingdom from the return of the Small Gods."

His heart swelled as he spoke, and a lifetime of experience and emotion flooded into him. How many times can a son disappoint a father? Words sharp as knives had injured him time and time again, expressions of discouragement, accusations of failure. He'd never grow in the king's shadow and his kin before him, didn't expect to have a chance to until he and Danya discovered the scroll. Now the opportunity to prove himself existed. After losing his way, forgetting his identity and purpose, and finding himself locked up in Juddah's barn, these revelations laid out a distinct future ahead of him.

He sat straighter, pulled his shoulders back. A smile tilted his lips. He'd save the kingdom and show everyone his value, leave his father no choice but to be proud of him.

"There's but a small problem, right, Trenan?" Ive raised his hand, a dagger Teryk hadn't seen him draw held loosely in his finger. He pointed it toward the one-armed man. The master swordsman glared at him.

"What's he talking about?"

Trenan's eyes found the prince, his expression softened, but he chose not to answer. The weapons merchant clicked his tongue twice, shook his head in mock disappointment.

"You don't want me to tell him, do you? I feel it's better if it comes from you. What do you think, swordmaster?"

Trenan didn't speak, so Teryk turned his attention to Danya.

"What does he mean?"

She shrugged, but the set of her mouth and the tilt of her brows suggested she might know.

They're lying. None of them believe I can save the kingdom.

He rose, arms and legs flooded with the adrenalin of anger. Wasn't it demeaning enough his father didn't judge him capable of being a man? Now his sister and the soldier who'd raised and trained him had lost faith in him, too... if they'd ever had it.

"Tell me what he's talking about, Trenan. I command it."

The master swordsman lowered his eyes, bowed his head.

"My prince," he said so quietly Teryk strained to discern his words. "You are not the firstborn child of the king."

For an instant, the statement made little sense, and he thought Ive might have broken contact with him, but he felt his grip on his shoulder—looser, but present. Understanding dawned as he remembered things he had no right to remember, and Teryk's brow furrowed, his jaw tightened.

"What are you talking about? Explain yourself."

Trenan inhaled a slow, deep breath between his lips, let it out the same way. "The king is not your father, Teryk." He paused, swallowed hard. "I am."

Everything took on a red hue around him. His pulse beat in his ears. He looked from the soldier to Fellick, then Evalal, and finally Danya. None of them appeared as surprised as they should have been. Suddenly, his life made sense. A recollection of a hidden courtyard passed through his thoughts. He let it go.

"Does he know?"

"I..." Trenan began but then stopped, seeming to reconsider his response.

"Does he know?"

"He doesn't, but I believe he has always suspected."

Muddled, painful memories congealed in his mind. Everything fell together: his father's derisive comments; his parents' obvious preferential treatment of Danya; the care with which Trenan had trained him. His lips pressed into a bloodless white slash across his face, his eyes narrowed. The master swordsman might have looked after him, taught him and watched out for him, but he'd also deceived him for his entire life.

I'm not the firstborn. The prophecy isn't about me.

His lower jaw moved forward and back, grinding his teeth as his mind unwound the deceptions of everyone he'd ever held dear like unrolling a tangled ball of yarn. He recalled stolen glances between Trenan and his mother, unnoticed when they happened but living in his subconscious. He remembered his father's unearned flashes of anger, the stealthy looks, whispers and laughter of the queen's guards when he walked past. Even Fellick and Ive knew, and he didn't remember them being part of his life.

Did everyone know this secret? Everyone but him?

I have been such a fool.

He'd believed the words inscribed on the scroll capable of redeeming him, offering him the path he longed for to prove himself. But the dream lay dead, stolen from him by the people who said they loved him but lied to him for so long.

His chest tightened, his breath shortened. Trenan spoke, drawing his attention, but the pounding of his heart in his ears hid the words from Teryk. He dragged his gaze away from the treacherous swordmaster, past the squat and powerful Fellick, the lithe, concerned Evalal, until his stare rested upon his sister. Her mouth moved, but to him it made no sound. He recognized his name from the way she shaped her lips, nothing else.

He continued staring at her, his mind working through his rising anger, his disappointment. If Trenan sired him, then he wasn't the heir to the throne, and the scroll did not refer to him. The revelation placed Danya as firstborn and destined to save the kingdom while he languished. With the truth out, the king would disown him...if he let him live.

"How could you do this?" he said, the question rumbling in his throat.

Danya's eyes widened, her head moved side to side. Her lips continued shaping words but Teryk heard nothing over the roar in his ears as his anger hardened into rage.

"You stole it from me. I'm meant to be the world's savior. Me."

He leaped forward, his body taking over and moving of its own accord. He snatched the knife from Ive's hand with so little effort, he might have thought the man handed it to him. His bare foot fell on a sharp rock sending pain shooting through his sole; he ignored it, the sensation suffocated by his blinding anger.

The world around him slowed.

Trenan stood, face contorted and mouth open wide as he shouted unintelligibly to Teryk. Fellick shifted, blocking the master swordsman. Evalal's body tensed, but she remained as unable to move as Danya beside her.

Teryk's vision narrowed, everyone disappearing from his view as it dwindled until he saw his sister, the blade in his hand, and nothing else. He heard naught but his heart slamming against his ribs, felt only the rage coursing through his limbs and filling his chest, thought about how his destiny—his one chance at a meaningful life—had been wrenched from him.

The point of the dagger pierced the skin of his sister's—half-sister's—throat. A tiny mist of blood fell onto the blade as it slid deeper. Her face twisted, surprise leaving it as it transformed into a mask of sadness, pain, disappointment.

I won't disappoint anyone anymore.

The full length of the knife thrust into her neck until the hilt pressed against her and the tip broke the skin on the opposite side. Danya convulsed, blood bubbling at the corners of her mouth. She stared into her brother's eyes, unspeakable dismay glistening at the edges of her eyelids. Her lips moved as though she wanted to speak, but her words became a cough spraying crimson droplets across Teryk's hand and forearm. Sticky redness ran along her chin; she coughed again, choking on her own life-giving fluid.

Teryk yanked the knife out of her throat, a thick, red gout following it out, running down her neck and staining her shirt. He took a step back, his vision of everything around him opening again. Beside Danya, Evalal's mouth hung wide, her face twisted as she wailed. Farther to his left, Trenan struggled against Fellick's hold to no avail. His sister teetered in her seat for a few heartbeats, tears spilling from her eyes, tinting pink as they mingled with the blood on her chin and jaw.

She shifted, her shoulder tilting toward him, as though she wanted to reach out and touch her brother, but her bindings prevented her from doing so. Her expression betrayed a longing to connect one more time. Teryk glared at her, batted her attempt away, his anger not in the slightest satisfied despite the bloodletting.

She pitched forward onto the ground, head coming to rest against his ankle. Blood gushed from her throat, splashing across his feet and turning the dirt to grisly mud.

Teryk lowered the knife and watched her life draining from her. The rage in his chest drained away along with it, his awareness of sounds returning—Evalal's sorrowful wail, Trenan saying the princess' name, Ive clicking his tongue.

"Tch, tch, tch. Look what's happened here. No more firstborn child. A shame, I say. A shame."

Vaguely aware he understood the man's words when he shouldn't, the blade slipped out of Teryk's slackened hand, thudded against the ground beside his foot. He crouched, used his fingers to brush the hair plastered to his sister's forehead away from her face and looked into her eyes staring ahead, her life flickering out in them like a candle in a stiff wind.

"Danya?" He stroked her cheek with his fingertips. "Danya?"

His rage disappeared, the memories of disappointments and failures displaced by adventures they'd gone on together, laughter shared. None of the blame for this belonged to her—she didn't choose who fathered him, or that she'd be the chosen named in the prophecy. It wasn't her hand which inscribed the ancient words upon the scroll, nor did she leave it for them to find. Truly, she loved him and supported him whenever he needed her, when no one else did. And now he'd betrayed her, ended her life.

"What have I done?"

Teryk leaned forward until his forehead touched his sister's. The energy she'd always possessed, the light that shone from within her, disappeared, extinguished by his instant of unfathomable, unreasonable anger. His heart shrank inside his chest, tightening, shortening his breath until tears ran from his eyes.

"What have I done?"

XLIII - Vesisdenperos - Return

*T*HE SCULPTOR OPENED HIS eyes as though waking from a long sleep, but understood this wasn't the case. His eyelids didn't open, but his awareness, his consciousness. For many cycles of the moon he'd hidden within his clay creation, carried around like a satchel full of essential contents waiting for the proper time to be untethered and used. Did the golem itself realize he dwelt inside it, dormant, awaiting his summons? Doubtful. The sculpture likely knew nothing beyond his assigned duty: retrieve the Small God and return with him to Teva Stavoklis.

Many things returned with his sight and awareness. A group of priests made up the circle, gathered around an ancient stone and wood altar where a figure lay. A chanted incantation rang in his ears and drops of rain splattered on the hard clay surrounding his consciousness. Beside him stood Kuneprius, his friend and mentor, the closest thing he'd ever had to a father. An agonized and despairing expression twisted his features as his hands came down, plunging the knife they held into the chest of the gray man lying on the holy table.

In that instant, Vesisdenperos realized the significance and timing of his wakefulness. This prone figure before him was a Small God from behind the Green, the very thing he and Kuneprius dedicated their entire lives to retrieving.

We did it.

He wasn't yet able to experience joy—at least not the fulfilling, physical side of it—but his consciousness swelled with pride.

But why does Kuneprius not appear overjoyed?

He possessed no control over the clay body and couldn't redirect his gaze to his friend to assess why this might be the case. Instead, the dun eyes watched the Small God's blood seep out of its corpse. It collected in cracks and channels in the altar's surface invisible until they brimmed with the bright red fluid. They directed it to a short trough cut in the altar before the golem. It filled slowly, steadily. The mythical being reached out, dipped its fingertips into the liquid.

A shock ran through the unnatural body, and it tensed around Vesisdenperos as though the muscles in this creature that didn't truly have such things tightened. The sculpture lifted its hands, touched the smooth tips of its fingers to its face and drew four lines along each cheek. This accomplished, it returned to the trough, this time cupping its palms, allowing them to fill. It raised them again, tilted them so the thickening fluid cascaded onto its chest, flowed down its abdomen. The golem placed its hands on the splash of red, dragged them across its torso, mixing the blood with its mud flesh.

A tremor shook through the monster, a jolt of energy Vesisdenperos' own detached consciousness recognized. Then the living statue did something he'd designed it not to need: it drew breath.

The incantation swirled around the sculptor and his clay vessel, filling the night air as droplets of rain pattered on priest's robes, on tiled floor, on the Small God's cooling flesh. Hidden beneath these sounds, he heard the strained sobs of his mentor, the sorrow Kuneprius struggled to hide but failed. With no power to influence the living statue's actions and observe his friend, the creature instead tilted its head back, raised its gaze skyward.

As Vesisdenperos might have expected, a layer of cloud obscured the night and trapped souls of the Small Gods. How he wished to see them. It had been so long since he gazed upon the evenstar and the others, offered his prayers. If only the sky above provided a glimpse, the faintest glimmer, the shallowest glow.

As if in answer to his thoughts, a light broke through the cloud cover. It appeared tiny at first but grew and expanded as it hurtled through the firmament. Vesisdenperos stared along with the golem, seeing through the creature's eyes, hearing the priests' chant grow and change through the living statue's ears. The High Priest's voice stood out amongst them, his tone excited, bordering on manic as he led his followers to the moment for which they'd waited so long.

The glow rushed toward them, aimed at the temple of Teva Stavoklis, and the sculptor experienced the unexpected notion he should flee. Not by himself—he'd gather his mentor in the golem's powerful limbs and carry him from danger as Kuneprius had kept him safe for so many seasons turning. But as he considered scooping his friend up in his arms, the living statue instead raised them skyward, as if welcoming the onrushing light with an embrace.

For the first time since his awakening, Vesisdenperos experienced a palpable sensation, physical rather than simply a thought. The mouth he didn't possess went dry; muscles not attached to his bones tightened; a heart not his own sped. Fear gripped him, made him wish to be anywhere but here, prompted him to want to be anyone but himself.

The light grew to the point of blinding. The sculptor screamed a scream no one but he heard, and then the luminescence touched him.

It didn't strike the golem with great impact but enveloped him, spreading buoyancy and sensation over, through, around the living statue, penetrating it so Vesisdenperos himself experienced its warmth. The clay man's vision clouded. The priests gathered near him disappeared, swallowed by yellowish-white light overtaking everything. It leeched color from the tiles underfoot, the blood on the golem's hands, melted sky and walls and altar to the wax of a candle made of the world.

And then Vesisdenperos wasn't alone.

Kristeus, Kuneprius, and the other men remained beside him, hidden in the overpowering glow, but the sculptor realized he no longer had the inside of his creation to himself. The clay vessel holding his essence now contained that of another, too.

A figure stepped out of the light, emerging naked and shaking like a bather might do when stepping from the mist of a waterfall. It started out a silhouette, a dark outline against the bright background. Its hunched shoulders and lowered head gave it the appearance and demeanor of a man who'd seen the seasons turn many times. But as the thought crossed the sculptor's mind, the form raised its chin, inhaled a deep breath that seemed to inflate it. Then he drew upward, straightened, appeared to grow.

It stepped forward, and the light that had swallowed everything gathered around him, revealing the robed priests, the altar, the temple, the sky.

All but Kuneprius had fallen to their knees. He continued standing beside the golem, sagging, arms dangling at his side as his head tilted down far enough his chin touched his chest. The others either didn't notice or paid him no attention. The Small God's body lay upon the shrine in the same place as before the light came to overtake everything. Vesisdenperos hadn't detected the smile tilting the dead man's ashen lips, but it sat his features as if he welcomed death.

"He doesn't welcome it, but he understood its inevitability."

The now-glowing figure stepped around the table and the corpse upon it without a sideward glance, approached the golem. His features appeared clear and visible and, though it wasn't a face the sculptor had ever seen before, he realized who stood before him.

"Lord, Ine'vesi," he said, his words spoken by the sculpture's lips.

"Yes, child. You have done well."

The evenstar laid his hand on the living statue's shoulder, and energy flowed through Vesisdenperos, and excitement. He put his other palm on the creature, and the sculptor redirected the golem's eyes, saw Ine'vesi's fingers sink into the clay. It caused no pain, only exaltation.

The One Who Watches From the Sky stepped forward, sinking into the golem like a red-hot dagger pressed against a block of lard. Vesisdenperos felt a change. The living statue grew around him, altering his point of view so he looked down on the priests from on high—not because they knelt but because he stood twice the height of the tallest of them. He swelled within the clay, taking up more space though he knew he now shared it.

He glanced to his right, at Kuneprius, who had raised his gaze and stared up at the golem with both astonishment and stark terror reflected in his features. The sacrificial blade lay shattered on the ground at his feet, its role complete. Would the same thing happen to his mentor and handler now he'd completed his job?

"Arise."

The lips and tongue of the statue formed the word, but its mouth spoke with the combined voices of the evenstar and the sculptor. The single utterance rattled the stone and wood altar, shaking dust from its joints and the rope holding it together. Priests gathered at the feet of their god raised their heads, clambered to stand.

"Arise, my faithful, for the return of the Small Gods is nigh."

<<<<>>>>

The end of Book 4

The fight against the rise of the Small Gods continues in *The Twilight Fades (the Fifth Book of the Small Gods)*, available at your favorite book retailer

Afterword

Hello again, readers.

I have to admit, writing can be a little bit of one of those love/hate things. While the joy of creation is undeniable, there are times tings just don't flow as well and authors have to just trust the process. I don't believe "writer's block" is a thing—any pause in the creative flow merely needs to be worked through—but it can be frustrating, nonetheless. The funny thing is, the stuff that gets written when one is simply "forging ahead" is often as good or better than everything else. Sometimes the best stuff arises out of adversity.

Speaking of adversity, things aren't looking great for out heroes, are they? I hope you want to see what happens. If so, you can find out in the fifth book of the Small Gods, **The Twilight Fades.**

Visit Bruce online ay www.bruceblake.net for
FREE SHORT STORIES and to stay
updated on new releases

Also By Bruce Blake

Curse of the Unnamed epic fantasy:

The Book of Shadow
Shadow Scarred
A Shadow Upon the Land
In the Shadow of the Dragon - coming July, 2023

Khirro's Journey epic fantasy:

Blood of the King
Spirit of the King
Heart of the King

The Books of the Small Gods epic fantasy:

When Shadows Fall
The Darkness Comes
And Night Descends
When Ravens Call
The Twilight Fades
And Kingdoms End

The **Icarus Fell** urban fantasy series:

On Unfaithful Wings
All Who Wander Are Lost

Secrets of the Hanged Man

Blood of the King (Khirro's Journey Book 1)

A kingdom torn by war. A curse whispered by dying lips. A hero born against his will.
With a vial of the king's blood in one hand, and a sword of legend in the other, one soldier sets out on an odyssey that will change his life... or end it.

Forced into the army, Khirro never wanted to fight. And with the monarch dead, any hope for the kingdom's survival hangs by a slender thread.
But when the king's shaman charges Khirro with a curse, he's compelled to undertake a journey to the haunted land in search of the outlaw necromancer. And if he fails... the very walls of the fortress itself will fall to the blood-crazed undead.

Can Khirro complete his quest in time to save his realm from a brutal end?

"Blood of the King is a masterpiece. It is as close to perfection as I would consider a book to be."- Ella Medler, author of *Blood is Heavier*
"Blake has a knack for bringing you into the story"
"Mr. Blake's writing is masterful and clear, he draws you into his story and when it's finished you feel like you're leaving an old friend."

The Book of Shadow (Curse of the Unnamed Book1)

Llyris Fildarae is an outcast tainted by a sliver of magic in a world terrified of the supernatural. Loathed and distrusted, she uses her ability to control a magical Unnamed to survive.

Caedric Carpera is desperate to save his son from a deadly illness. He enlists Llyris to locate a lost tome containing secrets capable of healing him, but its location is a mystery that's already claimed lives. Thrust into a hostile world, Llyris and her companions risk everything to find the relic and return before the child's sickness prevails.

But who is the enigmatic old man who appeared out of nowhere to set them on this dangerous expedition? And what does he really want?

Only a perilous mission to an untamed land can save the boy and reveal the truth.
Except some truths are too shocking to be exposed.

"Bruce Blake has written a hell of a book and I am eagerly awaiting the sequel!"
"I'm usually a chapter per night type, but I couldn't put this book down."

On Unfaithful Wings (Icarus Fell #1)

To some, death is the end; to others, a beginning. To Icarus Fell, it should have been a relief from a life gone seriously awry.
But death had other plans.
Icarus doesn't believe that the man awaiting him when he wakes up in a cheap motel room is really the archangel Michael, or that God's right hand wants him to help souls on their way to Heaven. Icarus doesn't believe there's a Heaven, so why should they want his help?
But the man claiming to be the archangel tempts him with an offer he can't ignore--harvest enough souls and get back the life he wished he'd had.
It seems Icarus has nothing to lose, until he botches a harvest and the soul that went to Hell instead of Heaven comes back to make him pay by threatening to take away the life he hoped to win back.
To save the wife and son he already lost once, Icarus will have to become the man he never was. Somehow, he will have to learn to believe.

"The next book in this series cannot come out soon enough for this reader. Not just my favorite Kindle book of the year, but one of my favorite books ever."
"I loved this book."
"Bruce Blake's On Unfaithful Wings is a great urban fantasy novel. I love good character development in a story's protagonist and Blake nails it with Icarus Fell. I found myself rooting for him from the get-go and laughing out loud at some of his observations."

"On Unfaithful Wings was an impressive first novel. All of the characters were interesting and engaging, but in particular the main character and his struggle to reconcile with his new identity/job. This is one of those stories that stays with me long after I read it and I'll be on the lookout for more from this author."

"This is just, simply, amazing. Icarus is one of the best characters I've ever "met", chock full of virtues and faults and doubts and worries and a simple HUMANNESS that comes through so clearly, I almost expect to run into him around the next corner."

"Icarus Fell is a flawed man but a wonderful character. From the moment I started reading On Unfaithful Wings I was pulled along by this interesting character and wanting to know what would happen next."

About the Author

Bruce Blake lives on Vancouver Island in British Columbia, Canada. When pressing issues like shovelling snow and building igloos don't take up his spare time, Bruce can be found taking the dog sled to the nearest coffee shop to work on his short stories and novels.

Actually, Victoria, B.C. is only a couple hours north of Seattle, Wash., where more rain is seen than snow. Since snow isn't really a pressing issue, Bruce spends more time trying to remember to leave the "u" out of words like "colour" and "neighbour" than he does shovelling.

Bruce has been writing since grade school but it wasn't until the mid-2000's he set his sights on becoming a full-time writer. Since then, his first short story, "Another Man's Shoes" was published in the Winter 2008 edition of *Cemetery Moon*, another short, "Yardwork",was made into a podcast in Oct., 2011 by *Pseudopod*. Since then, he has concentrated on writing novels, publishing the **Khirro's Journey** trilogy (*Blood of the King, Spirit of the King*, and *Heart of the King*), three books in the ongoing **Icarus Fell** urban fantasy series (*On Unfaithful Wings, All Who Wander are Lost*, and *Secrets of the Hanged Man*), and the **Books of the Small Gods** series (*When Shadows Fall, The Darkness Comes, And Night Descends, When Ravens Call, The Twilight Fades*, and *And Kingdoms End*). *The Book of Shadow* is the first book in the **Curse of the Unnamed** series, to be followed by *Shadow Scarred, A Shadow Upon the Land*, and *In the Shadow of the Dragon*.

Bruce has many more projects simmering on the back burner, so stay tuned.

Visit Bruce online at **www.bruceblake.net** for
FREE SHORT STORIES, signed copies,
and to keep up to date with new releases